JUST ENOUGH LIGHT

Visit us at www.boldstrokesbooks.com

By the Author

Hostage Moon

Show of Force

Rules of Revenge

Just Enough Light

JUST ENOUGH LIGHT

by

AJ Quinn

2016

JUST ENOUGH LIGHT

ISBN 13: 978-1-62639-685-2

This Trade Paperback Original Is Published By
Bold Strokes Books, Inc.
P.O. Box 249
Valley Falls, NY 12185

First Edition: July 2016

Credits
Editor: Ruth Sternglantz
Production Design: Susan Ramundo
Cover Design By Sheri (graphicartist2020@hotmail.com)

Acknowledgments

The process of creating and writing stories largely takes place in a solitary world, with countless hours spent dreaming, researching, writing, editing…and then repeating the cycle as often as necessary. All before a manuscript finds its way into the hands of an editor.

But much to my amazement and gratitude, writing has also opened previously unknown doors through which incredible people from all over the world have entered my life. Readers, other writers (yes, I mean you, Paige)…and my chosen family, who came into my life through my very first book.

So I will always be profoundly grateful to Radclyffe and Bold Strokes Books for providing the platform from which my stories can take flight. To Ruth, Cindy, Sandy, Connie, Sheri, Lori, Toni, and all the others who work so tirelessly to make everything possible. And especially to you, the readers, who continue to allow me to enter your lives through my stories. Thank you for your emails, your words of encouragement, and your support. It's both an honor and a pleasure to share this time with you.

Dedication

To my chosen family…forever in my heart.

PROLOGUE

It had to be a dream.

A really bad dream.

There could be no other explanation, Kellen reasoned, as the wind whipped around her and icy rain pelted her face. The sharp stings nearly blinded her, soaked her. She blinked, struggled to focus, and forced some even breaths, in and out, as she tried to make sense of what was happening. But it was as if a fog had enveloped her brain causing her thoughts to collide.

There'd been a call.

She distinctly remembered that much. A call coming in about three climbers—one seriously injured—somewhere on the north face of Devil's Tower.

It was an area she knew well. Steeper than a lot of the other climbs in the area, technically difficult, and most of all, intimidating. The approach was both steep and exposed, made more challenging by the ever-changing weather and a prevalence of rockfall, with most of the pitches between 5.9 and 5.10 plus.

Extractions from Devil's Tower were always difficult. The terrain made any rescue operation dangerous and even a minor accident could be potentially disastrous. And if the injured climber had any internal bleeding, it could mean death within two hours. So it was serendipity that Kellen had a SAR team in the immediate vicinity. And just like that, a training exercise turned into a real-life rescue mission.

While pilot and navigator worked on pinpointing the injured climber's location, Kellen recalled getting ready. Rigging up and hooking to a winch cable in the back of the bright red Sikorsky helicopter. She could feel the helicopter shudder—caught in the changing air currents—and heard Annie tell Sam to pass north. Turning her attention from the discussion continuing on her headset, she concentrated on adjusting the harness and got ready to be lowered down to the mountain ledge.

It was at that point that things stopped being quite so clear and time took on an eerie, slow-motion feel.

She remembered dropping her deployment bag containing everything she'd need to stabilize and prepare the injured climber for transport. Remembered pivoting on the skid until she was facing the inside of the helicopter and giving Annie and Ren, working the winch, a thumbs-up, indicating she was ready. And she could clearly recall vigorously pushing away from the skid to begin her descent.

If she had wanted to, Kellen could have rappelled from the helicopter with her eyes closed. Her actions were ingrained, body memory reinforced through years of continuous, repetitive training and real-life experience. She knew the drop rate was supposed to be roughly eight feet per second, and as she descended, she released the tension on the rope and moved her brake hand out at a 45-degree angle to regulate her descent.

But in the next instant, she felt a burning pain, high in her shoulder. Her arm became numb, her hand stopped responding, and she could no longer maintain her hold on the brake. She knew the consequences. But she could do nothing to prevent what was happening.

She knew she was falling and there was nothing but unforgiving rock directly below her to break her fall.

❖

When Kellen opened her eyes again, she was sprawled on her back on a cold slab of rock. The freezing rain was now mixed with wet snow, and if possible, it had gotten colder.

There was a faint ringing in her ears, but beyond that, nothing. She blinked in confusion and tried to move, but immediately stopped and nearly screamed as pain shot through her. Dazed, disoriented, unable to think clearly, she looked straight up and watched what could only be the winch cable as it swayed in and out of her vision.

So this was what real fear felt like.

She swallowed it back, exhaled slowly, and watched the icy air frost her breath. She knew that on a dark night, and especially in snow, perspectives became distorted so she tried harder to concentrate. Tried to follow the cable up until it disappeared in the fog and mist. Logic dictated it was still attached to the helicopter. But as she stared, it seemed as if the cable was connected to nothing more substantial than the thick gray clouds.

This wasn't happening. It was part of a dream.

It had to be.

But it wasn't. She remembered falling.

How long have I been here?

She pushed the question aside, knowing it was only a matter of time before the team would come for her. They were good. The best. And they knew what to do.

Even as the thought occurred, she was certain she could hear the cold air pulsing through the giant blades of the rescue helicopter somewhere above her. But by now, her head was hurting so badly it was hard to focus. Hard to think at all.

She fought off a wave of dizziness as bitter cold seeped into her bones, and slowly began testing her limbs, knowing the team would need to know how she was. Slowly, she tested her arms, fingers—

Her right arm was no longer numb. There was a burning sensation high in her shoulder, but it was manageable. But as she continued testing her limbs, she choked back a scream when she tried to move her left hand. A mistake. Nausea and darkness closed in. She could feel excruciating pain in her left wrist and knew it was broken. A mixture of adrenaline and shock made her shiver, but she pushed through it. Tried to stay above the pain as she gingerly tested her legs.

And felt nothing.

She tried not to panic as a cold fear passed through her. She wanted to scream. Wanted to weep and rail against the unfairness of it all until she was wrung dry and the fear left her. But she couldn't. Wouldn't.

The snow was falling more heavily now, but she could still hear the beat of the helicopter. And then she heard her name over her com link.

"Kellen?"

Annie? Her vision faded, her teeth chattered, and her world narrowed to that one sound. The knowledge that Annie was near stemmed the tide of pain and fear flowing through her, but it was a struggle to get any words out. Her breathing was coming in shallow gulps, her voice labored and weak.

Then Annie was there. Others were there as well, but she kept her focus fixed on Annie, who had dropped to her knees beside her and was gently brushing snow and her hair out of her eyes.

"I'm here, Kel. We've got you. Now try to hold still, sweetie. We're going to get you out of here as quickly as possible. In the meantime, I need you to focus, okay? Can you tell me what hurts the most?"

She felt Annie's hand clamp on her shoulder, anchoring her in time and place, and Kellen focused on that with everything she had. She tried to do as Annie asked, but it was getting harder to breathe. She shivered violently and felt someone palpating her neck.

What was the question? What hurt the most?

She tried to formulate a response and struggled to get the words out. "My head hurts…really bad…there's something wrong with my shoulder…I'm pretty sure my wrist is broken and maybe a couple of ribs." She swallowed painfully and forced herself to continue. Forced herself to say the words she didn't want to think, let alone say. "Annie. Oh God, Annie, I can't feel my legs—"

She heard Annie saying something and became aware of a penlight flashing in her eyes. Felt someone put a neck brace on her, and the prick of an IV needle. Someone was speaking, but the words simply flowed around her, meaningless and disjointed.

"…head injury…shoulder bleeding…legs…"

"Annie?"

"I'm here."

"Promise me…the girls…you'll look after them…"

She couldn't say anything else as a cold numbness filled her. Embraced her. But it didn't really matter. She'd done all she could.

One last time, she tried to focus, tried to keep breathing. But it was a losing battle. Her vision blurred and narrowed.

Became a dot of light.

Got ever smaller.

And then blackness.

Chapter One

S itting on the side of a snow-covered mountain road with a blown front tire and no cell service, Dana Kingston was put in mind of T.S. Eliot's thoughts on the end of the world. And she would have laughed if she could have managed it. But at the moment, the most she could manage was a small, strangled sound—a sound remarkably resembling a whimper.

What am I doing?

She'd been asking herself the same question for over two thousand miles. Since leaving New York on a cold and gray early January morning.

It really was a rhetorical question, because she already knew the answer.

At the end of her journey was a small town called Haven, Colorado. A recreation-friendly alpine community, population 6,200, although the town reportedly got its fair share of the millions of tourists that visited the Rocky Mountains each year, with skiing being the main winter attraction.

Located high in the Colorado Rockies among some of the state's highest peaks, Haven boasted more than five thousand acres of skiable terrain, along with acres of biking and hiking trails, apparently all within walking distance of downtown. Add an abundance of lakes, streams, and rivers, and it also became a fisherman's paradise.

And there, in a former mining town born during the Colorado silver boom, an opportunity awaited her that sounded frighteningly ideal. Almost as if it had been created with her specifically in mind.

Even better, if everything worked according to plan, she would settle into a life that would be as far removed from the life she'd known as she could get and still be on the same planet—or the same solar system for that matter. Far removed from everything and everyone she'd known. Making it everything she wanted.

Releasing a strained laugh, Dana shivered and watched the snow rapidly accumulating around her.

When she'd checked out of the small roadside motel that morning, the sky had been a perfect blue and the roads had been clear. Just over three hours into the drive, the clouds had moved in and a light snow had begun falling. But despite the lowering clouds, Dana had been enjoying her first foray into Colorado, awed by the spectacular displays of light and shadow. White snow and misty lakes. Dark green ponderosa pine, blue-tinted Douglas firs, and snowcapped mountains.

By the time the famed radio voice of the Rockies began issuing heavy snow warnings for higher elevations, Dana hadn't been at all surprised. At most, she'd felt a mild concern. But she hadn't felt any real cause for worry. Not even when the road became narrower and began twisting and turning back on itself and the surface grew slick with snow and ice. Or when the gusting winds increased and swirling snow further reduced visibility. She'd simply downshifted while her wipers worked furiously.

She'd grown up on the East Coast, after all. During her student days, she'd driven through some of the worst winters New England could offer, and though admittedly some time had passed since those days, it was like riding a bicycle. *Wasn't it?*

She never managed to answer her own question, because that was when the left front tire on her BMW blew and it all went to hell.

It sounded like a gunshot. Dana flinched and the acrid taste of fear rose in her throat as the car began to spin. Slowly. So slowly. In the curious way time has, it suddenly seemed to move forward in the most infinitesimal increments as she fought to regain control. The car slid through yet another blind curve before she was able to bring it to a lopsided halt at the edge of the road.

In the process, she stalled the engine and scattered her belongings. But she didn't care. She was simply grateful the car had opted to grab on to the deeper snow on the shoulder of the road. The alternative would have been to disappear down the steep drop-off she could just make out a few feet ahead, and she didn't want to begin considering what the consequences of that option might have been.

Releasing a shaky laugh, she leaned her head back, closed her eyes, and tried to gather her scattered wits. Then she began to shiver.

In the shadow of the mountain, the wind gusts had a cold edge, like a knife. Razor cold. But she knew her reaction had nothing to do with the chill in the air.

She shivered again.

I am so screwed was Dana's next cogent thought when she opened her eyes and considered the bright blue cast covering her right hand. The hand she'd broken three weeks earlier during what turned out to be her last shift in the emergency room.

Her mother had called immediately, having somehow heard what had happened through a mysterious grapevine that kept her informed at all times of all things Dana.

If you'd come back where you belong—in Boston, working for your father—this would never have happened. You know I'm right, Dana.

Her argument was an old one, but it was one her mother brought out without fail at every opportune moment.

Dana knew her parents had always wanted the best for her. Of that she was certain. And she had been raised to do what was expected of her without argument. Over the years, that had meant Harvard—her father's alma mater—for undergrad, medical school, and residency.

It had taken until the end of her residency before she realized she'd been so busy living the life her parents wanted for her, she'd forgotten to ask herself what she wanted. And though she still wasn't certain what that might be, she did know one thing for certain. She had no interest in going to work for her father.

In that moment, Dana had decided it was time to reclaim her life.

Finding herself at a crossroads, she'd left Boston and accepted a position at a hospital whose claim to fame was having the busiest emergency department and level one trauma center in New York City.

A very tough place by anyone's standards. But she had learned and thrived in that chaotic environment where no one cared she was Davis Kingston's daughter. It had also afforded her the time to learn more about herself and to decide what path she wanted to follow. And the path she'd chosen had led her here.

She allowed herself only another minute or two to dwell on the past before the pragmatic side of her nature took over, stilling her riotous emotions. Releasing a sigh of resignation, she reached for her cell phone. If nothing else, common courtesy dictated she call the woman she was scheduled to meet in Haven, where she would start her new life.

Annie Parker.

She'd met Annie three months earlier—a meeting arranged by a neighbor who also happened to be a headhunter. Annie had arranged to fly into New York and, over coffee, had told Dana about the position she was looking to fill.

What she offered was exciting—a chance to be part of setting up a combination medical clinic and emergency triage center from the ground up. The center would be part of a mountain search-and-rescue training center, high in the Colorado Rockies. It would also provide basic health care and medical services to the people living in the region. As the medical team lead, she would have final say on staffing the center. And if everything worked out, the offer included an opportunity after six months to become a partner.

Coffee had stretched into lunch. And then into dinner.

Search and rescue alone doesn't pay the bills, Annie had said. *That's where the idea for the school originally came from.*

She went on to explain that since its inception, the school had grown beyond their original vision, becoming one of the highest ranked search-and-rescue training centers in North America.

The plan to add the triage center had been fully endorsed by the communities the SAR operation served and would only enhance their success rate.

By the time they'd finished talking, Dana and Annie had both known she'd be moving to Colorado as soon as her contract with the hospital ended.

Now she would have to apologize to Annie and tell her she'd be arriving a little later than planned. She'd explain what the problem was. And then she would beg, if necessary, in the hope Annie could find someone to come to her aid.

Not the most auspicious of beginnings. But it couldn't be helped. It was an accident, a temporary setback, and nothing more.

That was when she discovered she had no cell signal. She'd no doubt lost it sometime back, when she left the interstate and headed farther up into the mountains. No doubt there was a rational explanation like the snow-laden trees were too tall or the surrounding mountains too steep. Or maybe the storm had defeated local service. It didn't really matter.

Staring once again at the cast covering her hand, she quietly released a string of words that were half expletive, half prayer. She knew it would be all but impossible for her to manage to change a tire. The best she could do was hope someone would come along before too long—not that she'd passed anyone in the last couple of hours on this lonely stretch of road.

On the plus side, she had a near-full tank of gas, a couple of apples, some trail mix, and a box of crackers in her backpack. She'd be able to keep warm and wouldn't go hungry. On the downside, she could already feel the onset of a headache from caffeine withdrawal. Where was a Starbucks when you needed one?

Dana restarted the car and turned on both the headlights and emergency flashers in case someone came along the narrow road. Hopefully they'd see her in spite of the snow. For the moment, there was nothing else she could do, so she settled her head back, allowing her thoughts to drift while the radio provided a blur of background noise.

Maybe if she counted to ten she wouldn't be here anymore, in a snowstorm in the middle of nowhere with a flat tire. *Right*. Or maybe if she clicked her heels three times, she'd open her eyes and find she was really in Oz with the Tin Man and the Scarecrow. Or maybe she'd find—

A sharp tapping on the car window drew her attention, startling her. Disoriented for a moment, she had no idea if she'd just been musing the time away or had actually fallen asleep.

"Are you all right? Do you need help?"

The low smoke-edged voice had her turning her head to look, but she couldn't make out her rescuer through the frost- and snow-covered glass. Almost giddy with relief, she lowered her window and immediately got a face full of brutally cold, wet snow.

A wry groan escaped Dana as she attempted to clear the snow from her face. She was also fairly certain the next sound she heard—coming from the direction of her would-be rescuer—was low and amused.

Aware she was the source of this stranger's amusement, Dana found herself even more curious to identify who had come to her rescue. She blinked several times, bringing a blurred image into focus, only to get lost in the vision looming above her.

A vision with windblown hair the color of a moonless night sky, Ray-Ban aviator sunglasses, and a snow-dampened face. Make that an *exquisite* snow-dampened face. Lean and sharp angled, with a slight teasing smile on a mouth that invited trouble and just a hint of a dimple showing on one cheek.

Dana stared. She couldn't help herself. And then she shivered as snow unexpectedly slipped inside the collar of her sweater. But the shock of it, cold and wet against her skin, at least assured her she wasn't dreaming.

"Do you need help?" the vision repeated, her low voice wrapped around a laugh, her breath frosty in the air. "Are you stuck?"

Nice smile, seeming sincerity. Somewhere between one heartbeat and the next, Dana found her voice. "Stuck? I'm afraid it's worse than that. I'm supposed to meet someone in Haven, my front tire's blown, and as you can see"—she waggled her cast—"I'm at a bit of a disadvantage."

❖

"Yes, I can see that." Kellen barely contained a smile. "Other than that cast, did you hurt yourself in any way? Did you bang your head or twist anything?"

"No. I promise. Nothing at all. A caffeine withdrawal headache is about the worst of it."

Kellen chewed on her lower lip and tried not to laugh. "Sorry to hear that, but first things first. Do you have a spare? And by chance, is it a real tire, or is it one of those wretched space savers?"

Her words drew the woman closer to the window, allowing Kellen to see her more clearly. Fair hair pulled back in a simple ponytail emphasized the structure of her face, feminine and flawless. She had slashing cheekbones, a dusting of freckles, and a distractingly nice smile. And her eyes—a warm, espresso brown—sparked with humor.

"Yes, I've a spare in the trunk. And it happens to be a real tire. I made sure of that before I hit the road."

"Good thinking, because quite frankly, trying to drive on anything less in these conditions would be quite dangerous, and you don't look particularly crazy."

"I'm not. At least I don't think so."

"Good to know." Kellen knew from experience the storm would get worse before it was done and, with little time to spare, she quickly cobbled a plan together. "Okay, here's what I'd like to suggest. Let's get you out of your car and into my Jeep. That way, you can stay warm and dry while I deal with your tire. In spite of the conditions, it shouldn't take me all that long and I can have you on your way before you know it."

The smile faded, which was really too bad, in Kellen's opinion. In its place, she saw an expression she couldn't quite read. But she could hazard a guess. "I'm not a maniac," she assured the woman mildly even though, to the best of her recollection, no one had ever viewed her as strictly harmless.

"Oh, it's not that," was the quick response. "Okay, maybe it's a little that. But it's also…can't I just stay here and try to help you? I may not be able to do much, not physically, but the least I can do is keep you company. It seems only fair since it's my tire that's flat."

Snowflakes scattered as Kellen shook her head. "I appreciate the thought." She added a smile for emphasis. "But it's really not necessary and there's no point in both of us being cold and wet. So why don't you grab your coat and let's get you settled in my Jeep. I promise I'll change your tire as quickly as I can. And if you need an added incentive, I've got a thermos of really good coffee in the Jeep."

The brief change in her expression indicated the woman was still prepared to argue, but at that moment a shiver visibly ran through her. In the next instant, she shrugged into her jacket, opened the door, and denim-covered legs came into view as she stepped out of her car.

That they were nearly the same height came as no surprise. Kellen had already noted legs that went on forever and filled the faded denim to perfection. What did come as a surprise was the fact that she'd noticed.

What the hell was that?

The direction her thoughts had just taken—well, it had been a long time, a *very* long time, since she'd noticed much of anything.

Annie would be thrilled, she mused, assuming she told her about this. Annie had all but given up on her. Had told her on a number of occasions to stop brooding and get back into the game— only more bluntly.

The bastard that hurt you didn't kill you, but you've withdrawn so much he might as well have.

Kellen didn't take offense at the harsh-sounding words. That was simply Annie's approach. Blunt and direct if she felt it was called for.

As with most things in life, Kellen knew it would happen when it happened. Without any pushing and prodding from others, no matter how well-intentioned or caring the friend might be. But who knew her first sign of interest in anything beyond work in over a year would come on a snow-covered road in the middle of nowhere? Let alone with a complete stranger.

When the woman slipped and almost went down on one knee, Kellen quickly reached for her. "Keep this up and I'm going to think you're accident-prone."

"And I'll think you're the proverbial Good Samaritan. The white knight going from place to place rescuing damsels in distress." She smiled, possibly trying to ease any sting in her words. "Chances are we'd both be wrong."

"Not entirely," Kellen said softly, surprising herself with her candor. "But that's a discussion best left for another place and time. Right now there are more pressing concerns, like getting your tire changed before the weather gets any worse. More to the point, I'm quite used to this weather, these conditions, while at a guess you're a little out of your element. So please. Let me do what needs to be done."

Their gazes locked as they studied each other. An intense, prolonged stare with neither seemingly prepared to give way. But then surprisingly, Kellen saw acquiescence.

"I'd argue with you, but I don't think it would do any good. More to the point, it would be foolish, since all you're doing is trying to help me."

There was no further argument. Just simple acceptance of the arm Kellen had offered.

Kellen felt her arm gripped by a strong hand. She nodded and a half-smile fleetingly touched her mouth as they began to move, with only the snow and ice crunching under their feet to mark their progress.

Just before they reached the bright green Jeep, Kellen hesitated. "I guess I should have asked before now…um, you don't have any problem with dogs, do you? Are you afraid or allergic or anything?"

"Dogs?" The smile was back, albeit a bit confused. "No. I like dogs just fine and they usually like me. No allergies. No childhood trauma, or at least none that I can recall."

"Good to know," Kellen said. "That means you should have no problem with the troublemaker you'll find in the backseat. He's a fair size and may look fierce, but trust me, it's all an act. He's really quite friendly. He's just a little put out because I got to go out in the snow—which he happens to love—and I left him behind."

As soon as Kellen opened the passenger door to her Jeep, a large dark head emerged from the dim interior and the German shepherd's big body wiggled with delight at her return. But then, almost immediately, a low warning growl began humming deep in the dog's throat.

"Bogart, no." Kellen spoke firmly. "Friend."

"Dana," the woman said. When Kellen turned toward her, she continued. "It's my name. Dana. Just thought it might make the introductions easier."

"Sorry, Dana. I seem to have forgotten my manners. I'm Kellen and this is Bogart." Turning back to the dog, she spoke softly once again. "Bogart, this is Dana. She's a friend."

Bogart's intelligent eyes looked at Kellen. Quivering like an overstrung bow and watching her avidly, he drew his head closer and tentatively nudged Dana's palm with his nose as he sniffed her hand.

"Bogart—"

The dog promptly offered a massive paw to a clearly delighted Dana. "Hello, Bogart. I've never seen a long-haired shepherd before. Lord, you're just beautiful, aren't you?" Dana's comment was accompanied by a still-cautious head scratch.

Bogart's tail twitched enthusiastically.

"Now you've done it."

Dana froze in the process of stroking Bogart and looked up nervously. "What? What did I do?"

"Sorry, it's just that Bogart's a great dog and he generally loves everyone." Laughter threaded Kellen's voice. "But he's also got an ego the size of these mountains and you just told him he was beautiful. So you've probably just made a friend for life."

"Oh. Is that all?" Dana visibly relaxed and resumed rubbing Bogart's ear. "I think I can live with that."

Although she trusted Bogart implicitly, he was still young and Kellen knew he could be overenthusiastic and bowl over the unwary at times. So she remained close, standing by while Dana got into the front passenger seat, and making sure she was truly comfortable with the dog, who had thrust his head between the two front seats and was awaiting another rub.

Kellen grinned, lightning fast. "The coffee I promised is in that thermos," she said. "Help yourself. Cream and sugar's in the glove box. And if for any reason you want me—"

"I'll just whistle…" Color immediately washed Dana's cheeks as she no doubt realized what she'd said. "Oh God."

Kellen grinned. "Don't worry about it. It's okay—"

"No, it's not. I can't believe I just said that to a near-perfect stranger, let alone the woman who's been kind enough to save me from spending the rest of the day stuck on the side of a mountain."

"Wow, you think I'm near perfect?" Kellen teased Dana gently and brushed off her apology with an easy laugh. "Don't worry about it. And it just so happens, Bogart and I really like Bacall," she added, before closing the door and heading back through the deepening snow to the BMW.

Chapter Two

The Jeep, insulated by the blanket of snow that was still falling, cocooned Dana in a warm embrace, shutting out everything except the faint sound of the wind. She blew warm air on her hands and made herself comfortable, then reached for the large thermos Kellen had indicated and gratefully poured a cup. The aroma of fresh-brewed coffee that immediately filled the passenger compartment was mouthwatering.

Cradling the cup, watching wisps of steam curl upward, Dana inhaled the fragrant scent one more time before taking a sip. Her eyes closed in sheer delight as she savored the taste—a delicious mocha laced with dark chocolate. Sheer heaven, she thought, and sat back to enjoy every last drop.

True to her word, it didn't take Kellen long to change the flat tire. Even so, Dana felt a profound rush of relief when a chill blast of wind announced Kellen's return. Her gaze rested on Kellen's face, flushed from the cold, while dark hair fell across her forehead, wet and tangled and untamed. "Damn, you look half-frozen."

"Not really. Actually, I don't mind this weather." Kellen paused, removed her sunglasses, and slipped out of her wet sweater, leaving her in a navy long-sleeved T-shirt. "I feel better already."

Blue. Her eyes were a brilliant blue.

Dana felt an unexpected shot of lust whisper along her nerves as she absorbed all the details—the dark flecks swimming in a sea of blue, the thick dark lashes—and found herself captivated by the tiny laugh lines before the sunglasses slipped back into place. Damn, she really was stunning.

She reigned in a libido she'd thought had gone permanently dormant, cleared her throat, and forced herself to speak. "Can I do anything to help? Maybe pour you some coffee?"

"Actually, I'm good. All I need is a minute or two so I can get some feeling back in my fingers, then I'll pull up as close to your car as I can get. Once you're ready to go, just signal and I'll head out in front of you. Bogart and I know these roads like the back of my hand, so you just need to stay close and follow my lead. And if you get nervous or have any problems, all you have to do is flash your lights. I'll pull over immediately. Okay?"

"You don't have to, but I really do appreciate it."

A few minutes later, Dana was once again ensconced in her BMW, following the taillights on Kellen's Jeep. Somehow it made the remainder of the trip much more reassuring, the blowing snow and the winding road less terrifying, and the time flew by.

Perhaps that was why it came as a surprise when Kellen signaled and pulled over as they crested yet another hill. Curious, Dana watched her let Bogart out of the Jeep and figured she probably wanted to let the dog stretch his legs and burn some of his boundless energy after being confined in the Jeep for so long. But as she slowly looked around, she realized what was happening. Kellen was simply giving her time to absorb the view.

It was an impressive sight. Releasing a sigh of gratitude and appreciation for her continued thoughtfulness, Dana leaned back in her seat and tried to take it all in.

Haven lay before her in the gathering gloom. It was a postcard-perfect scene, the town blanketed by the now softly falling snow and framed by towering snow-draped pines and the dark looming mountains.

Could I live here?

The scent of a wood fire hung in the air, mingling with the sharp, clean scent of snow and pines, and Dana could see golden welcoming lights spilling from windows as she rolled the idea around in her head. The thought held even more appeal now that she could see the town more clearly.

She asked again. *Could I live here?*

Definitely. There was no question.

She sensed rather than saw Kellen approaching, with Bogart dancing excitedly at her heels. Dana lowered her window and waited until Kellen drew up beside her.

"So what do you think?"

Dana sighed contentedly. "It's perfect."

"Glad you think so. As you've probably surmised, that's Haven straight ahead. You'll find it's a town that likes to stay up late and wake up early. People will tell you it's especially so during ski season, but really, it's like that all year around."

"It doesn't sound all that different from New York, so it shouldn't be a hard adjustment for me to make." The irony amused her.

"I think you might find a few differences." Kellen laughed. "For example, Main Street is the only street in town that's end-to-end shops, bars, restaurants, art galleries, and spas. But the good news is if you want or need something and can't find it on Main Street, someone will be happy to order it in for you. It's that kind of town."

"I think I love it already."

"I'd like to see you still feel that way a couple of days from now."

Dana grinned. "I'm open to suggestion."

"Well, you said you've come from New York, and maybe you already know this, but we're pretty high up in the Rockies. Actually, we're among some of the state's highest peaks. So, I'd like to suggest you try to take it easy for a day or so." She paused and pushed up her sunglasses. "The altitude can affect people differently, so you should try to stay hydrated, eat carbs, and let your body get used to being at this elevation."

"I will. And thank you." Dana's breath caught as she stared up into Kellen's eyes. She licked her lips. "Not just for the advice, but for everything you've done. Introducing me to Bogart, changing my flat tire, providing incredible coffee, then leading me here and making sure I made it in one piece. I really can't thank you enough."

"Not a problem. Bogart and I enjoyed meeting you and helping you out."

"I enjoyed meeting you both as well." Uncharacteristically at a loss for words, Dana looked down at her hands before meeting Kellen's gaze once again. "Um, so I was wondering. I—I plan on being around for a while. Possibly even for good. So maybe I could buy you a drink sometime, as a way to say thanks. Or even dinner?"

Kellen silently studied her before giving a slow nod. "Sounds nice," she said and started to ease away.

"Wait. Kellen? I don't know how to get in touch with you."

"That's a problem with an easy resolution." As Kellen spoke, a ghost of a smile appeared. "Do you have your cell phone handy?"

Dana passed Kellen her cell phone and watched her input a number. "That's not going to connect me to the local pizza place, is it?"

Kellen's laugh was soft and low. *Sexy.* "Not to say Up the Creek doesn't make some of the best pizza in town, but that would be mean. I believe a woman should be honest if she's interested. Besides, Haven is a small town and you'll discover pretty quickly I'm easy to find."

Dana watched Kellen's retreat as her long strides took her back to her Jeep. She saw her hold the door open letting Bogart scamper in, then slip into the driver's seat. A moment later, the Jeep eased back onto the road, heading for Haven.

By the time Dana restarted her engine and slipped back into gear, Kellen was gone. She'd somehow managed to disappear in a small town with one main street and what appeared to be a warren of side streets. Driving slowly through town, Dana briefly admired the old-fashioned light posts before turning her attention to each side street that she passed. But she saw only historic buildings, quaint low-rise hotels, and high-end condos.

There were plenty of SUVs and four-wheel-drive vehicles in sight. Plenty of people carrying skis or shopping bags, strolling in and out of the shops and restaurants. But there was no sign of Kellen or her bright green Jeep.

Shrugging off a sense of disappointment, Dana pulled over and found herself staring at her phone. On impulse, she reached for it and, with her heart beating faster, dialed the number Kellen had entered.

"Were you testing to make sure the number I gave you was real?" Amusement laced Kellen's voice.

Dana felt her face grow hot and she released a resigned breath. "I'm sorry. I just—I don't know what I was thinking. How did you know it was me?"

"Call it instinct. Or caller ID." Kellen laughed softly, warm and amused. "It's all right, Dana. You don't know me well enough yet to know you can believe what I say."

Dana wasn't sure what else was said. But by the time she hung up, she was feeling better and able to focus on following the simple directions Annie had given her, determined to make it to her destination.

Drive straight through town...you'll come to a Y...left takes you higher up into the mountains. You want to stay right, and when you can't go any farther, you'll be here.

Annie had been correct. The road ended at a driveway and a sign that read: *Alpine Search-and-Rescue.*

Parking her car near the front door by a sign that identified the main office, Dana took a deep, satisfied breath and looked up with pleasure at what would be her home for the foreseeable future. The rustic construction—natural woodwork, stone, and glass—made the buildings seem as if they had sprung from the hillside fully formed.

Like the mountains surrounding them, the buildings were a fitting part of the whole. When she stepped inside, she found the same sense of rightness and, more surprisingly, felt a sense of belonging.

The large front office featured beamed ceilings and smooth plank floors, and was filled with obviously handcrafted furniture.

One wall promised incredible vistas from floor-to-ceiling windows, while in another a fire burned in a large stone fireplace, filling the office with a welcoming warmth.

The girl at the desk, tall and in her late teens or early twenties with dark blue eyes and nearly black hair, looked up as Dana approached. "Dr. Kingston?"

"That's me, but I'd prefer to be called Dana, if that's all right."

The girl smiled shyly and for an instant an image of Kellen flashed in Dana's mind. A sister?

"Dana works. I'm Cody. Annie asked me to let her know as soon as you got here. I think she was starting to get worried, but we told her you'd probably just been delayed by the weather. If you leave me your car keys, I'll bring your bags to your cabin and make sure you've got enough firewood."

My cabin? Dana handed her keys to Cody. An instant later she was gone, disappearing through a doorway with only the echo of footsteps to mark her passing.

For a moment, Dana stared at where the girl had been. But with no idea how long she might have to wait, she shrugged and walked over to the windows, using whatever time she'd been granted to acquaint herself with her surroundings.

Much as she expected, the building housing the front office indeed provided spectacular views of both the town and the towering mountains. The snow had all but stopped, and she suddenly understood why Annie had said she would quickly fall in love with this place. With her eyes fixed on a distant mountain peak, Dana couldn't imagine a more incredible sight.

The landscape spread out before her—fields of endless white, forests of snow-draped trees with their branches hanging low to the ground, and the dark, jagged peaks of the mountains, outlined against the pewter sky.

It was perfect. Tranquil. And exactly what she needed to counter the chaos her life had been for the last few years. She sighed contentedly and, almost of their own accord, the knotted muscles in the back of her neck began to relax.

As she stared at the panorama, she tried to recall what Annie had said about housing. Somehow Dana had imagined it would end up being a tiny apartment in town, and after sharing a small flat in New York with two other doctors, just having a space to call her own would have been fine. But having a cabin to herself? That sounded unbelievable.

"Dana?"

She turned to find Annie standing directly behind her. Her dark hair was pulled up in a loose knot, there was a warm smile on her face, and she was casually dressed in jeans and a bright red sweatshirt that read: *The difficult we do immediately. The impossible takes a little longer.*

Dana liked the sentiment. She grinned widely, and as she moved toward her, she extended her hand. Annie took it, then drew her into a welcoming hug.

"I'm so glad you're finally here. I've spent the better part of the day trying to picture the little girl I hired from the East Coast driving through these mountains in a snowstorm, and I have to tell you, it wasn't a pretty picture."

Dana laughed. "I'm fairly certain I don't qualify as a little girl anymore."

"I don't know about that." The corners of Annie's eyes crinkled as she gently smiled. "But if you don't mind me asking, what have you been doing with yourself since I last saw you? What the devil did you do to your hand?"

Dana stared for a moment at the cast on her right hand, feeling unreleased emotions burning her throat. She remembered the commotion in the ER as a wounded and bleeding prisoner got away from his police escort. She remembered the crazed look in his eyes as he grabbed her and demanded she give him drugs for his pain. And she remembered finding herself on the bottom of a scrum with two police officers, a couple of hospital security guards, and her would-be patient on top of her.

When she looked up, Annie was studying her with quiet concern. "A small accident during my last shift at the hospital," Dana murmured. "The good news is the cast can come off in a couple of days."

"So that's your story and you're sticking to it?" Annie chuckled, but a hint of real sympathy softened her tone.

"Yup. Mm-hmm."

"Well, all right for now," Annie conceded. "But as soon as you're settled in, I want you to make an appointment to see Gabe. He's one of our paramedics and also serves as our resident physical therapist. He's young but he's good and we have great expectations for those hands of yours. He'll make sure you're in top working order in no time."

"Sounds like a plan."

Annie's smile slowly faded as she continued to study Dana's face. "You really were much later than I thought you'd be. Late enough that I was getting worried. Did you have any problems on the road?"

Dana attempted a casual shrug, but only half succeeded. "A bit. My front tire blew about an hour or so out of town."

"I know that stretch of road." Annie's eyes narrowed a fraction. "Not exactly the place I'd choose for a blow-out at the best of times, let alone in a snowstorm. And you with a broken wing. How on earth did you manage to deal with that?"

"An angel came to my rescue."

"Pardon me?"

Dana's smile widened. "You won't believe this, but an amazing, gorgeous woman appeared out of nowhere. She served me the most incredible chocolate-infused coffee I've ever tasted and changed my tire for me while I stayed warm and dry in her vehicle. And if that wasn't enough, she drove in front of me all the way into town to make sure I didn't have any more problems."

"That sounds wonderful. I'm so glad you were able to get help. And you sound slightly smitten. How did you let this paragon get away from you?"

"Yes. Me too. Maybe. And actually, I didn't let her get away. Not completely, anyway." Dana's mouth twisted into a wry grin. "Before she went on her way, I told her I'd like to buy her a drink—or dinner—to thank her for helping me out. And I'm happy to say she said yes."

"And you hadn't even gotten here yet? You New Yorkers certainly move fast. But I had a feeling about you and I'm pleased if it gives you yet another reason to want to stay here. So you're going to call her?"

Dana started to laugh. "Of course. I just think I should wait until I get a bit settled. In any case, she did say she'd be pretty easy for me to find, so I assume that means she's a local."

"Even better. What's her name? Maybe I know her."

"Her name's Kellen. Nice, don't you think?" She paused and couldn't help but notice the state change in Annie's expression. "Annie? Is something wrong? Is there a problem?"

"Dana?" Annie's voice sounded rational and calm. "What did Kellen look like? Can you describe her for me?"

"Of course." Dana was surprised by the question, but she could read nothing in Annie's expression. "She's a little taller than me. Long, lean body. Has dark hair down to her shoulders, an amazing face, and killer blue eyes. Actually, she looks a lot like Cody, the young woman I met at the front desk. And she had a dog with her. A—"

"A black and silver long-haired German shepherd named Bogart."

"You do know her." Dana swallowed.

Annie nodded and a smile reappeared on her face. "I would hope so. Her full name is Kellen Ryan and you're right. She is local and she is gorgeous. She also happens to be my dearest friend as well as the managing partner here at Alpine Search-and-Rescue."

"Annie?" *Oh, shit. I'm so screwed.* Concern and embarrassment edged Dana's voice. "Annie, please tell me I didn't just hit on my new boss and ask her out for drinks."

Annie started to laugh and once she started, she couldn't seem to stop.

"Annie, damn it, please. This isn't funny."

"Oh yes, it is," Annie replied, still laughing. "But it's not you I'm laughing at, Dana. It's Kellen. More to the point, it's the fact that she said yes. You have no idea how happy knowing that just made me."

Dana inwardly groaned. "I'm glad you're happy."

"I am, believe me." Annie paused and tried to take a calming breath. "I'm sorry. It's just that I've been worried about Kellen for too long. And technically, just so you know, she's not really your boss."

"She's not really my boss?"

"I know you're confused, but I promise I'll explain everything. For now, why don't we go into town for dinner? My treat. Everything sounds so much better over a glass of wine. And once you're settled, I'll make a point to have you over for dinner so you can meet my partner, Lesley."

"Lesley?"

Annie nodded. "Lesley Marlow. She's a writer."

"Oh God. Are you kidding? I think I have every book she's published. I think she's wonderful."

"I think so too." Annie paused then grinned. "Maybe we can invite Kellen as well."

❖

When Kellen pulled in to the main parking area at Alpine, the first thing she saw was a sleek black BMW 650i. She smiled as she drove past, heading behind the main building and past the recreation center before turning right onto a winding lane. It was narrow and sheltered, with towering trees on both sides, their branches bent under the weight of the recent snowfall. But it was wide enough for her Jeep to get through, which meant the girls—Cody and Ren—had done a great job of clearing it for her.

She'd have to do something special for them as a way to say thank you. Maybe plan a training session on the climbing wall they loved so much. Fun with ropes, followed by a night out at Up the Creek. Pizza, music, and a few games of pool. The longer she thought about it, the more it sounded like a plan.

Bogart started to bark as she reached the secluded cabins they'd had built on the property. She'd been pleased with the end result, glad they'd managed to maintain as natural a setting as possible, leaving each cabin shielded from the others by a wall of trees. It made for a perfect place to relax and enjoy the wraparound deck at each cabin, with nothing more than birdsong and the occasional chipmunk to break the silence.

Or dogs.

No sooner had she pulled in front of the last cabin and let him out than the cabin door opened and Cody and Ren raced out, their laughter as Bogart greeted them sounding like music to Kellen's ears.

Ren, with auburn hair and moss-green eyes, was growing more lovely with each passing day as she gained confidence. She was also the more openly affectionate of the two, evidenced by the bone-crushing hug she gave Kellen.

"I missed you. Next time, just so you know, I'm going with you. That way, I don't have to miss you. Now, what did Doc Susan say? Is Bogart going to be okay?"

Cody, whose dark hair and blue eyes were enough of a mirror image of Kellen that they were often mistaken for sisters, hung back a little. But only a little. "It's good to have you home, Kel."

"I'm glad to be home." Kellen smiled. "And Bogart's going to be fine. You know I only took him to Denver because he behaves better for Susan when he's getting checked out than he does for Jen here in town."

Cody and Ren nodded, and on the surface, they seemed happy enough. But Kellen instinctively felt something was off—with both girls. "Okay," she said as they entered her cabin, leaving Bogart to burn up some of his boundless energy outside. "Which one of you is going to tell me what's wrong?"

The two girls looked at each other and immediately busied themselves, bringing in firewood from the deck and building a fire to warm up the cabin. Finally, Cody looked up. "How do you do that?"

"You should know by now I can read your minds." Kellen grinned before conceding, "But only to a point. Now tell me what's going on. What's got the two of you upset? Did something happen while I was gone?"

Another prolonged silence followed, during which neither girl would make eye contact with her. Kellen's nerves began to twitch before Cody spoke once again. "A cop came by yesterday. He was asking for you."

Kellen stiffened. She knew her smile slowly faded, but she hoped she didn't allow any of what she was feeling to come through in her voice. "Did he say what he wanted with me?"

Cody shook her head unhappily while Ren looked almost on the verge of tears. "He just said he needed to talk to you right away. Said that it's really important. But he wouldn't tell us why. Probably thought we were just dumb kids."

"Kellen, are you in trouble?" Ren asked in a small voice. "Do we need to leave?"

At least, Kellen thought wryly, they no longer seemed to worry that she'd leave without them. To anyone else, it might not seem like a lot, but it was definitely progress.

Then she turned and glanced at the small front closet. The one that held a backpack with carefully chosen items. Jeans, T-shirts, some cash, several passports. Just in case she ever needed to leave in a hurry. In case she ever needed to run.

It was a habit she'd not managed to break, even after all these years of being settled in one place. Here. The first place that had ever felt like home in too many years to count. How could she expect to help the girls move forward when she hadn't been able to help herself?

"Kellen?" Ren's voice broke through her tangled thoughts.

"Do you want to leave?" she asked softly.

Both girls shook their heads. "No."

"Good, because I don't want to leave either," she said. A rush of emotions swept over her and she held out her hands. Both girls reached for her and she pulled them into her arms, holding them tight. "This is our home. No one—no cop—is going to tell us differently. Trust me. I'll talk to Annie and find out what she knows. Then I'll talk to this cop. And if there's a problem, I'll take care of it. Fix it. Just like always. Okay?"

Both girls nodded. There was gratitude on their faces, not something Kellen ever wanted to see. But she would deal with that later. For now, she could feel their fear start to dissipate, and that was all that counted.

A long moment passed before Ren spoke again. "The new doctor Annie hired arrived this afternoon. I didn't see her, but Cody talked to her. Her name's Dana and Cody says she seems really nice."

"She's also hot," Cody added with a grin. "Of course, she's older than us. I think more like your age. Maybe you should check her out. Then, if you like her and she likes you, maybe—"

Kellen narrowed her eyes. "Maybe what?"

Surprisingly, both girls giggled. "Maybe then you won't have to be alone all the time. You need someone, Kel. Like I have Ren."

Kellen scratched a nonexistent itch on the back of her neck and released a soft laugh. "How can I possibly be alone when I've got the two of you looking after me?" She looked from one girl to the other, realized that in spite of the teasing they were actually serious, and decided she needed to quickly change the subject. "How about we go to town for some pizza?"

CHAPTER THREE

The music playing as Dana walked into Up the Creek was just right. Loud and lively enough that she could feel it in her blood, low enough that people could still have conversations. The scent of barbecue and the sound of laughter filled the air, and the decor was truly eclectic—antique ski gear on the walls, comfortable chairs and love seats set up in groups, tables filled with pitchers of beer and platters of wings.

Perfect.

"I hope you're not disappointed," Annie said. They'd been seated in a relatively quiet corner near the back by the pool tables and dartboards. A server brought them two frosty mugs of beer and left menus behind. "There are quite a number of really good restaurants in town, but for some reason, I thought—"

"This is perfect, Annie. Exactly what I wanted and I didn't even know it."

"I'm glad, because more times than not, this just happens to be where most team members come when they want to unwind."

Deciding to wait before ordering, they chatted easily over their beer. Annie explained more of the organizational structure at Alpine. She also introduced her to various locals who stopped to say hello. It seemed everyone had an opinion about the clinic, and there was also a great deal of pride in how Alpine's growth and success had put Haven on the map. Especially from financial backers like the mayor and her wife.

"I have to say, this is the most gay-friendly town I've seen outside of Provincetown," Dana murmured. "In some ways, I feel like I've fallen down a rabbit hole."

"It's a great place to live and let live." Annie smiled. "And no offense, because I knew the moment I met you that I'd offer you the position, but the fact you were quite open about yourself didn't hurt."

"No offense taken, because I knew the moment I met you that I wanted the opportunity you were offering. I just didn't want there to be any misconceptions or disappointments."

As far as Dana was concerned, she'd already spent far too much time dealing with the aftermath of disappointing people. Enough to last a lifetime.

She could still see the carefully controlled disbelief on her parents' faces and hear the disappointment in their voices when she'd announced she was opting not to follow her father's footsteps in cardiology. And then she'd exacerbated the situation by moving beyond their sphere of influence and control to New York and taking a job in an inner-city hospital emergency room.

Her mother had sighed and told her she was being selfish. For what? Dana wanted to know. For refusing to continue pushing her own happiness aside for them? For wanting to live her own life, on her own terms, putting her own interests first?

Even though it was an old refrain, the hurt still cut deep. It wasn't that she didn't care about disappointing her parents. She did. But she'd waited a long time before asserting control over her own life and now they would all have to find a way to deal.

"That sounds like someone else I know," Annie said. "And speak of the devil..."

"What?" Dana turned her head and saw Kellen standing just inside the door, radiating energy and talking to the hostess, while the two girls who'd come in with her shook snow off their parkas.

Dana immediately recognized one of them. Cody, who'd been working the front desk. The other girl looked to be around the same age—late teens, early twenties.

"Do you mind if I invite them to join us?" Annie asked.

"Not at all." It was close enough to the truth. "I know Cody, Kellen's young doppelgänger, but I've not met the other girl."

Annie clearly found the description amusing. "Doppelgänger's an apt description for young Cody in that she can be just as stubborn as Kellen. The other girl's Ren. You'll seldom see one without the other, and if you see Kellen, the girls are seldom far behind."

Dana knew the instant the group headed their way in response to Annie's wave, and found herself watching Kellen's reflection approaching in an antique mirror on the wall. Dressed in jeans and a navy blue long-sleeved Henley, Kellen's eyes were bright with amusement and she was laughing at something one of the girls said. The sound of her laughter whispered along Dana's skin.

By the time introductions were completed, Cody and Ren—clearly a couple, judging by the possessive way they touched—had taken the love seat across from Dana, leaving Kellen no choice but to drop down beside Dana, under the watchful eyes of everyone at the table.

Kellen groaned softly.

Concerned, Dana turned to face her. "Are you okay? Is something wrong?"

Releasing a low laugh, Kellen shook her head. "Not exactly, as long as you don't mind having your every move watched and critiqued."

Dana glanced at the girls, who were momentarily distracted while checking out the menu. "I'm not sure I understand."

"I'm sorry. But once they get something in their heads, there's no stopping them."

"Should I know what you're talking about?" she asked. "What specifically do you think is in their heads?"

"Matchmaking."

For an instant, Dana simply froze, staring at the wry grin on Kellen's face. "Matchmaking?"

"That's right. Surely you've heard of it? It's the process of matching two people together—"

"I know what the word means." Dana frowned at her. "I just don't understand what it has to do with us. You and me. And why it matters to the girls."

"It matters to the girls because they're in love and therefore they think everyone should be." The faintest smile curved her lips as Kellen explained, "Apparently, they got it in their heads that I shouldn't be alone around the same time you came along, and it gave them ideas. We're both of a certain age—"

"Thirty-five."

"Thirty-two, so close enough. We also both happen to be unattached—um, you are unattached, aren't you?"

"Of course. I'm quite single. Sweet Jesus, I wouldn't have asked you out for drinks if I wasn't."

Kellen's smile widened and she leaned in closer. "There is that, although I need to tell you. This impromptu gathering doesn't count. I believe you still owe me drinks. And maybe dinner."

"All right. I'll give that some serious thought," Dana countered, faintly surprised that Kellen was flirting with her, and pleased at the same time. "In the meantime, what are we supposed to do about... expectations?"

"That depends. Mostly, I suggest we take it one day at a time. The girls will eventually get bored and move on to something else. And in the meantime, you and I will get to know each other, learn to work together, and end up somewhere along the continuum between hating each other and falling madly in love."

"That simple?"

"Yup. Life is complicated enough. Most of the time, it's best to take it one day at a time. Kind of like survival," she said softly. "And here's your first clue to surviving in the new environment you find yourself. The girls eat fish and eggs, but not meat or chicken, so we're ordering a vegetarian pizza. But if ribs or chicken wings are your thing, like they are Annie's, go ahead and order. It won't present a problem."

Dana raised her eyebrows. "And you? What side of the great meat divide do you fall on?"

"I'm much like the girls. I must say I love fish, especially salmon, but I don't eat meat of any kind. That said, I'd never judge someone else by what they like to eat and, heaven forbid, I'd never stand between Annie and her teriyaki chicken wings."

"I'll have to keep it in mind. You know, in the event I invite you for dinner."

"Touché." Kellen tilted her head back and raised a brow. "So tell me, Dana. Do you play pool?"

"Yes, but I haven't played in ages, and with this cast, I'm likely not going to be very good."

"Good to know." Kellen grinned and leaned closer once again. "And there, see how easy this is? Just like survival. We'll have a game in a bit, but because we're going to be working together, I feel I should warn you. Cody is a bit of a pool shark, so watch out for her."

❖

Over the next couple of hours, Kellen consumed more pizza than was strictly necessary, but she'd lost track while sharing in the laughter and banter at the table. She'd have to add twenty laps in the pool to her workout routine in the morning. But she had to admit, it had been a long time since she'd had such an enjoyable evening, so it made the prospect of an additional workout well worth it.

The warmth of genuine affection, small talk, and lots of laughter were like a balm for her soul, enabling her to push aside the detritus of the past that had been stirred by Cody's earlier comment. About a cop looking for her. And by Ren's fear that they would have to leave this place that had become a home for all of them.

The girls looked like they were having fun. And, in spite of her own innate reticence and wariness with strangers, she was finding Dana not just attractive, but remarkably easy to talk to.

Eventually, Cody stood and issued a teasing challenge. "Who's up for some pool? Kel?"

"Sure." Kellen turned to Dana and extended her hand. "Shall we take on this youngster and show her how it's done?" She couldn't read the expression on Dana's face but was pleased when she accepted the hand she'd offered and allowed Kellen to help her up. "You mentioned it's been a while. Do you want to practice a bit first?"

Dana grinned. "I doubt it will do me much good, so why don't we just go for it. What are the stakes?"

Before Kellen could respond, Cody jumped in. "How about a dollar a ball? Does that sound okay?"

Kellen frowned and stared at Cody, but the young woman ignored her while Dana considered the possibilities. "Fifteen balls, fifteen dollars. I think I can manage that." She accepted the cue Cody offered her and began to chalk it.

"Why don't you break, Dr. Kingston," Cody said, clearly feeling gracious, while Kellen racked the balls. "The game is eight ball. Do you know it?"

"Thanks, I'd be happy to break. And if you remember, you agreed to call me Dana." She looked at the table. "Eight ball? If I remember correctly, once I break, I'll be assigned either stripes or solids, assuming I sink something."

"That's right," Cody responded with a small grin and rattled off the rest of the rules.

"Sounds about right." Dana took a moment to steady herself, then bent over the table and took her first shot. She sank three balls on the break. Moving around the table, she leaned over, narrowed her eyes to determine the best angle, and neatly sank the next ball.

She picked up her beer, took a quick sip, and went back to work. Assessing her next move, and the one after that, she proceeded to run the table, knocking in a succession of solid balls with ease.

"Nice run," Kellen murmured.

"Thanks." Dana chalked her cue one more time and called her final shot, striking the eight ball and sending it cleanly into the corner pocket. "I believe that's fifteen dollars each of you owes me."

While the others cheered, Kellen started to laugh and wrapped one arm around Cody's shoulder. "Cody, I think we've just been hustled."

❖

Shortly after the pool game ended, the unexpected evening also came to an end. Kellen settled the bill with the hostess, gathered the girls and their coats, waved and headed out into the cold.

Dana and Annie followed more slowly, shivering as they climbed into Annie's SUV. Stars were beginning to show through the wisps of cloud overhead and they both sat looking up as they waited for the vehicle to warm up, lost in their own thoughts.

"You're going to be so good for her," Annie said, breaking the comfortable silence.

"Oh Lord, Annie." Dana didn't bother pretending she didn't know what Annie meant. "Don't tell me you're going for the less-than-subtle matchmaking, too? And you can stop grinning while you're at it."

"I'm sorry," she responded, but she didn't sound sorry at all. "I need you to know, it wasn't ever my intention to set anything up this evening or to make you feel uncomfortable in any way. But I have to admit, I thought what the girls were doing was cute."

"Cute?"

"They love Kellen and just want what's best for her, as do I. And you did tell me you hit on her before you had any idea who she was, so you had to be interested."

"I did. She's smoking hot." She met Annie's eyes calmly so she would know she spoke the truth. "I was. And no one made me feel uncomfortable."

"Good. I'm glad. And I did tell you how pleased I was that Kellen showed some interest in return, didn't I?"

"Yes, you did," Dana said with something like a sigh. She opened her mouth to speak but stopped, knowing Annie wouldn't understand the doubts that came from years of dancing to someone else's tune.

"Don't think about it too much. Tonight was a good start. For everyone. We're all going to be working closely and it generally works best if we can get along. That's all that matters for now." Annie's brow creased. "I do have one question for you, though."

"Yes?"

"After spending some time with Kellen and the girls, and hopefully recognizing that they come as a package deal, are you still interested?"

There was no question. It was a hell of a package. Caring, compassionate, intelligent, and sexy with a heart-stopping face.

Dana looked down at her hands for a moment. "The simple answer is yes, but I'll be honest and tell you I don't know what that means."

"It means whatever you want it to mean."

Dana considered her words. "Annie, Kellen and I really don't know each other. An initial interest on both sides doesn't mean we'll fit well, if at all. And while I wouldn't mind taking a chance, finding out more, everything seems to be happening too fast."

"New job, new place, new interest?"

"Yes. I find myself in unfamiliar territory and I think I'm afraid I'll make the wrong decision. Make the wrong move. I need to find *where* I fit first, get my feet planted firmly under me, and that doesn't leave much time for anything else. Like finding out *who* might fit with me."

"Can I share a bit of personal history?"

"Of course."

"My mother once told me she knew my father was the one for her within an hour of meeting him. They were living together a month after they met. I laughed it off at the time. And then I met Lesley. I felt it instantly, but I wasted ten years we might have enjoyed together fighting who I was and what I thought was expected. Believing my choices would hurt the people I loved only to discover my parents just wanted me to be happy." Annie reached over and squeezed Dana's hand. "It was your instincts that brought you here to Haven, Dana. Keep trusting them."

Chapter Four

Kellen awoke with a start. There was a scream trapped in her throat, her heart was pounding, her skin was damp with sweat, and Bogart's cold nose was pressed against her hand. Bringing her back. Reassuring her. Grounding her.

Bogart nuzzled closer. Without saying a word, she scratched his head and let him know she was all right, although the taste of fear lingered. She'd wondered once how he knew, but decided gifts weren't necessarily meant to be understood, only accepted.

Eyes gritty from too little sleep, she blinked several times and waited until her vision adjusted to the relative darkness that enveloped her. The cabin was filled with shadows blurring the details, the only source of illumination provided by the glowing embers of the fire she'd built a couple of hours ago.

She didn't need more light than that to know only ghosts stirred in the stillness. But she stared at her hands nonetheless, reassuring herself the blood she'd seen moments before had only been there in her dream.

She'd known from past experience it was likely going to be a rough night. Ever since Cody had mentioned the cop that had come by asking for her, there'd been too much adrenaline and energy crashing around inside her. Too much fear. Too many memories. Too many consequences.

There was also more than a bit of annoyance, because she'd yet to deal with the issue head-on. Yet to ask Annie what she might know. And it wasn't as if she hadn't had a chance. But after coming back from dinner with the team the previous evening, she'd pleaded tiredness and called it a day.

She'd walked with the girls as far as their cabin, then tried all the usual tools at her disposal, much as she did when things got rough. She headed to the recreation center. The gym was a source of personal pride and boasted state-of-the-art equipment and a challenging climbing wall, while the newest section included a selection of auto belayers, which meant she could work alone.

She spent time on the climbing wall. Swam laps in the pool. Did everything she could to wear herself out so the nightmares would be kept at bay. But nothing had helped. Not even warm thoughts of the new doctor. Dana Kingston, of the fair hair, incredibly deep brown eyes, endless legs, and gentle humor.

In the end, Kellen headed back to her cabin with Bogart. Hoping for the best. But when she finally managed to fall asleep, her demons crept out of the shadows where they'd been waiting for her.

That was the problem with memories. They lived in her mind and there was no outrunning them.

Her saving grace was Bogart. He'd pulled her out of the nightmare that held her in its grasp. Stayed beside her while the beat of his heart drove the remaining images away. Just like he always did.

Kellen knew most people would find it strange, at best, if they knew the truth. But for some inexplicable reason, she had a connection with Bogart. She'd sensed it from the moment she spotted him on the interstate. He had just escaped the rear wheels of a southbound semi and stood shaking on the side of the road. Young, emaciated, half-frozen.

Not that different from the girls, the first time she laid eyes on them.

She'd pulled over and somehow rescued him. Barely dodging a speeding SUV, she managed to grab him, coming away with nothing more than torn jeans and skinned knees. She'd then tucked the shivering pup inside her sweatshirt, sharing her body heat with him while she took him to see a vet she knew in Denver.

Susan had shrugged when she saw Kellen at her door with a bedraggled puppy of questionable parentage in her hands. Without saying a word, she examined the pup thoroughly and declared him surprisingly healthy, albeit malnourished and underweight. Together they'd then cleaned him up and discovered that beneath the filth was a likely purebred German shepherd puppy, maybe eight weeks old, with bright trusting eyes. The pup had looked up at the two women and had unerringly chosen Kellen. Crawled into her arms, licked her neck, and promptly gone to sleep.

In that moment, she knew he'd chosen her as much as she had chosen him. Just as she knew the two of them would be going home to Haven together. He needed a home. And she had one to share.

Bogart had paid Kellen back for his life a thousand times over. He'd grown into an incredible dog. Beautiful, intelligent, and tireless. Along the way, he'd insinuated himself into every aspect of her life, taking to canine search-and-rescue training as if he'd been born to it.

But more important, he had an innate ability to sense her moods and could bring her out of a bad spell with a lick or a nudge of his nose. Even when she'd been hospitalized. Somehow Annie had pulled off a minor miracle, convincing the staff that it would be in the best interest of both patient and dog to allow Bogart into her room. And there he'd remained, watching over her, comforting her, until she was strong enough to leave the hospital.

Unconditional love, Kellen thought wryly. She would have laughed if anyone had told her she'd ever get unconditional love. And not only from Bogart, but from Cody and Ren, who offered it to her each and every day in so many different ways. As did Annie, for that matter. Pretty damned amazing, especially for someone who'd grown up not knowing love of any kind.

Resigned to the truth that sleep would not be returning, Kellen crawled out from under the duvet and padded on unsteady legs to the kitchen. Trying not to think or do anything beyond what had become an everyday routine. She turned on the coffeemaker she'd prepared before going to bed, fed Bogart, and let him out. Then with nothing left to do, she headed to the shower.

Once there, sitting on the tiles with her knees drawn up against her chest and her head pressed to her knees, Kellen let the water beat down on her and hoped it would wash away the remnants of her dream. Hoped it would wash away the blood and the fear and the horror. She deliberately blanked her mind, concentrating on her breathing until she was conscious only of the heat enveloping her, cocooning her as it wrapped heated arms around her.

But she was still cold.

Twenty minutes later, she'd prepared a thermos of coffee and was dressed with silk long johns under her jeans, thick socks in her boots, a black turtleneck, and a black down-filled vest. She opened the door and was hit by a brief, fierce surge of passion.

Haven was still shrouded in darkness as she inhaled the cold air infused with pine. She felt it chill her face. Saw the remnant of the moon still visible in the sky. Felt the pines and spruce trees surround her, tall, but not high enough to block the beauty of the rugged mountains.

At thirty-two, she had traveled extensively. Lived in large cities and small towns, slept in alleys, in cars, and under bridges. She had never before understood how anyone could feel connected to one place.

But here? As she stood mesmerized by her surroundings, she felt sheltered. Protected. And here she welcomed the dawning of a new day. She stood still. Let her senses swim and enjoyed the bite of the cold as she listened to the sound of the silence.

And then her radio squawked.

Automatically reaching for it, Kellen mentally prepared herself to face whatever the new day was bringing.

Dana awoke, not to the familiar sounds of car alarms and sirens and traffic, but to birdsong. She lay still for a moment, listening with pleasure to the lilting call near her window before opening her eyes.

The morning sun streamed through the slatted blinds, painting pale stripes of gray over the tumbled bedding, and letting her know she had slept much later than usual. But she didn't care because she also realized she was smiling and, try as she might, she couldn't remember a time in her past when she'd awoken every day with a smile on her face.

The air that she breathed was still and cold, but under the duvet she was cozy and warm all the way to her soul. Content.

Not surprising, she thought, because her first week in Haven had been filled with hard work and unexpected moments of fun and laughter, as she got to know the new people in her life. Consequently, for the past week, she'd enjoyed the most peaceful nights' sleep she'd experienced in a very long time.

Maybe because she knew she didn't have to get up and face long lines of people with gunshot and knife wounds waiting for medical attention in the ER.

Far more likely because she knew while life in Haven was still quite foreign to her, that couldn't detract from the feeling she'd had since her arrival. The feeling of homecoming.

It helped that the people she'd met so far neither knew nor cared about who her father was or what the expectations had been for her before her arrival. All they cared was she was the newest member of the Alpine team, a qualified doctor bearing Annie's stamp of approval, and someone ready to add medical skills and expertise to their expanding search-and-rescue efforts.

Even more surprising, all they seemingly wanted in return was for her to approach her new life in Haven and everyone she encountered with acceptance and an open mind as she got to know them.

Stretching lazily, Dana scratched her arm, finally blessedly cast free, and turned to thoughts of one person in particular, the enigmatic head of Alpine Search-and-Rescue. She already knew Kellen was someone who was going to make her new life a hell of a lot more interesting than she'd envisioned. Definitely someone she was looking forward to getting to know much better.

She thought back to a singular moment after a team meeting, watching as Kellen chewed a bite of pizza, half closing her eyes in sensual appreciation as the flavors danced across her tongue. It was the first time in her life Dana had experienced jealousy. And of a damned slice of pizza, no less.

But behind the confident stride and sexy smile, she also sensed a very private woman when she looked at Kellen, one not easily moved to trust. So it would take time. And that was okay. If she had an abundance of anything right now, it was time. Time to get settled, time to feel comfortable, time to figure things out.

The cabin, as it turned out, also strengthened her feelings of finding a home, having far exceeded any expectations she might have had. Spotless and cheerful, it had come furnished with a large comfortable sofa, a couple of overstuffed chairs, and a fully functional fireplace. She looked forward to spending quiet evenings in front of the fire while it snowed outside.

Cody had pointed out the propane heater in the corner of the bedroom, but had assured her that the fireplace would probably generate all the heat she would ever want or need. And Cody and Ren ensured she had plenty of firewood, neatly stacked on the deck just outside her front door.

It was a need for caffeine that finally drew her from the comfort of her bed. After a wonderfully hot shower, she quickly dressed in jeans and a heavy Irish-knit sweater. Quite a change from hospital scrubs, she thought, as she finished off her new look by putting on the hiking boots she'd bought while in town with Annie. She tried to remember if she'd ever owned hiking boots. Probably not, but Annie had said they were essential.

Thinking of essentials, Dana wandered into the kitchen, only to discover she was out of coffee. With a sigh, she grabbed her jacket and headed for the door.

She blinked when she stepped out of her cabin into sunshine and stared up, not yet used to the heart-stopping, magnificent view that surrounded her. The woods were beautifully inviting in the morning light, the black of the tree trunks and branches in stark contrast with the bluish white of the snow dusting the boughs and shawling the ground.

The air held a silence that was still alien to her and she drew in another breath, letting the scent of pine and crisp, clean mountain air fill her lungs, while the silence soothed her heart and her spirit. She wanted to laugh at the joy she felt just from the simple, clean scent.

As she started walking down the snow-covered lane toward the office, Dana spied what had to be animal tracks. A few she recognized as likely belonging to Bogart. Other tracks looked like maybe deer. And still others, she couldn't recognize at all.

She felt a keen urge to follow the tracks and explore her surroundings more than she already had, but first things first. She needed coffee.

And just maybe she'd see Kellen in the office and have another chance to get to know her better. Something she was looking forward to with admitted pleasure.

The river was angry. Swollen and dark, it was flowing faster and stronger than usual, thanks to the recent storm.

Kellen gritted her teeth. The water was bitterly cold and she could feel the icy temperature cut through her wetsuit, feel its sharp stings each time it splashed her face. She flinched as the pain registered. *Oh Jesus, that hurts.* It caused her chest to tighten as if gripped by a vise and was making it increasingly difficult to take a deep breath.

They'd been searching for a missing boy since dawn before finally spotting him. He was floating face down in the river. There was no time to waste and Kellen had plunged into the dark, frigid water the moment Tim had fastened the rescue harness on her.

Even then, she barely managed to catch the edge of the boy's jacket, holding on with all her strength before the current could carry him out of her reach. Somehow, she managed to secure him to the rescue rope, then wrapped her arms and legs around him.

Holding him against her chest, fighting to keep his head above water, something struck her side with a glancing blow, distracting her momentarily. A familiar childhood nightmare flashed in her mind. Monsters—in the closet, under the bed, under the water. It was only for a second or two, but enough that she slipped underwater.

She surfaced quickly, coughing violently, but could see what had hit her—one of several small trees the river had claimed.

She renewed her focus on the boy as the one solid reality in the tumbling, shocking, cold universe she was in, while trusting her team and the belay rope to stop them both from going downstream. She knew it didn't take long for hypothermia to kill, and she had no way of knowing how long the boy had been in the icy water.

Long enough, she feared.

He was completely unresponsive and his lips were blue. Kellen thought she might have felt a pulse, but it could have been wishful thinking. And he was so still, she wasn't even sure if he was breathing. But she needed to believe he was.

Even as she felt the beginning of a headache brought on by the cold, she found herself wishing there was more she could do. But she knew it was taking all she had just to hold their position and keep the boy's head above water. The world was fast becoming blurry, her arms ached, and she could no longer feel her hands or feet.

She was so damned cold. But she was equally determined to hold on. Time slowed to a crawl while she held the boy and waited. Almost seemed as if it had stopped. But finally help arrived.

Through the gray mist hanging like smoke over the river, she watched Jeff and Tim wade into the water, fighting against the fast-moving current as they moved toward her. Between them, they managed to get the boy attached to the tag line, then got him safely to the riverbank, where Kellen watched Gabe start CPR on the boy.

"Come on, Kel. You're turning blue. Let's get you out of here. Give me your hand."

She heard Tim's voice as if from a distance. Her headache had gotten worse, and as she slowly turned toward him, she connected with a hard, warm human hand that gripped her wrist. Beyond tired, she relaxed and was instantly buried in water. But Tim's hand was still there, solidly holding on, and she gratefully let him help her out of the water.

Chapter Five

As was becoming habitual, Cody was the first person to greet Dana at the office. "Good morning, Annie said to tell you she's in Incident Command."

Thanking her, Dana wandered down the hallway and listened to the muted sound of voices.

"Good morning," Annie said, looking up briefly. "Come on in. Help yourself to some coffee and grab a seat. We've got a missing thirteen-year-old boy, separated from his parents and younger brother while hiking before dawn this morning. We've had two teams out since first light—one in the air, the other on the ground on snowmobiles. One searching north, the other south of where the boy went missing."

Dana gratefully poured herself some coffee and thought the steam rising from the cup smelled like heaven. She grabbed the seat Annie had indicated and tried not to distract anyone as she watched over the rim of her mug.

It was then she realized she'd been so focused on overseeing the construction of the medical facilities that she was only now witnessing her first real search-and-rescue attempt. This was no simulation.

"We don't always know where to look," Annie resumed speaking a minute later, but her hands didn't stop working the keyboard. "But in this case, we have fairly reliable information about where the family was when they lost contact with the boy."

Looking over Annie's shoulder at a pair of computer screens, Dana could see lights blinking over what appeared to be a topographical map. But she had no idea what exactly Annie was seeing.

"Every team member has a transmitter as well as GPS on their radios," Annie explained without Dana needing to ask. "It lets us have both audio and visual on everyone in the field so we can track them."

Nodding, Dana continued to watch and listened to the intermittent radio transmissions coming in from the teams involved in the search. The sun was out, but the temperature was still hovering near freezing and she knew the recent storm had dumped a lot of snow on the terrain being searched.

But as she tried to envision where the search teams were, what they were seeing, she realized she had no frame of reference for what they were doing. She would make a point to ask Annie or Kellen to take her out with a search team. Maybe a couple of times—by land and in the air. That would help her better understand not only the physical demands on the teams, but the emotional and psychological demands as well.

"IC, team one, we have a sighting." The disembodied voice cut into Dana's thoughts, jarring her back to the present.

"Team one, IC," Annie said, studying a map on one of the computer screens more closely. "Can you confirm?"

The room grew strangely silent while they waited.

"Negative. Cannot confirm it's our target," the voice responded. "We're checking it out."

A short time later, Dana shared in the feeling of elation when team one confirmed they had located the missing boy. But the joy was short-lived. The next transmission indicated the boy was in a river. Facedown.

Dana could feel her heart pounding in her throat as she listened to the two teams synchronize their efforts in an attempt to reach the boy. She heard a familiar voice and realized Kellen was involved in the rescue, and that she was about to jump into a frigid, rapidly moving river.

She shivered at the thought. But as she watched and listened, more of what Annie had explained in New York began to make sense.

Alpine SAR was structured functionally into three inter-connected teams. Kellen headed the operations team and had overall responsibility for personnel, equipment, and operations from the time of a team's activation to its return home. She continuously assessed each situation as it unfolded, developed and implemented plans of action, and assigned resources.

Annie was the logistics team lead. She maintained Incident Command, their base of operations. She was charged with developing and maintaining communications plans and equipment, as well as managing communications with the sheriff's department and any other agencies involved in a search. She also managed logistical supply and resupply issues.

And Dana would be medical team lead. Her primary role was to oversee the new medical center once it was fully operational and provide onsite trauma management. That meant working closely with the paramedics that went out with the search teams and ensuring any injuries received prompt and appropriate emergency care before they were transported to a health-care facility for further evaluation and treatment.

She also had a second and equally important responsibility. She was meant to monitor the health of all Alpine personnel, which included not only the nutrition and hydration needs of the teams, but also their mental and psychological well-being. Looking for any signs of stress.

As an emergency medicine specialist, Dana knew all about the endorphin high. The post-rescue rush that left first responders amped. But emergency teams often found themselves thrown into situations beyond their control, and they also knew going in they were not going to win every time.

She remembered that from too many times in the emergency department. Feeling as if she'd been thrust into the middle of a battle zone. Fighting to save the life of yet another youth caught up in a turf war, believing he was invincible only to have his chest torn apart by bullets. Trying to put kids back together even as she watched their lifeblood flow from too many wounds to count and the light dim from their eyes.

Dana recognized she'd hit a wall in New York and knew she needed something different. Something that didn't involve moving back to Boston, working in her father's posh offices, and returning control over her life to her parents. She'd taken a risk when she'd accepted Annie's offer. But she was beginning to believe she just might have found what she needed.

Haven came with its own brand of drama. Here it was more likely to be a battle against nature. Storms. Floods. Fires. Avalanches. Even wildlife. More than enough to satisfy the adrenaline junkie in her, while equally enough to fill her need to make a difference. To help, even knowing she wasn't always going to win.

But knowing didn't make it any easier to deal when you didn't win.

Like today.

The tension around her became more tangible with each passing minute as they followed the rescue attempt from the warmth and safety of the dispatch room, from the moment Kellen jumped from the hovering helicopter into the freezing water until the boy was brought to the riverbank and CPR commenced.

Dana could also see and feel the increasing tension in Annie the longer Kellen remained in the frigid river, although her voice never betrayed any of what she was feeling. She continued to communicate calmly with the rescue teams, remaining externally calm and professional until well after an out-of-breath voice on the radio informed them the boy was dead.

Once the two field teams transmitted their intent to return to base, Annie asked the paramedic on board the helicopter—Gabe— to check Kellen and make sure she was all right. Then, after glancing around the room and making sure her team had support, she excused herself and left the room.

❖

The helicopter shuddered briefly as it lifted off, carrying team one and its sad cargo. Huddled under several blankets, Kellen barely noticed as silence filled her with the numbness of loss.

She couldn't stop shivering. Her headache had become full-blown, tensing the muscles in her neck. Her chest hurt, making it difficult to breathe. And her mind seemed incapable of concentrating on anything.

Alone for the moment with her muddled thoughts, she stared out the window, not really seeing the beauty of the snow-covered landscape passing below. Just doing her best not to think about the black bag carefully strapped in the rear cargo area.

She hated it when a mission failed to bring someone home alive. And thirteen—*damn*. That was way too young to wind up in a body bag as a result of misadventure.

By now Annie would have been in contact with the sheriff's department and the boy's parents. The parents, and someone from the county coroner's office, would be there to meet them once they landed, and the boy's body would be transferred into their care.

Kellen closed her eyes and continued to shiver.

"You might start feeling warmer in a week or so," Tim teased, placing a warm mug in her hands.

"What is this?" she asked moodily, staring at the mug.

"It's a hot toddy," he said. "Hot tea with a shot of Jack."

Kellen grimaced as she took a sip and felt the whiskey burn the back of her throat. "I hate Jack Daniel's."

Tim grinned. "Yeah, I know. But we were all out of cognac and you're going to drink it anyway. If nothing else, it'll help get you through the next little while—talking to the boy's parents and all."

Kellen took another sip and stared back out the window.

When?

More than anything, that was what she wanted to know. When had the boy died? Had they not acted quickly enough in getting him out of the water? Or had he been dead the whole time she held him in her arms, fighting to keep his head above water?

When?

"We all did everything we could," Gabe said, replacing Tim as he came and sat by her side. "We got here as quickly as we could, and even if we'd managed to get here sooner, it would have made no difference. It was over the moment he fell into the river. You know that."

As he spoke, he casually reached out and tried to check her pulse.

Kellen jerked her hand back. "Tell Annie I'm fine."

Gabe flashed a smile. "You may know that and I might even agree with you, but I figure if I can at least tell them I checked, that your pulse rate is fine all things considered, and that you're not hurting anywhere more so than usual, they'll listen to me. And maybe they'll give you enough room to do what you need to do when we land."

Kellen sighed and held out her arm. Felt Gabe's fingers, warm against her wrist, while his eyes assessed her. Looking for signs of new damage, no doubt.

"Your pulse is elevated, but that doesn't concern me as much as the fact you're a bit warm."

"Actually, I'm frozen all the way to my soul," she murmured.

"I hear you." Like the others on the team, Gabe understood, having been there a time or two. "But you're running a temp. Are you hurting anywhere more than usual?"

Kellen swallowed the last mouthful of tea as she looked at the body bag. "It's a low-grade fever. I drank some river water and my body's natural defenses are kicking in. So I'm good. Nothing hurts out of the ordinary. Just a headache. And certainly nothing compared to what his parents are going to be feeling."

"You're right," Gabe said thoughtfully. "I've never lost anyone close to me, but I would think it would be worse to lose a child."

"Not necessarily. Not all parents give a damn," she responded harshly before she could stop herself, as anger warred with old grief and heartache. She swore quietly, knowing she was tired and her filters were obviously not working.

"Shit." The muscles in Gabe's jaw pulled taut. "I'm sorry, Kellen. I wasn't thinking."

The air thickened, the silence deafened.

"I'm sorry, too." She wrapped her arms tight around herself, took a deep breath, and pulled hard on her emotions. It wasn't working. Nothing was working. But she was not going to take it out on Gabe.

She knew Gabe, much more than a lot of the others on the team, had a good idea what her childhood had been like. They'd talked some. Not a lot, just enough. And he was smart enough to have put the pieces together when Cody and Ren came to live with her.

They were survivors, she thought. The three of them. That had made them strong. And it was that strength she would use to get through what was to come—meeting with the boy's parents.

After that, she would need to find some time alone. To meditate. To ground herself. And to find some desperately needed inner peace.

Dana gave Annie a minute's lead time after she left Incident Command, then followed her out, finding her easily enough, sitting in her small office staring sightlessly out the window. "Can I do anything to help?" she asked softly.

"I love her, you know. She's the kid sister I always wanted but never had. And I don't want to lose her." A long moment passed. "I just wish she wouldn't keep taking risks. Like jumping in that damned river when she's not yet back to full capacity."

"Are we talking about Kellen?"

"Yes. She's always been known for lecturing the team on safety then taking chances with a devil-may-care attitude. Always the first to make a risky helo jump, rappel down a cliff, or belly crawl on an unstable avalanche field. But ever since she got hurt, it seems like it's been so much worse. And it's not just me that thinks so. The whole team is worried about her. But it's like she can't stop. She's too committed to the work. To the soul of it. It's almost like she's afraid if she slows down it might mean acknowledging she's not yet back at one hundred percent. Or worse, that she may never be."

Dana stared at her. Dumbfounded. "Are we still talking about Kellen? She's hurt? What did I miss?"

Annie sighed. "I'm sorry, Dana, you didn't miss anything. It happened just over a year ago. But it took the better part of several months post-surgery for Kellen to learn how to walk again. She's only been back full-time with the team for a month, and while she may have moved on, I seem to be the one having trouble with it."

Jesus Christ. Dana shook her head in shock and disbelief. "Annie? What happened a year ago?"

"The girls—Cody and Ren—they'd been working really hard. They'd just gotten their high school diplomas. Tim, Gabe, Sam, we'd all tutored them and I suggested we recognize what they'd achieved by taking them out on a training exercise. The kids loved the idea and everyone agreed."

Annie stopped and Dana let the silence slide for a couple of minutes before gently asking, "Are you okay?"

"Yes." Annie's voice cracked and she cleared her throat. "We'd only been out a short time when a call came in about an injured climber. As it turned out, we were virtually on top of where we were needed, and although Kel said it was a difficult approach, she and Tim had done a rescue from Devil's Tower before. There were also more than enough fully trained SAR personnel onboard, and if we needed any further incentive, we'd been told one of the climbers was bleeding rather badly."

Dana watched as Annie fisted her hands and swallowed. "So you went ahead with the rescue?"

"Yes. There was really no other decision we could have made. We were using the winch, lowering Kellen to where the injured victim was, when she suddenly dropped. No warning. It was like she let go. She landed on the mountain ledge she'd been targeting, but it was nothing short of a miracle that she didn't go over the edge into the misty abyss."

Dana tried to process what Annie was saying. "How bad? How bad was she hurt?"

"Her internal injuries were severe. During her first surgery, the doctors had to work just to contain the bleeding, get it under control. Then they had to deal with all her broken bones. God, Dana, she'd broken ribs, collarbone, shoulder, wrist, both legs...and she said she couldn't feel her legs—" Annie stopped abruptly, got up, and poured herself a cup of coffee, clearly using the time to pull herself together. She held up the carafe. "Want some?"

Dana shook her head. "I'm good, thanks."

It took three swallows before Annie was able to continue. "It didn't look good, and for what seemed like much too long, they weren't sure she would make it. For several days, she remained unconscious, with no reflex, no response. There was also a spinal contusion, and no one could say whether the initial paralysis was going to be permanent or temporary if she pulled through."

Dana swallowed hard, even though she knew the outcome had been a good one. The best one possible.

"It was difficult," Annie said, "on everyone. Endless days at the hospital, waiting. Praying to whatever God anyone believed in. And sleepless nights filled with incessant replays, and a never-ending desire to go back. To change the past. No one understood how the hell it had happened and everyone on the team began questioning… questioning *everything*. Second guessing. Did we do all the right things when we moved her? Make the right choices? Miss something crucial? We all questioned whether we should have done something more. Something different."

"Isn't that pretty much the norm when people are making split-second decisions about critical medical care?"

"Yes, of course," Annie said. "But this was different. This was the heart and soul of the team lying in a hospital bed in a coma. We were afraid we'd never see her alive again. Or if she somehow made it through, if she somehow survived, that she would never walk again. That was unimaginable. We're talking about a woman whose life revolves around hiking, climbing, skiing, and of course, SAR. And then on top of everything else, there was the investigation to contend with."

"What investigation?"

Annie met Dana's eyes. "It turned out it wasn't an equipment malfunction that caused Kellen's fall."

"Oh? Then what was it?"

"She was shot. Someone deliberately shot her."

CHAPTER SIX

Kellen wasn't sure whether it was the aftereffects from her prolonged dip in the river or her chaotic emotions that had her shaking. She shivered in the sunshine and her voice lost momentum near the end. But at least she managed to get through what she needed to do without embarrassing herself or her team.

She met with Roger and Andrea Donaldson, handled their outpouring of grief and rage, then gently arranged for the return of their son's body.

At some point during the soul-numbing process, she became aware of another man's presence. Standing in the shadows of pine and spruce as they pressed in. At no time did he intrude on the Donaldson family's tragedy. He simply stood there and watched.

But Kellen saw him. And recognized him. After all, it hadn't been that long since they'd last spoken to each other. Just as she now knew it wouldn't be long before they spoke once again.

This was the cop, she understood immediately. The one who had scared Cody and Ren into believing they might need to run. But Kellen knew he was no ordinary cop. No, the man with the military haircut, craggy face, deep-set eyes, and dark blue suit was an agent with the FBI. Special Agent Calvin Grant.

For an instant, she wondered if he'd finally found out who had shot her. If he'd found the person who had nearly succeeded in killing her and had stolen almost a year of her life.

But no. That would classify as good news, and good news wouldn't have Special Agent Grant hanging back in the shadows. Only bad news waited in the shadows.

They made brief eye contact while she spoke to the county coroner. It sent a chill through her already frozen body and left her hopelessly caught between conflicting desires. Fight and flight. She gave him full marks for not intruding, simply watching from a distance, his shoulders hunched against the cold.

But she didn't give him an opportunity to approach her. Instead, in the emotional aftermath that surrounded the transfer of a thirteen-year-old boy's body to the coroner and his parents, Kellen slipped away.

Easing slowly behind the main building, she cut through an interconnecting hallway between two buildings and back out again, whistling for Bogart as she ran into the woods.

Fear had a taste all its own. It also had a feel, like an icy fist reaching inside her, finding her broken places and twisting them. In that instant, Bogart appeared at her side out of nowhere. As if he knew she needed him. And then they ran together until they reached her cabin.

❖

Dana stayed in the background, still as a stone. The people around her, watching the helicopter land, were equally still. The three Donaldsons, the county coroner, and members of the Alpine team all stood in a solemn show of respect.

Kellen came out first. There were signs of fatigue on her face, and Dana caught a flash of something in her bruised eyes. Anger and sorrow. Then it was gone and they were simply blue.

She stood tall as she approached the family. Took a telltale breath and spoke softly to the grief-stricken couple and their remaining son. Remained calm when Andrea Donaldson railed at the God that had forsaken her son, slipped from her husband's restraining hand, and crowded into Kellen. Pounding briefly on Kellen's chest before collapsing in her arms.

Kellen remained beside them. Supporting Mrs. Donaldson on one side while her husband supported her on the other as their son's body was removed from the helicopter and placed in the coroner's vehicle.

Everything that happened did so according to plan. But at some point during the exchange, Dana heard a discordant note in her head that had nothing to do with grief. It caught her by surprise and she looked around, trying to determine what was off, what was out of place and didn't belong in the emotional tableau before her. And then she saw him.

He was standing shadowed by the trees that crowded the clearing. Late forties, tall and heavyset, with a military haircut and a dark blue suit, he couldn't have looked more out of place in a skier's mecca.

Her years working emergency departments in New York and Boston had her immediately pegging him as a cop, but not local or state. Something told her this was genus FBI. But it wasn't just his unexplained appearance that was troubling. What made Dana increasingly uncomfortable was the way he was watching Kellen. Much too intently.

She anticipated Kellen would make her escape shortly after her part of the script was complete. While attention was focused on the black body bag being transferred to the coroner's wagon. But there was no time to bask in the correctness of how she'd assessed the situation. As Kellen silently backed away before slipping behind the main building, the cop made his move, appearing determined to follow her.

That was when Dana made a move of her own, with no thought beyond intercepting the cop and giving Kellen the time she needed to disappear.

The only sounds Kellen could hear as she neared her cabin were her own harsh breathing and Bogart's panting. But apprehension continued to prickle on her skin.

Once safely inside, she immediately stripped off her clothes and crawled into the shower. But the heat from the water pounding down on her didn't seem to help. No matter how long she stayed there, she was still cold. Still shaking.

It didn't help that her throat was sore, her head was aching, and her mind was struggling to focus. She was also damn tired.

Too tired to face Calvin Grant and whatever news he might have brought to share. Or to answer whatever new questions he might want answered.

So where did that leave her?

The hot shower quickly became a distant memory, and despite the Navajo blanket wrapped around her shoulders and a roaring fire only three feet away, Kellen couldn't stop shaking. The sound of her breathing was suddenly too loud in her ears, although her lungs seemed incapable of drawing in a deep breath.

A moment later, inexplicably, her vision blurred and the room started to spin.

She bit her bottom lip, fisted her hands, and held herself rigid until at last, the room stopped spinning and appeared to right itself. Until everything looked the same as it had.

Solid.

Safe.

Except she felt anything but safe.

She rubbed her hands over her face, over her dry burning eyes. There were times she wished she could cry, but crying helped nothing. She'd learned that the hard way, long ago. Crying only gave her a headache and she already had one of those.

With a sigh, she stood, surprised at how unsteady her legs were. But there were things to do. Bogart, who'd been quietly keeping watch over her, needed to be fed. And before too long, the girls would appear. One by one or as a pair. Intent only on making sure she was all right.

Emotions swamped her at the thought. But that was all right. It was part of the reason she loved them, she thought, as pride stirred in her chest. She and the girls looked after each other. They'd made a family here, not of blood but of choice.

A family of misfits, sure, but they were her misfits as much as she was theirs.

A chosen family.

"I'm afraid I can't let you do what you're planning," Dana said, forcing the cop to take a step back or run over her.

He gave her a single innocuous glance and moved to get past her, issuing a low, rumbled, "Excuse me."

"You're following Kellen," Dana persisted. "I'm afraid I can't let you do that."

The cop stopped cold, his dark eyes squinting as he stared at her. "And who might you be?"

"This is Dr. Kingston." Annie's voice came from behind her. "Dana, this is Special Agent Calvin Grant. We met last year during the investigation after Kellen was shot. What brings you back, Agent Grant? Business or pleasure?"

Grant turned, what passed for a brief smile crossing his face. "Ms. Parker. Sadly, I'm here on business once again. But it's always a pleasure to see you. I met with your father just a couple of days ago. Told him I was heading this way, and the senator sent along his best."

"Oh?" Annie raised an eyebrow. "And how is Dad?"

"Still tough as nails on some of the old blowhards on the Hill," Grant responded with a grin that disappeared as quickly as it had appeared.

"He'll be pleased to know you said so," Annie said, her stance softening. "Now, if you wouldn't mind telling me, why were you about to follow Kellen before my colleague stopped you?"

Dana looked from Grant to Annie, trying to assimilate all the information she'd just learned in a brief amount of time. If Annie's father was a senator, it would explain the presence of an FBI agent during the investigation of what would have been an isolated Colorado shooting.

Putting two and two together, Dana realized she knew Annie's father. She'd met Senator Parker once at a fundraiser she'd attended in Boston. Left of center, outspoken, and quite charismatic. And she had no doubt he would have wanted to ensure his daughter was in no way a possible target.

"I was about to follow Ms. Ryan because I need to speak with her," Grant said. "It's rather urgent."

"Have you found her shooter?" Annie asked.

Grant shook his head. "I'm afraid it's not as simple as that."

"Then simplify it, Agent Grant," Dana said sharply. "I'm responsible for the well-being of everyone at Alpine. Both physical and emotional. And as you saw, Kellen has already had a pretty tough day. There was a thirteen-year-old boy in that body bag, and I'm not sure she should have to handle more right now."

"It's never easy and I'm sorry for the poor timing of my arrival, but it can't be helped," Grant responded quietly. "We have every reason to believe the person who shot Ms. Ryan is also responsible for the deaths of several search-and-rescue personnel over the past year. From what we've been able to figure out, he's been hunting. We've tracked him to Oregon, Wisconsin, New York, and most recently to Kentucky."

Annie's mouth opened, but all that came out was a hiss of breath.

Dana shook her head, denying things she didn't yet fully understand. But then denial ceased to work. "He's cycling back? That's what you think, isn't it? You think he'll come back, try again for Kellen."

Grant's solemn expression never changed. "There are no guarantees in my business, Dr. Kingston. But it's something we need to seriously consider, which is why I'm here and why I need to speak with Ms. Ryan."

Dana forced herself to distance her emotions and look at the situation from Grant's perspective. "I understand. But I'd like to check on Kellen first, to make sure she's all right. And if, in my opinion, she's not, I'm going to strongly recommend you postpone meeting with her until tomorrow. Give her a chance to get past today."

She felt Annie squeeze her hand, obviously concurring with what she'd just suggested.

Grant, on the other hand, looked less than pleased. His lips flattened into a hard, straight line and he appeared about to argue. But then he surprised them all, possibly even himself, as he conceded to her terms. "Agreed."

Chapter Seven

K ellen rubbed her legs where they continued to ache, felt a ridge left behind by too many surgeries to count, and thought of the other scars on her body. On her back, on her legs, on her arm. Her hand automatically sought out the scar on her shoulder, left behind by a bullet out of nowhere. It was now covered by ink. A phoenix rising from the ashes. But she could still feel the scar.

Time had taught her that scars weren't true healing. They were simply an end to the bleeding. As time passed, wounds scarred over. Some eventually became faint silver lines, faded with age and alive more in memory than reality. Like the thin scars crisscrossing her back which raised questions she refused to answer. Others—like the ones from the incident at Devil's Tower—were much more recent and still quite visible.

They were all physical reminders of the paths her life had taken. But sometimes, when she reached out and touched them, she was surprised not to find her wounds still bleeding.

Bogart whimpered and nudged her hand.

Grateful, as always, she patted the space beside her, a rare invitation for Bogart to get up on the sofa. She didn't have to ask twice. Bogart jumped up and instantly crowded her. She laughed briefly when he licked her face, while he responded by wagging his tail as she stroked him.

"What are we going to do?" she asked him softly.

She'd been here in Haven for ten years. Somehow, she'd built a business and a home. She'd made friends for the first time in her life. People in town knew her by name. And when an old acquaintance contacted her about a pair of homeless girls, running scared and living on the streets in Seattle four years ago, she hadn't thought twice about bringing them here where they would all be safe.

She'd been so confident then that it was the right thing to do. This place had become her sanctuary. It would be theirs as well.

Now she was not so sure. Memories pushed in, images she didn't want to see. Numbly, she balled her hands into fists.

Had she stayed in one place too long?

She thought again of the backpack in the front closet. It would be so simple. Grab it, take Bogart, and disappear. With enough cash and different ID's at her disposal, she could slip away and nobody would ever find her. Not unless she wanted them to.

It would be so easy.

Easy for her, maybe, she corrected herself unhappily. But not so easy for the ones she'd leave behind this time. The girls, who had come to mean so much to her, would be devastated. Then there was Annie, her friend and business partner, and by extension Annie's father, the senator. They'd accepted Kellen, believed in her at a time when no one else ever had, and had backed the notion that became a first-class search-and-rescue operation without hesitation.

And there was the team she and Annie were building together. Kellen wasn't surprised when her thoughts drifted to the newest member of the team. Dana. She indulged herself for a moment while a different set of images flashed in her mind. Silky blond hair, a dash of freckles, warm eyes, a full bottom lip. And not just attractive. Intelligent. That was Kellen's greatest weakness when it came to women.

The fact she was the first woman in far too long who had caught her interest made her wonder why. Why Dana intrigued her so much. And why now, when she would most likely not have a chance to see where it could go.

There it was. That was what was new, what was different, she realized.

She'd never had anything or anyone important to leave behind before. Now she did, and for possibly the first time in her life, she wasn't certain she could just walk away. Especially when she wasn't prepared to say good-bye forever. Because she knew from experience that was what walking away meant. The knowledge left her feeling sad and off balance and tired.

"So what are we going to do?" she asked Bogart again. But she still had no answer.

She continued to sit there, for minutes or maybe hours. Hugging her knees to her chest. Staring into the fire, unseeing. Stroking Bogart. Wondering how much time she'd have before a decision was forced upon her.

Even as she fought it, exhaustion took its toll. Her eyes lost their sharp focus and all thoughts faded as her eyelids grew heavy and sleep pulled her under.

Dana remained with Annie and Grant, standing in silence until the county coroner's vehicle pulled out onto the main road, with the Donaldson's car following close behind. Once the rest of the team slowly scattered in twos and threes, Dana turned and, without saying a word, led the way to Kellen's cabin. The air was still and cold, the path quiet except for the thin cry of the snow being compressed beneath their boots.

Kellen's Jeep was still parked near the front of her cabin and there was smoke rising from the chimney. But as they climbed the steps toward the door, there was no sound, no visible movement or other indication anyone was inside.

Maybe she hadn't returned?

The silence pushed in from all directions while Dana deliberated what to do. Then she heard a scream. Hoarse and tortured.

Deliberation shattered and fear clutched her heart in a tight fist. Before Dana could react, Grant had his gun out and was pushing the front door open. An instant later, they all froze, staring at Bogart who stood on the other side of the door. The hair on the dog's back was raised in a silent flag, while he bared his teeth and growled a low and threatening warning.

"Bogart. It's okay, boy. Friend," Annie called out urgently, trying to draw the dog's attention before adding in a whispered hiss, "Agent Grant, put your damn gun down."

Bogart ceased his growling but held his ground. With the taste of fear still lingering, Dana looked around for Kellen. Wondered why she hadn't told Bogart to stand down.

A heartbeat later she saw her, sitting on the sofa. Her hair was damp, her eyes were wide and unfocused, her face pale. With her arms wrapped around herself, she was slowly rocking back and forth, and she was clearly struggling to breathe.

Not willing to wait a moment longer, the doctor in her had Dana pushing past Annie and Grant in her rush to get to Kellen. Half expecting the bite that never came as Bogart allowed her to pass.

"It's all right, Kellen. You're all right." Moving closer until she was less than arm's length away, she kept her voice soft, but it shook with repressed energy as she continued to speak. Whispering a litany of reassurances, saying anything that came to mind, while she gently picked up Kellen's wrist and checked her pulse.

For an endless moment, she could hear Kellen's breathing, harsh and ragged. Watched her continue to gasp for air. Over and over again. But then slowly, so very slowly, her breathing began to steady.

"That's it. Just relax," Dana murmured. "Annie and I are here and nothing's going to hurt you. It was just a dream."

"Just a d-dream," Kellen repeated as she managed another breath. "Just a bloody dream. I know. I'm all right now." She snapped her fingers and Bogart immediately went to her side, nuzzling her hand with his nose.

A moment later, Annie walked over behind Dana, holding out a glass of water. Dana took the glass and put it in Kellen's hand, wrapping her fingers around it and guiding the glass to her lips. "Drink it, Kellen. You're running a fever and can't afford to get dehydrated."

"I can't."

"Yes, you can. It was just a dream and it's over now, so drink the water." Crouching, Dana watched her steadily until Kellen nodded. She then watched her slowly empty the contents of the glass, sip by painful sip, while Annie came and sat beside her.

Kellen looked up when she finished, appeared as if she was about to say something. Maybe thanks. But then her eyes widened and the empty glass slipped from her fingers. Dana knew she'd just caught sight of Calvin Grant. And as she bent to retrieve the glass, Kellen's expression—one that had been so filled with emotion only an instant before—closed down.

"Special Agent Grant." The words burned in her sore throat and she worked at maintaining her composure, at least on the outside. She could keep her expression blank. Knew how to shut things out. How to separate. How to survive. "I saw you at the landing pad and guessed you were waiting to see me. And now it seems you've found me with a little help from my colleagues, so we might as well get this over with. What can I do for you?"

"Ms. Ryan, we need to talk."

"Obviously. Why else would you be here?" Kellen struggled to concentrate while feeling hot and cold simultaneously. "It's clearly not to tell me you've caught the man who shot me. If that was the case, you would have already told me. And since I've already told you what I know, which is nothing, why is it we need to talk?"

There was an infinitesimal tensing of Grant's big body. Bogart evidently didn't like it any more than she did and immediately issued a low warning growl. Even after a soft word from Kellen, the dog held his ground and his ruff remained spiked as they both watched Grant and waited.

"The man who shot you—he's been busy. As near as we can tell, he's killed at least four SAR personnel, in Oregon, Wisconsin, New York, and most recently in Kentucky. We still don't have any idea who he is and haven't come close to catching him. But we believe he's working his way back to Colorado. Back to you, Ms. Ryan."

As Kellen's heart rate increased, Bogart whimpered, pressed closer, and licked her hand. "It's okay, boy," she murmured, but the words rang hollow in her own ears.

Beside her, Annie placed a hand on her leg and squeezed gently, which she took for a silent show of support. Dana caught her gaze. She continued to hold it until Kellen began to feel uncomfortable. Dana saw too much, Kellen realized and was the first to break the connection.

With no choice remaining, she turned back to face Grant, hesitated, then asked, "Me specifically or anyone on my team?"

"You. Specifically."

Kellen's mind raced with questions and insane possibilities she had to consider. "Why me?"

"It's what the experts back in Quantico believe. I can give you all the psychobabble if you want me to, Ms. Ryan, or I can keep it simple."

"Simple, please. And if we're actually going to have a conversation about someone who wants to kill me, can you at least call me Kellen?"

Grant nodded. "Kellen, the experts believe after he failed to kill you, he went out and practiced. Perfected his craft, if you will. And now he's ready to come back and remove the only failure from his record."

"Me."

"Yes. The simple truth is we can only guess at what's motivating him. He could simply be angry, because SAR services failed to save someone important to him or because he tried for SAR and failed to make the grade. Both scenarios are equally possible and we've got people going through every documented search across the country covering the last ten years. Looking at cases where at least one victim died. They're also combing through the records for SAR training programs across the country, looking at anyone who got cut."

Kellen instinctively knew there was more. It was almost as if he was watching her. Waiting. Trying to determine the right moment when he had her off balance enough to spring whatever else he was holding back.

"Or maybe he's someone from your past."

Apparently the moment was now.

Grant spoke softly, but there was an edge of something—impatience maybe or anger—in his voice. "Because that's where things get really interesting, in my opinion."

"How so?"

"Everyone leaves a paper trail as they go through life. So would it surprise you to know that before you rescued a senator's daughter roughly ten years ago, other than a student enrolled at the University of Colorado, there's no record of a Kellen Ryan anywhere that matches your description? No birth record. No parking tickets. Nothing whatsoever. Kellen Ryan simply doesn't exist before then."

Kellen felt as though he had hit her with vicious blows rather than simple words. How strange that any reminder of the past could hurt and make her defensive. "That's crazy—"

"Is it? Then why don't you show up in any records? And here's the thing. We all know if you have enough money or know the right people, anyone can buy a new identity. You can get forged documents as good as the real thing, have them entered into a computer system, and use the information that's been planted to get a driver's license. Credit cards. A passport. And if you use them long enough and nobody raises any flags or asks any questions, you have a new life."

Kellen felt Annie's hand, still on her leg, begin to shake. She swallowed hard and forced back a surge of questions of her own, hating the way her heart pounded against her ribs, leaving them bruised, battered. "Tell me, Agent Grant. What is it you want?"

"What do I want? I want to understand what the hell is going on. Maybe by understanding, I can identify whoever is out there killing people and trying to kill you in the process. The truth is people don't appear out of thin air unless they have something to hide. So I need to understand. Are you running from something? Is someone trying to hurt you? I know you're not in witness protection because I checked. Tell me who you are and who's after you and I'll do everything I can to help."

No.

Her head hurt, throbbing and pulsing as cold reality seeped in. She narrowed her eyes against the pain. "Will you answer one question for me?"

"Of course. I need you to know, I'm not your enemy."

Kellen shrugged, not certain if she believed him. Not certain it mattered. What was important, what she needed to ask was, "Are any of my…my colleagues…are they at risk if they're around me? Near me? Is there a chance that any of them could get hurt if this person tries for me again?"

"Can they become collateral damage? Is that what you're asking? Out in the field, on a rescue, where even a slight shift in the wind can alter the direction of a bullet? I'm sorry, but the answer is yes."

Kellen closed her eyes, guilt trickling through her.

Annie chose that moment to speak. "Then we won't let her go out in the field."

Nearly simultaneously, Dana added, "We'll ground her until this is resolved."

Kellen's eyes flew open again. "You can't do that."

"I'm sorry, Kel, but yes, she can," Annie said gently. "In her role as medical lead, Dana can ground anyone she feels isn't in peak condition, mentally or physically. Anyone who could be a danger to themselves or the team. And if it was needed, which it isn't, I would back her on this one."

That was all it took.

One moment Kellen felt ready to fight, in the next she went very still. Completely shut down as something deep inside—maybe the trust she'd managed to build—shattered like shards of ice. Running her hands over her face, she pressed her fingers hard against her eyes.

"All right, then. I'm grounded." She didn't raise her voice. She didn't have to. Keeping her emotions on a very short leash, she turned away from Dana and Annie, squared her shoulders, and lifted her chin to face Grant, using up her last reserves of energy. "I also have nothing to say to you. All I want is to be left alone. And since for now this is still my cabin, you can all let yourselves out."

"Kellen—" Annie pleaded.

"Bogart." The word was soft, but carried unmistakable strength. The dog immediately issued a low growl in his throat as he stood by her side.

Annie and Dana looked at her a moment longer, then quietly followed Grant out of the cabin.

CHAPTER EIGHT

Well into the evening, Dana struggled to understand what had happened and tried to determine the best course of action. With no success. She couldn't stop seeing Kellen, how devastated she had looked when they'd left. Rage and grief had burned equally in her eyes. And with her skin flushed with fever, she'd also looked more fragile and more vulnerable than Dana thought possible.

What Grant had disclosed—it was simply unthinkable, and somewhere there had to be the truth. Answers. But she knew finding them was going to be the challenge. And there was always the possibility that some questions would never be answered.

Cody and Ren clearly knew something was wrong. Anytime she saw them over the remainder of the day there had been no shy smiles. No laughter. They simply went about their business and made no eye contact with anyone other than each other, before disappearing altogether.

In the meantime, she still had no answers. Only questions.

Ignoring the debate raging in her head, Dana turned her depleted energy to finishing the work on the medical center, overseeing construction and working until she was too tired to think. She then spent the rest of an endless night tossing and turning. Wishing she'd done things differently. Wishing she understood how someone could simply not exist prior to ten years ago.

But outside the realm of fiction, she had no frame of reference for how someone could simply change their identity and become someone else.

Dana considered the similarities with her own situation. She too had ended up in Haven hopeful of a new start. But that was where the similarity ended. She hadn't wanted to disappear. Not exactly. Rather, she'd been looking for a place where people would actually see who she really was.

She'd never been comfortable around people who thought they were better than everyone else because of their socioeconomic status. She'd encountered the breed often while growing up and had always been angered by people whose innate arrogance made them believe they could claim her as one of them. Simply because she came from wealth. Because her father was a highly respected and sought after cardiologist. Because her mother was a partner in a prestigious law firm.

They failed to see those things didn't define her. Just as her parents failed to see her move to New York and then to Haven wasn't intended to punish them or eradicate her past. Instead all she wanted was some distance. Some breathing room. A place to sink roots of her own and be all the things she hoped to be. A doctor. A friend. A lover. A soul mate.

Long before the first light of day bled through her bedroom window, she gave up any pretense at sleeping. She quickly showered and dressed, then headed to the office, not surprised to find a hollow-eyed Annie struggling to make coffee.

Placing a gentle hand over Annie's, she said, "Go sit down. I'll finish this."

She cleaned up the grounds Annie had spilled, rinsed the pot, and finished making the coffee, waiting as the water ran through the machine and the aroma of coffee filled the air. Once two mugs were filled with fresh brew, she brought them to the desk where Annie sat, mindlessly toying with a carving of an eagle that had previously sat on her window ledge.

"Kellen made this for me, the first Christmas we were business partners," she said. "I knew she had no money, that everything she had she'd been pouring into making Alpine a success, and I wasn't expecting anything. So I was stunned when she gave it to me. It was so incredibly beautiful and I hadn't known wood carving was something she liked to do, let alone did so well."

"It's amazing." It also explained the web of scars she'd noticed on Kellen's fingertips. Fine, pale white scars.

"Yes, it is. She told me that when she'd lived on the streets, she hadn't wanted to panhandle. She didn't like to ask for anything. But she could make carvings—large and small—and sell them, make enough money to survive. It was a business transaction, in her mind, rather than a handout."

Dana tried to process what she'd just heard. All the disparate pieces that made up the whole story. "You knew."

"That Kellen had lived on the streets? Yes. She told me, very early on in our friendship. Not a lot, just that she'd been a runaway. That she'd celebrated her thirteenth birthday under the Golden Gate Bridge. She never said why and I didn't press. But I should have."

"Why?"

"I'd seen some of the scars she has. I knew someone had hurt her. Hurt her rather badly. But I didn't put it all together, that she might still be hiding from someone. I didn't know she'd changed her name, her identity. She should have told me."

"But she didn't."

"No. I know for a fact my father had Kellen checked out, around the time we became business partners. But all he would tell me was she posed no threat to me and, in fact, he thought we would be good for each other. I wish he had told me more. Maybe then I could figure out how to help her."

"Does that mean you still want to help Kellen?"

Annie's eyes widened with surprise. "Of course. Don't you?"

There was no hesitation. "Yes."

"Good." Annie surprised her and grinned weakly. "I'd hate to have to fire you instead of making you a partner."

Dana stared at her as the words filtered into her tired brain. For an instant, their eyes locked. And then they both started to laugh.

"Could I ask you something? Grant said—"

"He said Kellen saved my life."

"Yes."

"She did. That's how we first met." Annie's focus visibly faded a little as she remembered. "I was here with a group of friends from college. We'd gotten together because we were all turning the big three-oh and for some unknown reason, we decided we needed to do something adventurous to commemorate the event."

Dana laughed. "Let me guess. The decision was made over drinks?"

"Of course. Then someone—I can't remember who anymore— suggested since we were here, our adventure should involve something outdoorsy, like hiking in ice and snow. None of us had any real experience beyond things we'd done in college, but we all agreed and set out the next morning. Except none of us had bothered to check the weather forecasts, and as luck would have it, we somehow got separated just as a storm hit." Annie shrugged as the memory sent a visible shiver through her. "Lesley and I had just gotten together during that trip. Finally admitted our feelings for one another. And when everyone got back to the lodge and they realized I hadn't made it back, Lesley decided she wasn't willing to take any chances."

"What did she do?"

"She called my father."

"Oh Lord." Dana bit her lip. "Have I told you I've met your father?"

Annie smiled. "Then you can imagine the kind of stir the senator created when the SAR team called off the search for his only child, saying conditions were too dangerous and they needed to wait until the weather improved. He was in the midst of threatening hell and damnation when this skinny twenty-two year-old kid volunteered to go and find me. Everyone thought she was crazy, but she told my father she knew these woods like the back of her hand. She said she'd bring me back and then she just wandered off into the storm."

Dana shook her head. "She hasn't changed much, has she?"

"No. It took her a while to find me. I'd sprained my ankle badly and the storm was rather fierce, so she dug a snow cave just big enough for the two of us. We shared body heat, trail mix, and dreams until the winds finally let up. We were almost all the way back, with Kellen bearing most of my weight, when a couple of rangers found us. They quickly bundled me up on the back of a snowmobile, but Kellen refused a ride. Said she'd make it back on her own and then disappeared as quickly as she'd appeared."

"I don't understand. She didn't come back with you?"

"No. And you should have seen my father when he discovered the rangers had left Kellen behind to return on her own. He had the secret service combing the woods, looking under every rock and tree until they found her. It turned out she'd been living in the woods while doing her degree at the University of Colorado, which is how she knew the territory so well." Annie sat for a minute, thinking, remembering. "But she wouldn't come back with them. Said knowing I was safe was all the thanks she needed. So the secret service kept an eye on her until my father could get there to meet with her. And as it turned out, he got there just in time."

"She was getting ready to take off, wasn't she," Dana stated softly.

"You got it in one. She'd just finished packing and was none too pleased about doing it under the watchful eye of my father's entourage when the senator got there. She also wasn't too keen to come back to town with him, but my father didn't get to where he is without learning a thing or two about persuasion."

"What happened next?"

"He asked her to stay with us for a few days, and although it was clear she wasn't comfortable around so many people, she agreed. On her last morning with us, my father suggested she should be passing on her backcountry knowledge and rescue expertise to train future generations. She said it was something she'd dreamed of doing. And then he offered to back the endeavor, on one condition."

Dana frowned. "What condition was that?"

"He said she needed to take his wayward daughter on as a business partner and keep her out of trouble," Annie said with a laugh. "I happened to think the idea was terrific. I had a degree in business I wasn't using, and Lesley had found a cabin near town, the perfect location for a mystery writer to settle down in and write."

"So all's well that ends well."

"Yes," Annie responded with certainty. "Dana, I don't give a damn what Grant said. It was Kellen Ryan who saved my life and Kellen Ryan who helped build this business. I don't care who she was before that. I only care about who she is today. But I worry that on some level, she's always just a step from running. Disappearing."

"What do you mean?"

"She once shared that she keeps a backpack in her front closet, filled with essentials in case she needs to run. I may not like it, but I do understand having it there helps her feel better, so I don't interfere. Because it's simply a part of who Kellen is. And that's the same person I've known and loved for the last ten years."

Dana felt momentarily stunned by Annie's revelation. That after all these years, Kellen would still keep a go bag ready in case she needed to run at a moment's notice spoke of a level of fear she couldn't begin to understand. She also wasn't certain what it would take to turn things around.

Whether it mattered or not, they still had no idea who Kellen had been prior to meeting with Annie and her father. And there was still someone out there, hunting her. Wanting to finish what he'd started a year earlier.

There was also one other question that remained critical. If Kellen's pattern was to disappear, would she do that now? With a clear threat, would she run? Or would she stand and face whoever was coming after her, knowing she'd established strong bonds of friendship here, built a community. One that was prepared to stand by her. Fight with her and for her.

Kellen stretched and sighed as she awoke. The stretch pulled at a tube attached to her arm, and it took a handful of frustrating seconds for her to orient herself and for her eyes to focus. That was when she found herself staring at an IV.

What the hell? The realization came at the same instant she discovered two girls and a dog gathered beside her.

Bogart immediately drew near and nudged her hand with his nose. He then looked at her with *where the hell have you been?* in his eyes. Good question. How long had she been out?

Kellen scratched his head and looked at the girls. "What's going on?"

"Please don't be upset, but you've been really sick," Cody said.

Before she could think of an appropriate response, Cody pressed her palm on Kellen's forehead, then pressed it against her cheek. "I think your fever's finally gone down. But it was really bad and when it kept getting higher, we had to ask the doc to come and take a look at you."

"Oh?" Kellen struggled to remember. "When was this?"

"Um…three days ago. Please don't scare us like that again."

Letting out a resigned sigh, Kellen sank back into the mattress. She sifted through her memory, but her thoughts remained foggy. Disjointed. Like a flickering movie. Slowly, vague recollections took shape. She remembered the failed rescue. Holding the boy in the river. Flying the boy's body back to his parents.

And then she remembered Calvin Grant.

Damn. He'd talked about the man who had shot her. Speculated he was coming back after her. That she was a danger to her team. Worse, out of nowhere, he had raised questions about her past—or lack of one. In front of Annie and Dana.

If she closed her eyes, she'd swear that had only happened minutes ago. Or yesterday. But if what Cody said was right, that clearly wasn't the case. "Three days?" she whispered hoarsely.

"We've all been taking turns watching you. Cooling you down with cold cloths and ice like Doc D showed us," Ren said. "How are you feeling?"

Doc D? Now wasn't the time to question, because Kellen could see fear and concern warring in Ren's eyes. Could hear it in her voice. She took a quick breath and forced a smile onto her face. "I'm not sure. You know nothing keeps me down for long, but for some reason I feel like I've been run over by a bear."

"Bears don't run people over." A giggle escaped Ren and she began to visibly relax. "They might nibble, but they'd probably think you're too skinny and move on to something better."

"The doc said we needed to make sure you got fluids," Cody said and Kellen followed her eyes to the near empty IV bag. "She showed me how to change the bag and she came by a few times to make sure I was doing it right and to check that you were doing okay."

Kellen heard the pride in her voice. "So you're going to become a doctor now?"

"No. Dana told me how long she had to study and I can't see me doing that," Cody answered seriously. "But maybe a paramedic, like Gabe, so I can still go out with the team. That'd be cool and Dana and Gabe both said they'd help me study."

Dana had certainly managed a small miracle, if both girls had let her get that close to them. Kellen's smile was genuine this time. "I think you'd make a terrific paramedic. But then I think you both will be wonderful at whatever you choose."

"That's because you love us," Ren teased. "But I don't like needles. I just want to paint."

"That makes you very lucky then, because it turns out you have an amazing talent," Kellen said. "It would be a shame to waste it."

It had taken a lot of convincing before Ren had finally agreed to let them hang some of her wildlife paintings in the main office, and Kellen wondered when it might be a good time to let Ren know the small gallery in town wanted to start selling some of her work.

Everyone who saw them thought she was exceptionally talented, but Kellen understood. Ren struggled with self-confidence and got skittish when it came to letting people see her work. Ren was afraid to let strangers get too close, afraid they would see into her soul, and see what had been done to her by looking at her paintings.

All in good time, Kellen decided. Right now, she needed to dispose of the IV, take a long hot shower, and then indulge in some coffee. In that order. That would go a long way toward making her feel more human.

Thankfully, the IV catheter came out smoothly.

"What are you doing?" Cody asked.

"I really need a shower and this"—she pointed at the IV—"is not coming with me. Could you get me a Band-Aid? And if someone could manage to brew a large pot of coffee by the time I come out, I would be forever grateful."

"With chocolate?" Cody asked.

Kellen grinned. "Absolutely."

Cody nodded. "Okay, but I think Dana's going to be pissed you did that."

"Probably," Kellen said and wondered what the doctor would look like angry. *Hot*, that was how Cody had first described her. Dana would look hot, she decided with a smile.

❖

Hot didn't begin to describe how Dana was feeling when she stopped by the cabin and discovered her patient was missing. "What do you mean she's gone?"

Ren slipped quietly out of the cabin without a backward glance, but Cody held her ground. "Kellen's fever topped out at 104," she said, "but then it finally broke early this morning."

Dana sighed. "And—?"

Cody stared at the floor for a moment, then squared her shoulders and lifted her chin in a move that so mimicked Kellen it left Dana speechless. "After she showered, we shared a brew and she talked to us for a bit. She explained she needed some time alone. She needed to figure out what to do. Then she packed a few things and took off with Bogart by her side."

"And you just let her go?" Dana struggled to keep the disbelief and anger out of her tone. It wasn't just that Kellen had been weakened by her illness. There was danger in having her go off alone. It was palpable. Unrelenting. The terrain and the weather could be treacherous, unforgiving to a poorly placed foot or handhold. And there was a two-legged hunter, somewhere out there seeking her as his prey.

Cody took a step back. "Kellen makes up her own mind, Dr. Kingston. And you grounded her, so there wasn't much reason for her to stay."

Dana saw the hurt in the girl's eyes, heard it in her voice and in the fact she was no longer calling her Dana, but had reverted to her formal title.

"I'm sorry, Cody," she said gently. "I'm not angry with you. I'm upset at the situation. Kellen's been so sick and I'm worried about her because the fever will have left her weak and it could also come back. And I know she's the best at search-and-rescue. The only reason she was grounded was to protect her. The FBI thinks she's a target and we've got to protect her until they can find out who's after her."

Cody's stiff posture showed only faint signs of relaxing. "You don't need to worry about Kel. She knows what she's doing and she's got Bogart to protect her. And it's not like she won't be back. She'll come back as soon as she clears her head and sorts out how she's feeling."

"How do you know?"

"That's easy." Cody grinned, her face lighting up from the inside. "It's what she said and Kellen doesn't lie. Plus, if she was going for good, she'd have taken us. Me and Ren."

"She'd have taken you?"

Cody nodded. "Yes. Sorry, Doc, but I've got to go check on Ren. Make sure she's okay."

Dana stared at the front closet door long after Cody slipped away from the cabin, leaving her alone. It was less than five feet away and she wanted to open the door. Wanted to pull out and open the backpack Annie had talked about. Wanted to understand.

The best safety lies in fear. Wasn't it Shakespeare who had said that? Perhaps she was already beginning to understand. Without needing to open the door. Without violating Kellen's privacy.

Ten minutes later, Dana found herself in front of Annie. "She's gone."

Annie glanced up. "I assume we're talking about Kellen?"

"Of course we're talking about Kellen. The woman who's driving us all crazy. Yesterday she's running a fever of 104 and today she's gone walkabout. Never mind there's someone out there the FBI thinks is after her, wanting to kill her." She stared at Annie for a moment and realized how calmly she was taking this turn of events. "You're not surprised, are you?"

"She's not done it often, but Kellen has gone walkabout a time or two in the past few years. That's a great term for it, by the way." Annie smiled.

"So what are we going to do?"

"Nothing. We just wait." Annie's voice was as calm as her expression. "She'll be back when she's in a better place in her head, when she's ready to deal with whatever's going on. In the meantime, I've told the teams just enough to satisfy them. That Kellen's been grounded as a precaution because it appears her shooter might be coming back to finish what he started. They understand all too well she'll be frustrated, but they all support the decision. No one wants a reprise of the events from a year ago."

Dana swallowed hard and a soft groan escaped her lips as she looked out the window. The snow had been falling all day, with that slow steadiness and determination she was told made the natives in Haven and nearby communities check their supplies of candles and firewood. The kind of weather perfect for staying inside, not roaming through backcountry.

"Then I guess we wait."

CHAPTER NINE

As night descended, Kellen's arms ached, her head throbbed, and she was bone-deep exhausted.

Pain was something she could normally ignore. Another lesson she'd learned long ago. But what was different this time, and what she wasn't certain she could ignore for much longer, was the weakness inside her. The feeling that someone had carved a gaping hole in the center of her life and left her to bleed out.

That was what Calvin Grant had done when he'd raised the specter of the lost and broken child she'd once been. He'd shown her the threads of the past were impossible to completely sever. That she was only lying to herself if she believed she could eradicate the past.

Her past.

Over the years, she'd done everything she could to cover her tracks. To bury any connections to family. To her parents. She'd moved constantly, changed identities, and then moved again. Never certain whether or not her fears were warranted. Just knowing fear had always been there, a constant companion, a sliver in the back of her mind.

She shook her head slightly but couldn't stop the litany of what-ifs. She knew the girls were worried about her, but she couldn't afford to think about them right now. She needed time to clear her head, time to collect her thoughts before making any decisions. Otherwise she wouldn't be good for anyone, herself included.

It didn't help that she'd been running a low-grade fever all day. But she'd known instinctively when she'd left the cabin that an overnight trip on one of the numerous unmarked trails and time on her own would be just the tonic she needed to ground herself and regain some perspective.

The trail she'd chosen was a familiar one that began as a gradual climb. It followed several switchbacks that ran through a beautiful section of forest on a south facing slope, surrounded by several massive, sharp peaks. Then it changed, and after leaving the lower trail behind, the terrain became rugged and more difficult, with ungroomed typical backcountry conditions in the higher elevations.

That virtually guaranteed she'd be alone, which was what she really wanted. Other than Bogart, of course, who was playfully chasing shadows and trying to catch snowflakes in his mouth.

The climb was well worth the effort. As she came up and out of the trees and approached the summit, a postcard-perfect panorama lay before her. She closed her eyes and drew the scent of pine and crisp mountain air into her blood.

With the continuing fall of light snow, it had been a day without a sunrise or sunset. Instead, the day had stayed gray since morning. At some point, night had closed in without fanfare, and it was fully dark by the time she had her camp set up.

The spot she'd chosen was protected from the elements by trees but still provided clean lines of sight in every direction. No one would be able to approach her without her seeing them or having Bogart alert. It would be safe here, she assured herself, and she could take the time she needed to think things through.

Even better, the snow finally stopped and the sky had cleared. She started a fire, fed Bogart, and ate a freeze-dried meal of some kind—she could never really tell what it was by taste because they all tended to taste the same. Now she just needed to boil some water to make coffee.

Once it was ready, she and Bogart sat on a boulder and gazed skyward. There was a beautiful, clear, star-studded sky visible as far as the eye could see, and the only sound was the occasional distant howl of a coyote. It was so beautiful. Perfect. And in spite of everything that was going on, she felt her spirit lifting and all traces of weariness vanished as a calm descended on her.

On the second morning, while hiking with her camera and contemplating her next move, she was following some mountain goats when a movement somewhere above her started a rock slide. Small at first, it quickly gained momentum.

Her first instinct was to protect Bogart. She yelled for him, then had just enough time to mourn the imminent loss of her Nikon—one of the very few personal indulgences she'd allowed herself over the years—before she turned all her energy to surviving. Every muscle inside her screamed for her to move. Half stumbling, half sliding, she grabbed Bogart and dragged him with her behind a large boulder. Holding him close, she protected him as best she could with her body and covered her head with her arms, while rocks continued to rain down around her.

She wasn't certain how long it took, or if perhaps she'd lost consciousness at some point. But Kellen was eventually fairly confident everything had stopped moving and opened her eyes. She was overjoyed to find Bogart staring at her, his nose inches from her own. Laughing out loud, she reached and rubbed his head between her hands, reassuring him she was all right while he licked her face. Shifting to a sitting position, she grimaced as she conducted a quick assessment, but concluded she'd gotten off lucky.

She had a raging headache. That much was certain. She was also covered in an assortment of bruises, but she didn't think anything vital was broken. There was a lump on her head, only slightly bloodied, and she decided it could be ignored once she cleaned it. The worst of the damage appeared to be a deep laceration to her right thigh where the bleeding seemed to be the heaviest, and a smaller one on her left arm. The good news was there was no pain from her wounds yet, although she knew given time it could come.

Feeling faintly light-headed, but not certain whether it was the result of the blow she took to her head, blood loss, or simply a reaction to what had happened, Kellen began to make her way back to her camp. She was uncomfortably aware she was leaving a blood trail that would be far too easy to follow by both four- and two-legged predators and knew she'd have to move quickly. Get the bleeding under control, tear down her camp, and head back to the security of her cabin on the outskirts of Haven.

Once in her makeshift camp, she dug into her pack and pulled out a first-aid kit containing gauze, peroxide, and superglue, plus a needle and some suture thread. Laying everything out within easy reach, she removed her ruined clothes and examined the damage.

The cut on her arm would be fine with the superglue, she decided and set about cleaning and disinfecting the wound. Once it was clean, she opened the tube of glue and applied it as best she could to her arm, closing the cut. She then blew on it until it dried sufficiently.

Her leg was another matter, and she delayed as long as possible while she studied what turned out to be a pair of parallel tears, knowing it was going to hurt like crazy. The bleeding had slowed in one cut, but the second was deeper. There was no question both would require stitching. She was also beginning to shake as reaction set in, and she knew she had to act fast.

After cleaning the cuts and threading the needle, she found the first piercing into her leg stung ridiculously. Kellen sucked in a breath, concentrated on ignoring the burning pain, and focused on making two neat rows of tiny stitches. She kept it together until she snipped the last stitch, then allowed her body to go limp as her world narrowed to a single point of pain.

As another night approached, Dana finished interviewing a nurse practitioner with Annie, checked on the progress of the construction in the medical center, and then headed to Kellen's cabin, much as she had done for the last two days. Not that she expected Kellen to have come back unnoticed. She just wanted to be there when the wanderer finally returned.

She encountered the girls just as they were leaving the cabin. That they were equally concerned about Kellen was self-evident. Ren looked at her hopefully until Dana shook her head, indicating she hadn't heard anything new. "I'm sorry. I wish I knew something, but I don't."

"Maybe tomorrow," Cody replied.

"I hope so."

The girls wished her a good night then disappeared into the darkness, leaving Dana to let herself in. The silence of the cabin welcomed her and surrounded her with Kellen. With her belongings and her style, her carvings, and even her scent.

For the first few minutes, she busied herself rebuilding the fire the girls had started. She ate the sandwich she'd brought while standing up in the kitchen, then made some coffee and poured herself a hefty mug. After tidying the kitchen, she stretched out on the sofa, closed her eyes, and began what had become a nightly vigil. Waiting for Kellen to return.

She must have fallen asleep. There could be no other explanation because when she next opened her eyes Bogart was only inches away, looking at her curiously. When he licked her hand in greeting, Dana sat up, scratched his head, and looked around until she spotted Bogart's travel companion.

She stopped breathing. Had to force herself to begin again.

Kellen had shed her top and was wearing only a navy sports bra, bloodied and filthy jeans, and bruises. She was leaning over the stainless-steel sink in the kitchen and was sticking her arm under running water.

For a moment, Dana stared at her pale face and bloodshot eyes. She looked to be in pain and emotionally wrung out. But what worried her even more was Kellen had a great deal of blood on her—likely her own—and Dana had no idea how badly she was hurt.

"It's not as bad as it looks," Kellen said without looking up. She sounded so tired. Using her elbow, she shut off the faucet and raised her dripping forearm while she inspected the cut. "It should have stayed closed, but the damned glue didn't dry properly. Probably got too cold out on the mountain. Still, it looks clean enough, don't you think? More like a bad cat scratch than anything else, though it stings a little."

Stings a little? Nonplussed, Dana looked at the blood and water running from Kellen's cut and bruised arm. She stared a moment longer at the bruises covering her back, then looked down at her ripped and bloodied jeans. It made her wonder what horror lay beneath the jagged tears.

"Your arm could use stitching," she said, "but that's a guess. I'd also like to take a look at your leg."

"My leg's fine, but my arm—" She scowled at the cut. "I just wish the glue had held. The location of the cut made it impossible for me to stitch it myself."

"Stitch it yourself?" Dana searched her eyes. "Is that what you did with your leg?"

Kellen nodded and shrugged.

"Okay. Why don't I go get my medical bag? When I come back, we can decide what's best for your arm. After that, I'll still want to take a look at your leg as well as any other damage you may have incurred."

She looked at Kellen's face, a complex mixture of frustration, embarrassment, and unhappiness. Watched the lines around her mouth tighten and saw her look away before she looked back at her with shadowed eyes. "No need."

"Kellen—"

"No need for you to go get your medical bag, Doc. There's a fully stocked first-aid kit on the shelf in the front closet. It's in a tackle box. Not to say we're accident prone, but between the girls and me, it pays to keep one handy."

Dana smiled. "Damn, Kellen. I think I just might like you."

Kellen grinned. "You mean you're not sure?"

"Fishing for a compliment?" Not waiting for a response, Dana walked to the closet and opened the door. Her eyes were immediately drawn to a black backpack. This would be the backpack Annie had talked about. The one Kellen kept packed just in case she needed to run. The temptation to bring it down and ask about it was nearly overwhelming. But now was not the time. Ignoring it for the time being, she spotted the tackle box and reached for it.

"Dana?"

She turned and looked at Kellen, still standing by the sink. "Yes?"

"Thank you." She hesitated, trailing off as if searching for better words. "I'm not sure why you're here, but for some reason, it helps. So thank you."

"You're welcome. We can talk about why I'm here later. First things first." Dana brought the first-aid kit to the kitchen and set it on the table. "Can you get out of those jeans on your own or do I need to cut them?"

Kellen looked down at her bloodstained jeans and grimaced. She struggled out of them and a minute later stood swaying in her sports bra and boy shorts. Poised between movement and total collapse. "Not quite how I imagined getting out of my clothes with you," she murmured.

"You imagined getting naked with me?" Dana teased as she picked up Kellen's arm and examined the cut.

She took an audible breath. "Sorry. A couple of days in backcountry with no one around except Bogart, and I forget how to talk around people."

"No worries." Dana grabbed an alcohol wipe and cleaned the damage Kellen had done to her arm. The bleeding was minimal and on closer examination the cut didn't look too bad. Her skin was warm, soft. "Does that mean you didn't imagine getting naked with me?"

"No—I mean, yes. Yes, I've imagined it, but never would I have imagined having this conversation with you. Or anyone. And just so you know, you have no reason to fear the imaginings of my inner teenager." She choked out a laugh. "So can we please forget it?"

"Forget you want to get naked with me?" Dana finished wrapping Kellen's arm, all too aware of the simmering arousal she felt having a barely dressed Kellen this near.

And why not? Kellen was intelligent, passionate in her beliefs, and beautiful. A combination in a woman that was deadly to Dana's self-control. With effort, she turned her attention to Kellen's leg. "Sweet Jesus."

A deep crimson flushed Kellen's face. "I'm aware I'm a scarred mess—"

There are critical moments when the right or wrong word can irrevocably change the course of a relationship, Dana thought. This was definitely one of those moments.

"Kellen, darling, at the moment I'm not looking at any scars you might have. And were this any other more personal situation where I found myself with you inches away and nearly naked, I might be inclined to tell you just how damned beautiful I think you are," she said as she forced herself to return her focus to a set of parallel lines. Twin rows of tiny black stitches on a well-muscled thigh. "But right now I'm a doctor examining your leg. You stitched this yourself?"

Kellen swallowed visibly. "Yes. Why? Is there a problem?"

"Problem? No, I wouldn't say it's a problem. It's just that I've seen emergency department doctors unable to do as good a job. Where the hell did you get your medical training?"

"The street."

Chapter Ten

The girls hugged Kellen until her ribs ached when she stopped by their cabin and woke them up just before sunrise. But she wouldn't have had it any other way.

She made them an early breakfast and talked with them about what she'd seen and done until the sun peeked over the mountains and broke through the tall pines, leaving the sky streaked with pink. And then, ignoring the pull of stitches on her leg and the ache in her head, she took them with her and put them to work, helping her with the finishing touches in the medical center.

She was pleased with how much progress had been made since she had last checked in. The exam and treatment rooms were finished, as was the dimly lit room dominated by a huge X-ray table. And the small surgery gleamed. In fact, most of the work remaining was cosmetic and limited to the main reception area, the on-call room, and the small offices to be shared by the doctors, physician's assistants, and nurse practitioners that would eventually staff the clinic.

She put Cody to work painting the offices, then pointed Ren in the direction of the large blank wall in the waiting room. Ren stared at the wall Kellen had indicated before looking back at her. "A mural?"

Kellen nodded and smiled.

Ren continued to stare at the wall, wide-eyed. "Anything? Really?"

There was so much hope and pride in that one word.

"Really. Whatever you do, I guarantee everyone will love it," she answered. "There's your canvas."

For the next few minutes, they worked to cover the new wide plank flooring with a tarp and set out the paints Ren would use. She then left Ren to create something she knew would be unique as the girl herself and wonderfully spectacular, while she assembled and moved the filing cabinets, bookcases, and desks that would go into the doctors' offices.

Slowly, more help arrived. Tim, Gabe, and Sam came by, free because team two was on call. She got caught up on local news, learned they'd missed her, and that Annie and Dana were interviewing staff for the clinic all day. *Even better*, she thought as she put them to work helping her.

She found the competing scents of wood, paint, varnish, and coffee, plus doing physical work, the steady rhythm of it and the kind of concentration it required, helped anchor her mind.

It was just what she'd wanted. Needed. Then why wasn't it helping?

Because it definitely wasn't helping. She remained unable to generate any great insights or plans of action. At best, she confirmed what she didn't want.

She knew she didn't want to strike out on her own again.

As she and Gabe attached the hardware and hung the last door, she felt hot all of a sudden. Felt the need to go outside and stand in the cool fresh air. And it had nothing to do with the work she'd been doing all morning.

It was because of Dana Kingston. Just thinking about her.

It was rare that she found herself even remotely comfortable with someone she didn't know. And rarer still that she found herself wanting to get to know someone better, and just maybe letting someone get to know her. *Really* get to know her.

But her reaction to Dana last night had nothing to do with getting to know her better or being hurt and in need of medical attention. It had been far more elemental than that. The woman attracted her on so many different levels. And sooner or later, she would have to deal with it. She closed her eyes and rubbed the bridge of her nose. In between dodging the FBI and an unknown killer who wanted her dead.

Sure, she thought wryly. *I'll get right on it.*

❖

By the time Dana and Annie finished with the last scheduled interview, they were both smiling.

After a day filled with close but not quite right, the last candidate had been perfect. Elizabeth—*my friends call me Liz*—Shaw. A physician's assistant, midthirties, with dark red hair and intelligent eyes with laugh lines in the corners. Her references were excellent. And she was clearly not frightened by the prospect of practicing in a remote area.

"My last job was through USAID. We were in Nigeria charged with providing basic care—which translated mostly into HIV counseling and testing, and administering vaccinations."

"Why did you leave?"

"No choice, really. We got pulled out after the clinic we had set up was firebombed," she said mildly. "If you're interested, it means I'm available to start immediately."

Dana and Annie turned to each other, but it was obvious they were on the same page.

"Everything I own is in my truck," Liz added with an infectious grin. "Just tell me where I can park my stuff and I'm yours."

"Then let's get your things taken care of and we'll show you the clinic," Dana said, extending her hand in welcome. "I need to be honest with you. The clinic is a work in progress. But when it's finished, I think you'll be quite happy."

"I'm happy already."

Pleased, Dana led Annie and Liz to the main office only to find it strangely deserted. "Where is everybody?"

Annie paged the Incident Command room. In a moment, she had the answer. "It seems everyone is at the clinic."

"The clinic?" Dana prompted.

Annie shrugged but the corners of her eyes crinkled with humor. "Sorry. No idea. That's as much as I'm being told."

"Then I guess this is as good a time as any to show Liz what we've got."

In spite of the cold, the front door to the clinic was open, and as they drew near, the scent of paint and varnish grew stronger. Once inside, Dana could only stop and stare at the obvious improvements made since yesterday. The walls in the main reception area were freshly painted. The furniture was in place along with a couple of large potted plants.

But more noteworthy was an enormous mural covering the west wall. It was a stunning masterpiece featuring Haven and the surrounding mountains beneath a star-filled sky. "Oh, my God."

In the act of putting finishing touches on the mural, Ren froze.

Before Dana could move to reassure the girl that nothing was wrong, Kellen appeared. "It's all right, Ren," she said softly. "I think what the doc's trying to say is that she likes what you've done."

"Like it?" Dana choked. "It's the most incredible thing I've ever seen."

Ren turned to Dana, swallowing nervously while visibly fighting an innate desire to flee. "Really?"

"Absolutely," Dana murmured. "Nobody has ever done something for me like this before, and if you let me, I'd like to give you a hug to say thanks."

She didn't have a chance to say more. An instant later, she found herself wrapped in a bone-crushing hug while Ren buried her tearstained face in Dana's shoulder. Looking over the girl still clutching her, and aware her own eyes had filled, Dana's gaze drifted to Kellen, who was watching her with a gently amused expression.

After a moment, Kellen moved closer until she could begin to disengage Ren's octopus-like grip on Dana. "Come on, wild child. Go finish your mural while I show the doc what else we've been doing with her clinic."

Ren stepped back, wiped her face with the back of her hand, and gave Dana a tremulous smile. "I'm glad you like it, Doc D." She relaxed visibly when Cody appeared and grasped her hand as the crowd parted, allowing them both to ease away.

Kellen turned to Dana. "Thank you for what you just did. Ren is unbelievably bright and talented, and she's come so far from where she was. But she's still uncertain in a lot of situations, still dealing with a lot of ghosts."

"Not a problem, and if there's anything I can do to help, please let me know," Dana said softly. "It looks like you've been busy."

Kellen shrugged, smiled, and tucked paint-spattered hands into the front pockets of her jeans. "I heard you and Annie were interviewing, and I thought it might be an easier sell if you could give people a better idea of what we have to offer."

Dana smiled. "Well, your timing is perfect. Allow me to introduce Liz Shaw, the newest member of our clinic. Liz, this is Kellen."

Liz stepped forward and extended her hand, rolling her eyes when Kellen pulled her hand from her pocket and tried to wipe the paint on her equally spattered jeans. Both women laughed and shook hands.

❖

As they toured the clinic and absorbed all the work that had been done that day, Kellen felt Annie looking at her with a frankness she'd learned to expect from her. Allowing Dana and Liz to get ahead of them, Kellen stopped. "Okay, let's get it over with. What have I done?"

"You've done what you always do. You disappeared for days after being seriously ill. And when you finally come back, you spend all day working here, doing God knows what, to the point you're limping. Why do you always push yourself so hard?"

Kellen sighed. "Annie, love, I'm all right. I was only gone for two days and I recruited lots of help today, or we would have never gotten this finished. All of team one and a couple from team two have been here at one time or another. As for limping, it has nothing to do with today. I got caught in a bit of a rock slide yesterday and my leg got cut and bruised, so it's still tender."

"Cut and bruised?" Annie's eyes were suddenly worried. "How bad, Kellen?"

"Thirty stitches," Dana answered as she came up behind them. "But not to worry, I checked out all the damage she did to herself, and she's in surprisingly good shape, all things considered. And damned if she didn't do a better job of stitching herself than half the doctors I graduated from med school with."

"You put thirty stitches into your own leg?" Liz asked.

Annie groaned. "Oh, please, don't encourage her, Liz. Lord only knows what she'll do next. Thankfully, I think I've spied Gabe and Tim. Why don't we get your things moved into one of the cabins and get you settled. Kel, which cabin is ready?"

"Number two," Kellen mumbled, her eyes fixed on Dana.

"I'll catch you later, Liz," Dana added, as she met Kellen's gaze.

Kellen did her best to appear attentive and engaged when members of team two came by and made comments about the work they'd accomplished. But she was unprepared for the onslaught of volatile emotions stirred up by having Dana so near. Part desire, part wariness.

She wasn't ready for this. Not now when there was so much uncertainty, so much hanging in the balance.

"I need some fresh air," she mumbled and pushed past the people still standing in the reception area, admiring Ren's mural. The moment she stepped through the open door, the cold air hit her and helped clear her head, which was what she desperately needed. She stretched her tired back and drew in the scent of snow and pine trees and wood smoke.

"You're going to freeze, standing out here without a jacket," Dana said, coming up behind her. "We need to get you somewhere warmer."

Kellen shook her head and stood staring without speaking. It had started to snow, but all she could see were the crystals sparkling in Dana's hair. And in the shadows, it was as if the people and voices from the clinic simply disappeared.

"What is it, Kellen?"

"Come skiing with me tomorrow." She paused and gestured to the mountains that stood like sentinels over the town. "Let me show you places most people never see, where the snow is pure powder and the views will take your breath away."

Dana chewed her bottom lip. "You really know how to tempt a girl, don't you?"

"Is it working?" Kellen grinned suggestively. "What do you say? Will you let me take you out of bounds?"

There was no hesitation. "Yes."

With her gaze locked on the curve of Dana's lips, Kellen's grin faded. She hesitated, not quite certain how to proceed. Swallowed and slowly moved closer.

When Dana moistened her lips in anticipation, Kellen knew she could no more stop herself than she could stop her next breath. Slowly, she slipped her hands behind Dana's neck. Their faces lingered a fraction of an inch apart. And then Kellen pressed her lips against Dana's.

Dana gasped against her mouth, melted into her, and Kellen could no longer think as she slipped into a liquid heat. So soft. So sweet. If she had only this one kiss, she wanted to remember it forever. Every lick, every taste. Every whimper. Dana's lips parted and Kellen deepened the kiss. Drawing her closer, searching, coaxing, teasing.

She caught Dana's moan and used her teeth to gently nip on a lush bottom lip. She kissed her as though she never wanted to stop. And then she slowly drew her mouth away, let out a heartfelt sigh, and stepped back.

Dana opened her eyes and quietly regarded her with an unreadable expression. "Kellen?"

She couldn't answer. Couldn't speak.

"Are you all right?"

No. She was not all right. Need rocked her. It was base, primal. Heat swirled inside her, making her knees go weak and leaving a restless ache in its wake.

"Yeah. I couldn't breathe for a moment."

"And now?"

"And now I can." She took Dana's hand and drew the inside of her wrist to her mouth before placing a gentle kiss. "I'll see you in the morning. And don't worry. I'll look after getting you set up with equipment."

She reminded Dana again that her skis would feel different from anything she'd previously used, but because they were wider and shorter in length, it would also take less effort to make turns. "The motion is more a shifting of weight," she said and demonstrated what she meant. She waited and watched Dana copy her movements, ensuring she was comfortable.

Clearly reassured, she started them through some gentle trails, moving slow and easy while Dana got used to her equipment, and increasing the challenge gradually when she saw what Dana could do. Taking them near the bottom of one of the bowls, she taught Dana how to maneuver in deeper powder.

There were times when Dana admittedly lost focus as she watched Kellen execute textbook perfect turns. *She's so damned beautiful.* The high cheekbones, the smooth line of her jaw, the awesome smile…and the killer body. During those moments, it took little effort for Dana to imagine what was beneath the ski suit, all long and lean, smoothly muscled, and very naked.

Of course, those were the times when Dana ended up facedown in the snow or on her ass. But each time, Kellen reappeared by her side, pushed her goggles up to reveal eyes that rivaled the blue of the sky, and patiently helped her up. All without saying a word beyond ensuring she wasn't injured.

By early afternoon, Kellen noticed Dana was struggling a bit. She circled and stopped alongside. "How are you doing?"

"I'm okay. I think I just need a moment to catch my breath. I keep forgetting how high we are."

"No problem. We'll take a break and grab a bite. There's no need to push and if you're still tired after you've rested and eaten, we'll head back."

Kellen scanned the area before choosing a spot she knew for a well-deserved break. Leaning both pairs of skis against a fallen tree, she pulled out sandwiches and a thermos of hot chocolate from her backpack.

Clearly hungry, Dana unwrapped a sandwich and wolfed it down.

"Hey, slow down," Kellen teased. "There's plenty more where that came from."

"Good, because I find I'm ravenous. Must be all this fresh air and exercise." An instant later, she reached for another sandwich.

The sandwiches were consumed, the hot chocolate vanished, and they relaxed and talked about everything and nothing at all for nearly an hour. Noting the time, Kellen asked, "Since you have your breath back, do you want to ski a bit longer or would you rather head back?"

Dana smiled. "I'm ready for more if you are."

"I'm always ready," Kellen responded with a wicked grin.

The next hour and a half turned into the sexiest ski lesson Kellen had ever given. Standing behind her with her skis straddling Dana's allowed her to put her hands on Dana's hips or shoulders to correct her form. And with each breath, she inhaled the clean, fresh, and tantalizing essence of Dana's skin.

Kellen closed her eyes as the scent evoked a series of tangible images. The warmth of the sun on her face, a cooling breeze, clean mountain air, and unfettered freedom. That was what Dana's scent reminded her of.

"Kellen?"

She opened her eyes and realized they'd stopped moving. "Sorry. My mind wandered somewhere."

"No problem. But judging by the smile on your face, I hope you let it wander wherever it went more often."

That could be very nice, Kellen thought, as she began to lead the way home. It had been a good day, and with the shadows lengthening, there was no sense in taking any unnecessary risks.

The sense of bonhomie lingered until they were back, standing in front of Dana's cabin.

"Do you want to come in for that drink I promised you?"

"I've still got to take Bogart out for a run." She paused for a moment. "Thank you for today. I had a terrific time."

"Can we do it again?" Dana asked.

Kellen nodded. "Of course. In the meantime, try to soak in the tub so you don't get stiff. If I didn't have to go, I'd give you a rubdown. Maybe next time." She could only hope.

Dana awoke early, as had become her habit, still floating on the euphoria from yesterday's skiing. It would not be her last, she promised herself, as she got ready for the day. Her coffee, for some reason, was never as good as what Kellen made. So after giving up on yet another futile attempt, she grabbed her boots and jacket and wandered toward the office, hoping Liz hadn't felt abandoned yesterday.

She called out a cheerful good morning to Cody as she entered. Something was off in the girl's expression. She could sense it immediately but didn't know her well enough to interpret what the problem might be. But as she approached Annie's office, she couldn't shake a sudden and oppressive feeling of dread, so strong it left her momentarily dizzy.

She found Annie in her office. But she wasn't alone.

Two men in dark suits turned toward her as she stopped at the door, uncertain if she should enter. One of the men was immediately recognizable. "Special Agent Grant. Back so soon?"

"Special Agents Grant and Owen are here to meet with Kellen," Annie said, her voice indicating she was none too pleased.

"Why? Wasn't your last visit bad enough?"

"Dr. Kingston, it's not our intention to cause problems for Ms. Ryan," Grant said. "But there's been another killing. A SAR volunteer was killed at Yosemite two days ago."

"Whoever he is, he's escalating. But we've been unable to turn up anyone with a potential motive for these killings," Owen said, taking over the conversation. "It brings us back to Ryan and whoever she was prior to ten years ago. If the killer is someone from her past, then she's our only link. She needs to talk to us. Tell us who she was and what she's hiding."

Dana's thoughts troubled her and she turned to the only person who might be able to help. "Annie?"

"I've already checked," she said. "Kellen's in the gym putting the teams through their paces. We'll go and talk to her. And if she needs help, I've already spoken with my father. He assured me all it will take is one phone call and he'll have a team of lawyers here within three hours. We're not going to let Kellen get steamrolled. You have my word."

Grant grimaced. "Ms. Parker...Annie, you don't really need to get the senator or his lawyers involved. We're not looking to steamroll anyone, least of all Ms. Ryan. I empathize with the position she's in. But we need to stop whoever's behind these killings—"

"Not at Kellen's expense," Dana said.

"Exactly," Annie added. "That's why Dana and I will be present when you talk to Kellen. And if need be, we will shut everything down until my father's legal representatives can get here. Is that understood?"

Grant nodded while Owen looked less than pleased.

Kellen stood to one side, clipboard nestled in her folded arms, as she watched her teams go through this morning's version of the obstacle course she'd set up for them. Into the pool. Out, then up, over, and down the other side of a rope net. Back into the pool. The second station was an inverted rope climb. Back in the pool, then finishing with a single rope climb and ringing the bell at the top.

The teams went through in pairs—one from each team. It brought out the natural competitiveness in their blood, the need to be the best, along with a lot of good-natured catcalls. And after a sleepless night, watching them go through the familiar routine calmed her nerves.

"How are they doing?"

She turned to find Liz, the newest member of the medical team, closely watching the action. "They're good. The best. But then in SAR, physical fitness is a way of life."

"Does that include everybody?"

Kellen nodded and smiled. "Anybody who goes out on a rescue. So if you're interested in going out with the team sometime, I'm here every morning."

Liz looked at her intently. "Would you be interested in going one-on-one with me? Maybe let me know how far I've got to go to qualify?"

The challenge in her voice was unmistakable. Kellen had read the background documents Annie had provided and knew Liz had been a medic in the army before going to work for USAID. And just by looking at her, it was obvious she had stayed in shape. Kellen knew if she accepted a challenge it was always possible she'd lose. But she'd never passed up a challenge yet.

"Hey, Tim. Take the clipboard and stopwatch for me, would you?"

Tim walked over and grinned. "Are you going to have a go?"

Kellen nodded. "Tim, meet Liz, our new physician's assistant, who I believe just challenged me."

Tim's eyes widened. "You're kidding."

Liz shook her head. "I never kid when it comes to fitness." She flexed an impressive biceps for good measure.

"Um…Kel, are you sure you should be doing this?" Tim asked.

She answered by dropping her sweatpants to the floor, leaving her in knee-length spandex shorts that mercifully covered her latest stitches, if not all of her scars. Dropping her hoodie on top of the pants left her in a racer back tank top that revealed some of the faint crisscrossing scars on her back if anyone looked too closely, a tattoo of a phoenix covering a bullet hole, and a freshly bandaged arm. "Absolutely. Shall we go?"

Liz looked at the scars on her knee and the bandage on her arm as they lined up at the edge of the pool. "No disrespect, but are you sure this is a smart thing to do?"

Kellen grinned and dived cleanly into the water the instant Tim yelled go. When she got to the net, she climbed quickly, not bothering to place her feet on the ropes, relying completely on her upper body strength. She was flipping over the top when she saw Liz hit the bottom of the net.

She considered simply dropping to the floor, something she might have done a year ago. But she doubted her knees would handle the additional punishment and opted to climb down. Her decision enabled Liz to close the gap as she hit the water a second time. But Kellen made it up on the inverted rope climb and the gap stayed that way as they headed for the final rope climb.

In the end, Liz hit the bell only a couple of seconds behind her.

The teams gathered round, joking good-naturedly and making comments about Kellen slowing down with age. Kellen laughed as she extended her hand to Liz once they were back on solid ground. "Well done. You can come out with my team anytime."

"Thanks," Liz responded. "I'm looking forward to it."

She was still laughing when she saw Annie and Dana standing near the entrance of the recreation center. But her smile disappeared as she recognized one of the two men standing behind them.

Dana licked suddenly dry lips as she watched the ongoing obstacle course challenge. She attempted to tear her gaze away but couldn't. She'd actually been mesmerized from the moment Kellen tossed her hoodie and sweats onto the floor. The move left her in a tank and spandex shorts that lay smooth and tight on her skin, so that every muscle showed. Dark hair, blue eyes, dusky skin.

Perfect.

She couldn't say she was surprised to see Kellen taking part. Although she didn't know her well enough to predict her course of action with any regularity—something she planned to rectify as soon as possible—she recognized the competitive streak that ran through all the SAR team members. The desire to be the best. Doctors weren't all that different.

Her heart pounded in sync with each breath Kellen expelled as she completed each segment through to the final rope climb. Unrushed, despite Liz closing the gap between them. In total control of every movement she made. A perfect blend of grace, strength, and determination.

She looked glorious in victory, laughing joyously and extending a hand to her vanquished challenger in the true spirit of competition.

Dana also knew the moment Kellen saw the two FBI agents. One instant she'd been laughing, standing in the midst of razzing and cheering team members as she and Liz Shaw congratulated each other. In the next, her movements suddenly slowed. There was a perceptible stiffening of her shoulders and her smile vanished as she turned and cast a long, hard look in Calvin Grant's direction before looking away.

The team sensed the change and circled protectively around her, uncertain of the problem, but ready to defend her if needed.

Dana half expected Kellen would simply walk away in the opposite direction, knowing her team would cover her back and prevent the two FBI agents from following her. She continued to watch nervously as Kellen took her time putting her sweatpants back on. Saw her pick up her hoodie, stare at it, and keep it in her hand rather than put it on. Then she slowly made her way across the gym to where Dana, Annie, and the two agents were standing, stopping when she was less than five feet away.

Owen broke the silence. "You need to talk to us."

Kellen stared at him through narrowed eyes. "I don't know you. Nor do I have anything I need to say to you." She cast her eyes on Grant. "You I do know. And if there's anything we need to talk about, this isn't the way to do it." Without another word, she turned and walked into the changing room.

Owen made a move as if to follow her but was stopped as both Dana and Grant stepped in front of him.

"Dana, why don't you go in and talk to Kellen," Annie said quietly. "See if you can convince her to come to my office to talk. Let her know we'll support her in whatever she decides, and that the support includes my father. In the meantime, I'll take these gentlemen back to the office to wait for you."

Dana thought she heard Owen start to protest, but she didn't stick around long enough to listen. Leaving the disgruntled FBI agent for Annie and Grant to sort out, she followed Kellen. She could hear the shower running and dropped onto a wooden bench to wait.

It didn't take too long, but when Kellen finally appeared, the first signs weren't promising. Her hair was hanging wet, dripping onto a towel draped on her shoulders, but she was dressed in jeans and a turtleneck sweater. A frown appeared to have permanently settled over her brow and her body was rigid with tension.

Without saying a word, Kellen sat on the bench beside her and added socks and boots to what she was already wearing. Intensely aware of the temper radiating from her, Dana decided to play it light. "That was an amazing display you put on during the obstacle course. So tell me, do I need to protect my new PA?"

Kellen scowled. "You're thinking you need to protect Liz? You did notice she nearly beat me, didn't you?"

"Actually, my money was still on you." Dana smiled. "If Liz had gotten any closer to you, I was certain you would have found the energy you needed to go just a little harder and ensure you won."

"I'm touched by your faith." Drawing in a sharp breath, Kellen clenched her jaw. "Tell me, are you here as the Judas goat, sent to lead me to slaughter at the hands of the FBI?"

"Damn it, Kellen, of course not," Dana said. "You know better than that. I'm here as a friend. Now put away the lousy mood."

"Some people would say it's the only mood I have lately." She finished toweling her hair, tossed the wet towel into a laundry hamper, then shook her head slightly, so the dark locks fell in some semblance of order.

Dana tried, without much success, to ignore the sensuality inherent in Kellen's movements. "That tells me there are people who don't really know you."

"The same could be said about you."

The comment came perilously close to hurting. "Maybe," she answered honestly, "but unlike agents Grant and Owen, I'm working on rectifying the situation without browbeating or threatening you."

A ghost of a smile touched Kellen's lips. "I'm a situation?"

"You know what I mean." Dana groaned. "Now just listen to me for a moment. Can you do that?"

"Fine. I'm listening."

"Good. You need to know Annie and I aren't about to hand you over to the FBI and walk away. You should already know that, but that's a conversation for a different time. For now, I'm asking you to trust me when I tell you we'll both be there by your side while the FBI talks to you. And if at any point you're not comfortable with the direction the conversation is going, Annie's already told them the whole thing gets shut down."

"And then what?"

Dana gave her a wry grin. "And then everyone waits for the arrival of the cadre of lawyers Senator Parker has on standby. So come on. Game on, Ryan."

"I'm counting on lawyers and politicians to save the day?" Kellen laughed in spite of herself. "God help me."

CHAPTER TWELVE

Cody and Ren were in the hallway outside Annie's office, faces pale, eyes filled with fear by the time Kellen and Dana got there. She didn't know how, but Kellen was starting to believe both girls could somehow pick up on her emotional state by sensing disturbances in the universe. Just like Bogart.

There wasn't a lot she could do at this point, but Kellen touched them both, reassuring them through physical contact that she was fine, and that they would all be fine, even though it was possible nothing could be further from the truth.

She hated it. She'd never lied to the girls before and had no interest in starting now. But she didn't know how long she'd be tied up in Annie's office. Not that she could begin to imagine a positive outcome, but she didn't want them to worry needlessly.

"You won't disappear, will you?" Ren asked.

Surprisingly, it was Dana who answered. "Kellen's not going anywhere except back to work after we're done here. You have my word on it."

After the girls were gone, Kellen reached out and squeezed Dana's hand. "Thanks for that."

Dana smiled briefly, but there was no more time as they entered Annie's office and closed the door behind them.

Hands loosely held at her back, Kellen chose to stand near the window where she could look out at the mountains that normally soothed and calmed her. She blanked everything out of her mind but the moment. And then she waited for the first volley to be fired.

"Ms. Ryan, I understand this is difficult."

Turning to face the room, Kellen looked at Calvin Grant. "Special Agent Grant, although I appreciate the sentiment, you have no idea what this is like for me. But if I remember correctly, you previously agreed to call me Kellen."

"But that's not your real name, is it?" Owen interrupted. "So why don't you make this easier for everyone by telling us who you are?"

Kellen leashed her pain behind an inscrutable calm, even as a cold chill descended along her spine. "If this is the tactic you've chosen to use with me, I suggest you rethink your approach. Because I can tell you I've no interest in playing a role in your good cop-bad cop routine."

In the ensuing silence, Kellen could hear only the sound of her own shaky breaths.

"You're right. I told them it wouldn't work." Grant shrugged. "But we're desperate and willing to try anything. We've got a hell of a mess on our hands, Kellen. I don't need to tell you that. People are dying and we need to figure it out and stop this before someone else gets killed."

"Don't you think I know that?" Something gripped Kellen's throat, making it hard to swallow. Her heart started to race and she could hear nothing beyond the noise in her head.

Dana caught her shoulders, her strength apparent in her hold. "Kellen." Her voice was sharp, her hands tight. "Breathe."

And she did, desperate for air.

"Another," Dana said more softly.

As the panic in her lungs subsided, she pulled in air. Deeper this time, as the need to be alone slammed through her. Alone. Safe. Anywhere but here.

Somewhere the memories crashing through her mind could be held at bay.

please don't please don't please don't

Somewhere she could get her feet back solidly in the present.

Except in the present, Special Agent Owen was still talking to her. "Why don't you give us what we want?" he asked. "Tell us who you are."

Her stomach churned, the pressure in her chest increased, and she was beginning to shiver. *Don't lose it,* she told herself. *For God's sake, don't lose it.*

"Who are you protecting?"

"No one." She all but screamed out the words before her voice dropped to a near whisper. "I ran away when I was twelve and I wasn't worth looking for. Is that what you want to hear?"

"That just tells me your parents were dumber than I thought." Everyone turned as Senator Harrison Parker entered the room. "Stand down, Agent Owen."

He was, at sixty-four, a striking man. Tall and fit, with a full head of silver hair. He looked older than the last time she'd seen him. There were lines on his brow and bracketing his mouth. Lines that hadn't been as evident before.

But as he pulled Kellen against his broad chest, his hand gentle on her cheek as his eyes gazed down at her with a compassion she didn't want, the overwhelming need to accept the shelter he offered pounded in her blood.

The senator's hawk-like gaze swept over the room. "Special Agents Grant, Owen. Step out."

Kellen let her gaze skim over Owen, whose impassive brown eyes avoided hers as he got to his feet, while his hands balled into fists. Of course, the way things had just gone, she couldn't blame him for wanting to punch something. Or someone.

She eased from the senator's hold and moved back to the window and a view that at least offered the illusion of escape while Harrison Parker settled into the wingback chair Calvin Grant had vacated and looked around the room.

"Hello, sweetheart," he said to Annie. "Would someone care to bring me up to speed?"

❖

Dana moved closer to the window and kept her eyes on Kellen while Annie brought her father up to date. Annie never once asked the senator why he was here. There was no need. Harrison Parker had built his reputation as a man of action quite honestly. He would not send in his lawyers if he believed his presence could accomplish the same thing—or more.

Kellen remained silent while Annie answered the senator's questions. But that didn't worry Dana as much as how she looked. Ice pale. Her stance stiff. Her hands unsteady. Her eyes shadowed and echoing her pain.

"Kellen?"

She didn't immediately answer when Harrison spoke to her. Ten seconds turned into thirty and then into a minute. Finally, she looked up. "Why are you here?"

"When I first learned what was going on here, about the FBI raising questions regarding your past, I became worried that they would fixate on you to the exclusion of everything else. It seems I was right." He sighed. "I'm sorry they upset you."

"You know, don't you," she said in a flat voice. "About my past."

"Forgive me, Kellen, but you were going to be associating closely with my only child, a child I would do anything to protect. A child whose life you saved. And while I felt instinctively I could trust you, I needed to be very sure."

"How much?"

"How much do I know?" He gave her a gentle smile. "At a guess, most of where it started."

She drew back to study his expression. "What does that mean?"

"It means I know what your father did to you when you were a child. And instead of protecting and defending you, as she should have done if she was any kind of a parent, your mother threw you out. Left you to fend for yourself."

Dana heard Annie's gasp, but she could only focus on Kellen. She watched her run a hand through her hair and saw the weariness in the gesture.

"For years, my father used me as a life model for his art. Made me pose for him and for his friends. And then, then it wasn't enough to just look, so he raped me. Is that what you need me to say? Is that what the FBI agents want to hear? That my father had me pose nude for him and his friends, starting when I was seven. And then he raped me and beat me repeatedly."

"Jesus, Kellen. No," Dana whispered. "You don't have to—"

"You're wrong. The senator already knows what happened. Who I was. But the FBI…that's what they're waiting to hear. Maybe you are too."

Except Dana didn't want to hear any of it. Didn't want Kellen to dredge it all up. But it seemed Kellen had slipped into another place and time and had stopped listening.

"I hated it. I hated how his friends—how *he* looked at me. How he made me pose. I knew it was wrong, but I had no say. And then it all changed, and I couldn't stop him. It hurt, but no matter how much I begged and pleaded with him, or how much I fought back, he just kept holding me down. Kept raping me. Kept beating me." She stumbled over the last couple of words and stopped to take a shuddering breath.

"What happened afterward?"

"You mean when my mother finally came home and saw what had happened, what continued to happen? I thought—I thought she was going to help me."

"But she didn't?"

"No. I don't remember how, but somehow she got me into her car. But instead of taking me to a doctor like I thought she was going to, she drove me somewhere in the middle of the night. Somewhere I'd never been. She made me get out of her car, threw three twenties at me, and told me never to come back if I knew what was good for me."

Nobody said anything when Kellen fell silent, her eyes dark with introspection. Dana grew increasingly concerned, because defeated was the only word that came to the fore of her mind as she took in Kellen's slumped shoulders, her hunched posture. It was not a word she would have previously associated with the woman she'd been slowly getting to know.

Worse, she had no idea how to resolve the impasse. She could think of nothing to say that could make a difference. No words of consequence or comfort that could ease this much pain.

"My father..." Kellen said into the silence. "The day it happened, my father said it was my fault. That I'd been trying to seduce him for years and now it made sense why he'd always wanted me. He was only human. And I was just a whore for tempting him."

"Kellen?" Dana had heard enough. She wanted to help. But more than anything, she wanted to stop Kellen from bleeding out in front of them. She took her hand, held it firm.

"It's all right, Dana. Let me just finish this," Kellen said. She squared her shoulders against her obvious exhaustion and took a shuddering breath, but Dana noticed she didn't release her hand. If anything, she held on to it tighter.

"All right, but I don't understand. Why didn't your mother help you?"

"I think maybe because she was afraid it would ruin my father... their life...if people found out what he'd done. If she took me to the hospital like she should have, social services would eventually become involved and start an investigation. And then it would all come out. So it was far better for everyone if I simply disappeared."

"Not for everyone," Harrison said. "What happened to you after your mother forced you out of her car?"

"A stranger—a woman, she found me wandering alone on the street. I guess I looked pretty bad because she took me to a hospital."

Letting go of Dana's hand, she wrapped her arms around herself and squeezed. Struggled under a strong compulsion to hold herself together, to not let too much slip beyond her reach. "I remember all the pitying glances from the nurses, the whispered conversations of the doctors. I had to have surgery. The repeated rapes had...there were tears. After I woke up, the doctors wouldn't tell me much. They said all that mattered was getting my strength back. Getting better. And they asked me who had hurt me. Mostly, they just wanted to know my name and who had done that to me."

"What name did you give them?"

"I made one up. That was the first time. I gave them the first name that came to me, and just like that, I became someone else. I guess I've been doing that ever since."

"Why did you never go back? Why didn't you confront your parents or file charges?"

"I'm not sure whether this will make sense to you, but the loss of innocence, it can't be undone, no matter what you do or how hard you try. So there really was no point in going back."

Placing a gentle hand under Kellen's chin, Harrison made her look at him. "I understand. And Kellen? You need to know, I'm so very sorry."

She nodded. "I can see that. I can also see you knew all along, yet you never said anything. Never told me you knew."

"I decided I would let you make that choice. I decided if you wanted to talk to me about your past at any time, I would be there to listen."

"And you never told Annie."

"No, for the same reason. I know my daughter. And I figured if you ever felt you could trust someone—trust her—enough to share what had happened to you, Annie would be there to listen. She would stand by you and offer whatever you needed. But it wouldn't change the essence of your friendship."

Kellen turned to Annie. "And does it? Does it change anything between us?"

"Kellen Ryan, how can you even ask that?" Annie gave Kellen a shaky smile, her eyes swimming with tears. "I know you. I've known you since you saved my life ten years ago. You're my best friend, the sister I'd always hoped for, and I love you. Nothing can change that."

Looking as if the world had tilted under her and she hadn't found a way to regain her balance, Kellen merely nodded.

"At the time, was there no one else?" Dana asked. "No one you could turn to for help?"

"I'd been homeschooled, so other than my father's artist friends, I had virtually no contact with others. The hospital arranged for a social worker to come and see me. But I heard her talking to the doctors about putting me into a foster home while they tried to find out who I was and what had happened to me. I didn't think anyone would believe me if I told them what happened. Or that somehow they'd believe my father. That it was my fault."

She shrugged and gave a flicker of a smile. "I guess counting on others was never something that naturally occurred to me. Not at any time but especially not then. So I waited until there was just enough light to see, but dark enough for me to hide in the shadows. I slipped out of the hospital and ran. I don't think I stopped until I found myself here in Haven."

"I think I can understand, given what you went through," Dana said firmly. "But things have changed and you don't have a lot of choice this time. You know that, don't you? You're going to have to trust us to help you. We care about you, Kellen, and we're not going to let you down."

Kellen thought she had steeled herself, but in the aftermath of the telling, she felt emotionally and physically drained.

She hadn't planned to delve so deeply into the past. Not here. Not now. Maybe not ever. But she'd been fighting it for so long. Trying to hold it together. Trying to hold it all in rather than letting it bleed out for all to see.

And yet somehow, word by revealing word, a thin shaft of light had shone into the darkness inside her, and a glimmer of peace descended in her mind. Was this what she'd needed all these years? To speak the truth to someone who would believe and understand?

If so, it was a start. A good start. Even though she knew that beneath the liberating words, the fear still ran deep.

"Why don't you go back to your cabin and rest for a while?" Annie's eyes were soft with understanding.

"I can't." Her voice broke and for a heartbeat or two, she stared out the window, her jaw working tightly. "Unless I'm mistaken, there are two FBI agents waiting outside this office, and the moment I step outside, they're going to be all over me. Pushing for me to tell them everything."

Harrison cleared his throat, not unaffected by the exchange. "Kellen, tell me something. Do you think there's any real possibility that either of your parents is responsible for these killings?"

"You know who they are, don't you?" She didn't wait for him to acknowledge the truth of her statement. "Let me ask you the same question. Do you believe either of them is capable of being behind all these deaths? For the sake of killing a daughter they haven't seen and likely haven't thought about in nearly twenty years?"

"Nothing in life is ever guaranteed," Harrison said, turning his head to look straight at Kellen. "Personally, I believe your parents are much too selfish and self-absorbed to do anything that might in any way interfere with their lifestyle. Of course, knowing who your father is, I would have never thought him capable of doing what he did to you. Or your mother, for that matter."

"That's kind of what I thought."

"So my answer is that I wouldn't eliminate either of them from a list of suspects, but I strongly believe we'll find the answer elsewhere. I'm sorry to say we'll also need to take a look at the other families," Harrison said gruffly. "Cody's and Ren's."

"You're going to raise a lot of ghosts that might be better off left undisturbed," Kellen said. "No one becomes a runaway by choice. The girls were sixteen when I brought them here, and they'd already been on the streets for four years."

"Oh God. You're saying they were twelve?"

She heard the horror in Dana's voice but couldn't deny the truth. "Yes, just a bit younger than I was. What's important is we all survived what we encountered living on the streets, and it was far better than what we left behind."

"What did Cody leave behind?"

"Cody never knew her dad. There were men around, but never for long and never the same one. She's never mentioned whether there were any siblings, but I do know her mother died of a drug overdose. It happened not long after she tried to sell Cody to her boyfriend of the moment so she could buy enough to ease whatever demon was haunting her."

"And Ren?" Harrison asked.

Kellen closed her eyes as an involuntary shudder ran through her. "I'm sorry. Ren's story isn't mine to tell. Over the years, she's shared bits and pieces with me. I don't know all of it, but what I do know is bad."

"Don't worry about it," Harrison said. "My people can do their jobs and get me whatever information we'll need to determine if there's a connection. I'm sorry if too many ghosts are disturbed in the process. Sorrier still because I have to head back to Washington now. But before I go, I'm going to take care of the FBI. They won't harass you again," he said as he picked up his coat. "But I need you to do one thing in return."

"What's that?"

"Until this matter is settled, if anything comes up, if you need help of any kind, I need to know you won't run. Instead, I expect to hear from one of you. Do I have your word?"

"Yes, all right." She was shocked to hear herself say it.

As he squeezed her shoulder one last time, his eyes held only approval and warmth. "Be good to yourself, Kellen. You've got strong support here. There's no shame in leaning on them until this is over. Annie, love, why don't you walk me out to the car?"

After Annie and her father left the room, Dana turned to Kellen and smiled. "Wow. He's quite a force of nature, isn't he?"

Kellen nodded. "He is that. I just can't believe—"

"Can't believe what?"

"I can't believe he's known who I am from the beginning. And yet he still trusted me. Financially, by backing the business idea, and with Annie. He trusted that I wouldn't hurt Annie."

"He's obviously a good judge of character," Dana said. "If I can ask, what happens now?"

"At this point, I'm guessing you can ask me anything, Dana. But I'm not sure what you mean."

"Really? I can ask you anything?"

"Yes. And don't ask me why because that's one thing I can't answer. Just tell me what it is you want to know."

"All right, but I reserve the right to come back to this later."

Kellen would have laughed if she didn't hurt so badly. "Fine."

"I guess I'd like to know what happens now that the genie is out of the bottle. Do you stay as Kellen Ryan or do you start using a different name?"

Kellen didn't immediately respond as she struggled to find the right words. "I believe a life-altering experience changes you so much that going back to who you were is impossible. And who I was—that person, that life doesn't exist anymore. Time moves forward, not backward," she said. "I've used many names since I left home. And as the senator said, there are no guarantees in life, so only time will tell. But for now, I'm happy being Kellen."

"I'm glad. As it happens, I like Kellen Ryan. Quite a bit," Dana murmured. "But just to be clear, who you were? That life still exists. Time does move forward, but that doesn't mean the past goes away."

"I know. But it's not something I'm prepared to think about right now."

Chapter Thirteen

The call came in just after three in the afternoon. "Alpine, we've got a report of a slide near Baker's Pass. Witness reports at least six snowmobilers buried."

In the process of touring Liz through Incident Command, Dana stopped, watching and listening as the center switched into action.

"Dispatch to Ryan."

Almost immediately, she could hear Kellen's voice, "This is Ryan, copy."

"Kel, we've got a slide near Baker's Pass. Near as we can tell, it was triggered by some kids high-marking. We've got a hysterical witness saying at least six buried, but it could be more. Time three-oh-eight."

"Copy," Kellen replied. "Page out team one and whoever else you can reach. Tell Sam I'll meet her at the helipad with Bogart in less than two."

"You're letting Kellen go out?" Dana asked quietly.

"She's our best avalanche searcher and Bogart will only let Kel handle him," Annie responded. "I know there's a risk, but there's really no option here. We've got kids missing."

"Of course." Dana didn't think twice. "What can Liz and I do to help?"

"On an avalanche rescue? Honey, Kellen will take every person she can get and we're on the clock."

"What does that mean?"

"Every minute a person is buried in an avalanche, the chance of survival drops one to two percent. Are you up for it?"

The instant Dana and Liz agreed, they were handed bright red jackets, backpacks, and radios, then directed to the helipad. They got there just as the first helicopter lifted off. A minute after that, they were sitting inside the second helicopter along with several members from rescue team one.

Dana had flown before, but always on a large commercial airliner. Never on anything so small. And certainly never on anything that looked like it was skimming the treetops. But as she looked around and tried not to think about it, she caught the grin on Liz's face. "Bring back memories?"

"Oh yeah. Not all good, but I'm more than okay with this. It's no different than being on a roller coaster. Try to breathe, okay? You'll find it helps."

Dana grinned wryly. "Did I ever mention I'm not a fan of roller coasters?"

Breathing slowly and trying to relax, Dana listened to the pilot talking to someone, debating the best approach. Looking around, she noticed each member of the team had a different way of coping with the nervous anticipation as they found themselves en route to a rescue. Some sat quietly, some fidgeted, others chattered nonstop.

Dana turned to Tim. "Any idea what Annie meant by high-marking?"

"It's a sport after a fashion, I guess, when a person on a snowmobile tries to ride as far up a steep mountain slope as possible, then turns around and comes back down the hill without getting stuck or rolling their snowmobile," Tim answered.

"Whatever for?"

"The height of the arching track left in the snow sets the mark, and then everyone else tries to surpass the height of the original arch."

"God save us from alcohol-fueled games," Liz interjected.

"True enough, because it's not just the kids that get caught up in it," Gabe said. "The problem is that optimum high-mark terrain is typically in areas where avalanche danger is extremely high. And if you climb a slope from the bottom without first assessing the snow stability, you are playing a game of Russian roulette. That's why high-marking accounts for more than sixty percent of the avalanche fatalities involving snowmobilers."

"Sweet Jesus," Dana mumbled and shivered while muted conversations continued to flow around her. Drawing her jacket closer, she tucked her hands in her pockets.

Gabe smiled in sympathy. "Even with the heater on full blast, it's always cold traveling like this in winter. I think it's to make up for being too hot in the summer." He reached behind Tim, then dropped a blanket over her shoulders.

"Thanks."

Eventually, all conversation ceased as the helicopter banked, then landed with a gentle lurch. It stayed stationary long enough for everyone to get out before heading back to pick up more searchers.

Ducking until she was safely standing away from the helicopter, Dana got her first view of the massive field of avalanche debris. She wasn't certain what she'd expected, having never seen one up close before, but the field seemed enormous and looked like slabs of concrete that had been broken up.

Awestruck, she asked, "Is it always this big?"

"This is actually pretty average," Tim responded. "The average avalanche is two to three feet deep at the fracture line, about one hundred fifty feet wide, and will fall about four hundred feet in elevation. And the average duration for a slide of this size is less than thirty seconds. That means it catches and kills most backcountry travelers that happen to be in its path."

Dana stared back at the field with a greater sense of the damage it could cause. For an instant, she imagined what it had been like when the giant slab of snow and ice broke off and came down on a group of kids just having fun. Pushing the unwanted images from her mind, she looked around and spotted Kellen partway up, scanning back and forth over the field.

They hadn't spoken much since the senator left, taking the FBI agents with him. Kellen had mostly spent time with the girls and Bogart, and no one blamed her for wanting some time to regroup.

To heal the wounds that had been reopened. But Dana found herself missing her and wishing things could get back to normal, whatever that might be.

"What's Kellen doing?"

"Her first responsibility is for the safety of all field personnel, so she's assessing the risk of additional avalanches," Tim explained as he helped her take her avalanche beacon and probe from her backpack. "But she's also looking for any distinguishable tracks entering or exiting the slide area. Or any clues lying on top of the debris. Anything she didn't see when she and Sam did their flyover."

Moments later, Kellen worked her way down to them, quickly organizing, instructing, and dispatching groups of searchers, before stopping in front of Liz and Dana.

"Hey, thanks for coming out to help." Kellen cocked her head ever so slightly toward the avalanche field. "Are you ready for this?"

Kellen felt inordinately pleased when Dana answered, "Just tell us what you want us to do."

"According to the witness, some of the kids had beacons, so you're going to be looking for a signal indicating the rough position of a victim. If you hold your avalanche beacon like a compass, flat and straight out in front of you, it will give you both an idea of direction and distance to the beacon you're searching for." Kellen quickly demonstrated. "If you find someone, put your probe in to mark the position."

"What do we do if we find someone?" Liz asked.

"Call out on your radio then start to dig. Rather than going straight down on top of the victim, move slightly downhill and dig in horizontally to them. That way, you won't collapse any airspace they may have or cause snow to topple into a vertical hole on top of them. Once you've extricated them, you'll need to quickly check the victim for clogged airways and any life-threatening injuries." She stopped as she realized who she was talking to. "Sorry. Force of habit."

Dana and Liz both laughed. "No worries. How long do you think this will take?"

"Minutes. Hours. Days. Searches can go any which way. There's no predicting." Kellen shrugged. Beside her, Bogart started to whine with apparent impatience.

"Looks like someone wants you to get going."

Kellen nodded. "He knows he's here to work. He's trained to find human scent coming up from the snowpack and he'll search until he finds where that scent's coming up. He'll alert, then start digging where that scent's the strongest." She paused for an instant. "Stay sharp. I've posted a lookout for any secondary slides, but that doesn't mean you can take any unnecessary chances. And above all, don't make me have to look for you. Okay?"

Kellen walked away, aware both Dana and Liz were watching her. Beside her, Bogart barked, quivering with anticipation. "Okay, boy, ready? Let's search."

Bogart took off in the direction Kellen had indicated, while she followed more slowly.

The first victim was quickly found. Kellen started to dig him out, which was not easy as the snow around him was extremely hard and packed in. Others arrived to help, and before long, they uncovered a boy, maybe sixteen. He was shaking and scared, but able to communicate.

While she checked him over, he told her he thought there were two others close to him. "And I think there are a couple of others downslope from me. At least, that's where they were the last time I saw them."

A group of searchers, including Dana and Liz, immediately broke off and began to dig where the boy indicated, while Kellen and Bogart resumed the search for other victims. But it was not an easy task.

With time, they discovered two more victims, far apart and buried very deep in the snowpack. As luck would have it, they'd gotten tangled in debris from trees caught by the slide, which had created air pockets and enabled them to survive. But both were bleeding and had suffered a number of broken bones. And one complained of acute abdominal pain, suggesting internal damage as well.

Kellen sent Liz back to the clinic with the three wounded to oversee their transfer to a hospital in Denver. She would have preferred to send Dana, who was looking pale and tired. But as long as hope remained, any additional survivors would need the most experienced medical team she could provide.

Four hours later, the original group of searchers were cold, aching, and fatigued. Kellen knew she should have called off the search until morning. But no one wanted to stop. Not with two kids still missing.

Thankfully, they'd been joined by a group of fresh volunteers. Townspeople. Friends of the missing boys. They distributed hot coffee, listened as Kellen directed them by the glow of Maglites, then everyone silently pitched in.

Hope springs eternal. But it was still too late. Kellen knew in her heart that it had taken too long. Slowly and without formality, the focus of the searchers shifted from rescue mode to recovery until the final two victims were found. Unresponsive. Not breathing, no pulse. And nothing anyone could do would change the outcome.

Dejected, physically hurting, and tired, Kellen hung her head for a moment, trying to catch her breath, while Bogart leaned against her leg. Arms wrapped around her from behind. "Kellen, don't," Dana murmured.

She turned but stayed in Dana's arms. "Don't what?"

"Don't play what-if. *What if* you'd gotten to this spot sooner? *What if* these boys hadn't decided to high-mark? Everyone did their best. That's all anyone can ask. And as a doctor, I can tell you it wouldn't have made a difference if we had found those boys five hours ago. Not with the injuries they suffered."

"You're right, of course. Hell, that's the speech I give to searchers every time out. But it's still hard. And they were just kids." Kellen released a sigh. "How are you holding up?"

Dana laughed. "I could use a three-hour massage. Didn't you once promise to give me an awesome rubdown?"

Kellen tried to clench her raw hands and couldn't. "Damn. Would you take a rain check?"

"What the hell did you do to your hands?"

"I went through two pairs of gloves." Kellen grinned weakly. "Turns out I didn't have a third pair."

Too tired to think of food, Dana stood in the shower for a long time, then dressed in pajama bottoms and a T-shirt, lit a fire, and collapsed on her sofa. She welcomed the warmth from the bright flames, loved how the smoke scented the air. Half dozing, she was giving consideration to warming up a can of soup when she heard a soft knock on her door, followed by a sharp bark.

Smiling, she opened the door. Bogart bounded in and settled in front of the fireplace, leaving Cody, Ren, and Kellen at the door. The two girls held covered trays that smelled suspiciously familiar and wonderful, while Kellen held a large thermos in freshly bandaged hands.

"Sorry about Bogart. Some days he has no manners," Kellen murmured.

"Not a problem. Come on in," Dana said. "How did you know I was just thinking of food?"

"You're as bad as this one," Ren said indicating Kellen. "Thinking about food doesn't make it magically appear."

"Sure it does," Dana fired back. "You're here with food, aren't you?"

Kellen laughed. "Don't bother trying to argue, Ren. She's got you beat."

Ren grinned good-naturedly. "Okay. Cody and I have tomato soup and grilled cheese sandwiches. Kel has a thermos of brew."

"She means coffee," Kellen translated in response to Dana's questioning look.

"Brew. Coffee. Makes perfect sense to me."

While the girls uncovered the trays and filled cups with coffee, Dana watched the firelight playing on Kellen's face. For some reason, tired and relaxed, wearing well-worn jeans and a black turtleneck, Kellen had never looked as breathtakingly beautiful. It made Dana wish they were alone, and for an instant, she imagined taking her mouth in a long, slow, leisurely kiss she would feel all the way to her soul.

Sighing, she moved away. "Let's eat."

❖

Memory hit clear and fast, and fear rushed back in. She was twelve. Sitting in a sun-drenched living room, listening to birdsong coming from a tree just outside the window.

A man entered the room. Tall, broad-shouldered. Handsome. Striding toward her, calling out her name.

The sun momentarily blinded her, but she knew who he was. Her father. She felt his seething rage—and something else that made her instinctively afraid. He was muttering to himself. Saying things. Things she didn't understand.

An instant later, it no longer mattered. She tasted blood from her freshly split lip as he struck her, knocking her to the floor. She felt him tear at her clothes and kick her legs apart. Felt the pain as it exploded through her body. No. She screamed and tried to twist away. Panic gripped her throat and she fought, striking out with legs and arms. Her lungs tight, she tried to breathe. But it was hopeless.

Kellen jolted, instantly awake. Her breathing was hard and fast and her heart was pounding, but the images from the dream were already muddled and blurred.

Her sight clear of the fear that still jittered at the edges of her mind, she looked around, confused that she wasn't in her bed. Or even in her own cabin. It took a moment longer for her to recognize she was on Dana's sofa, wrapped in a blanket that held the clean, fresh, and tantalizing essence she thought of as uniquely Dana. And that Bogart's cold wet nose was nuzzling her neck.

She reached and stroked him, puzzled for a moment by the bandages on her hand, then remembered the painful search for the missing boys. Seven of nine was better than they'd had any right to expect. Or hope. But she was sad for the families of the two who would never return. A fatigue, heavy and deep, settled to the depths of her soul.

Wrapping the blanket around her shoulders for warmth, she went to the door and opened it. Beyond the front steps, the snow-covered trees looked more blue than white, while stars filled the sky. It was peaceful. Beautiful. The remnants of her nightmare receded. And when she felt the press of a soft feminine body against her back, the perfect scene was complete.

"How come you're up? Did you have another nightmare?"

Turning slowly, Kellen lifted the blanket until Dana was under it with her, sharing their combined warmth. "How is it you've known me for such a short time and yet you know me so well?"

"Does it bother you that I do?"

"I've no frame of reference for it, but…no. I don't think so."

"Good."

Stepping back inside, Kellen shut the door. "When I awoke, I found myself on your sofa with no memory of how I ended up there."

Dana laughed softly. "You and the girls brought dinner over. I don't think you managed more than two spoonfuls of soup before you fell asleep."

Kellen felt her face heat. "I'm sorry. I can't believe I did that."

"There's nothing to apologize for. You were exhausted. You slept while the girls and I ate, cleaned up, and took Bogart out. When we came back, you were still dead to the world, so we covered you in a blanket, the girls went back to their cabin, and I went to bed."

"I'm still—"

Dana pressed her fingers against Kellen's lips. "Don't, Kellen. You did nothing wrong. You were tired. You're still tired unless my eyes are deceiving me. And so am I. So why don't we just go back to bed. Anything that needs to be said can wait until morning. All right?"

Kellen nodded and slowly moved toward the sofa, only to be stopped by Dana. "What's wrong?"

"I said bed, Kellen. Let's go to bed." Dana reached up and cupped her cheek. "You're too tired and so am I. But I want you in my bed. And I believe you'll find your dog's already there. Nothing's going to happen tonight, if that's what worries you."

"Sorry about Bogart." Kellen laughed softly. "And for the record, it doesn't worry me."

Chapter Fourteen

L ate into the night, Dana gazed at the hollows and angles of Kellen's face. Long after she'd mumbled that she didn't want to dream anymore, she'd fallen asleep beside her. Facedown in an exhausted, limp sprawl.

"No more dreams tonight," Dana murmured. "Tell me what to do. Tell me what you need."

Kellen hadn't stirred. But at least her mind seemed quiet. For the moment, not troubled by whatever dreams and memories seemed to plague her. Dana took some satisfaction in that, as she closed the distance between them and drifted off to sleep.

But in the hazy light of morning, Dana awoke alone. The thought bothered her more than it should have as she breathed in Kellen's lingering scent. The bedding was cool to the touch, telling her she'd been gone for some time. With the memory of Kellen's scent still filling her mind, Dana got up, made the bed, and headed for the shower.

When she returned to the bedroom, however, it was to a different scent—freshly brewed coffee. She smiled as she spotted Kellen by her bed, having just poured some into a mug. And the steam rising smelled like heaven.

"Sorry. I guess I took too long feeding Bogart and taking him for a quick run. I'd hoped to find you still in bed, where you could enjoy coffee and this." She sounded apologetic as she pointed to a fat copy of the *New York Times* on the bed. "I'm not scheduled to work until this afternoon, and it's one of my favorite ways to spend a lazy morning."

"That would have been nice." Her stomach fluttered at the image Kellen's comment evoked, but she ignored it. "Since the bed's already made, why don't we light a fire and enjoy the *Times* and coffee on the sofa? We can split sections then share the crossword. And I can toast some bagels if you're hungry."

It pleased Dana to see Kellen's quick, amused agreement.

As they took opposite ends of the sofa with the paper spread out between them, she noticed Kellen's hands were still bandaged, but she was using them more freely. "Your hands seem better this morning. Do you want me to take a look?"

Quickly taking inventory for herself, Kellen shook her head. "No need. They'll be fine by tomorrow."

"Kellen—"

"Seriously, Doc." Kellen moved fingers and clenched her hands. "It all works. I'm using a salve that's got to be the best first-aid remedy I know. I learned how to make it from a Lakota healer I met when I was still living on the street. I've been using it ever since and I swear by it. So do the girls."

"You make it yourself?" Dana frowned. "What's in it?"

"It's a blend. A little this, a bit of that. Calendula, comfrey, plantain, and lavender."

"And it works?"

"Absolutely. Wait and you'll be able to see for yourself tomorrow."

"If you're trying to make me a believer in the medicinal benefits of roots and herbs, you won't have to work too hard," Dana said and started to laugh. "Of course, my father would be horrified."

The lazy, relaxing morning eased into a productive afternoon as Kellen and Dana worked with Annie and Liz, evaluating the request they'd received from two local doctors who wanted to move their practice from town.

"I think all we're missing is the dentist's office," Dana said with a laugh. "Should we just start advertising for one now?"

Everyone was laughing when Kellen's radio squawked. "Ryan, pick up."

The tone on the radio said it all. Instinctively, Kellen switched her two-way to cell mode and called Incident Command. "Who?" she asked as soon as her call was answered.

Any sign of banter was gone from her voice and she immediately felt three sets of eyes fix on her face, while she listened to news she didn't want to hear. Her knees nearly buckled and the edges of her vision grayed. "Okay. Have Sam and a chopper standing by, Nick. I'm heading to the helipad immediately."

"Where do you think you're going?" Annie asked as soon as she ended the call.

"There was an incident with the team searching for that lost hiker." She needed to be cold right now. Ice cold. "The bastard just shot one of my team."

"Kellen, you need to sit down," Dana said. "Think this through. If one of your people got shot, that means he's out there. He wants you. Please. Don't give him what he wants."

Kellen took a deep breath when the room appeared to close in. The back of her throat burned, but she wouldn't get sick. Couldn't get sick. So she lashed out. "I'm sorry, but this can't be helped. I'm going, and if you're not comfortable coming with me, then step aside so that Liz can come."

She could hear her voice, low and harsh, but she couldn't stop herself. She'd apologize later. "Decide now, Dana. The clock's ticking, I've a team member down, and Gabe's on his own trying to stop the bleeding. Please."

She saw Dana's face, pale and strained. Watched her swallow, then reach for her jacket and medical bag without saying a word.

"Who is it?" Annie asked.

"Tim." It hurt to even say it. And if she allowed it, everything would start to hurt. Her head, her stomach, her heart. Everything. So she couldn't let it happen. The pain—that would be for later when she was alone. Right now, she needed to work. Tim needed her focused and in control. She would give him no less than her best.

❖

Dana watched Kellen, coiled like a spring through the short flight, jump from the helicopter before it had set down. Ducking her head, she slipped on the ice and snow, then caught herself long enough to reach the team on the ground.

They parted as she approached, letting her through until she was kneeling on the snow next to Tim's bleeding head. Feeling for his pulse and reassuring herself he was still alive, she held his hand and talked to him even though he couldn't reply.

Unable to do more than race to catch up, Dana followed and knelt down beside her, dropping her bag beside Tim.

"He's going to be all right," Kellen said.

"Yes, he will," Dana assured her as she examined the wound more closely. "I know there's a lot of blood, but head wounds tend to do that."

She checked Tim's pupils and that his airway was clear, checked the IV Gabe had started, then examined the wound. It wasn't as bad as she feared. It was a deep crease along the right side of his head. And while there still were myriad possible complications, from a skull fracture to a brain injury to bleeding in his skull, she also knew a fraction of an inch difference, and Tim would be dead.

And if Kellen had been out with the team, she might be the one lying on the ice and snow. Seriously wounded. Possibly dead.

Dana didn't want to think about that. But she couldn't avoid it because it was likely what Kellen was thinking. Thinking if she hadn't been grounded, she would be the one lying on the ground bleeding instead of Tim. Her friend and teammate.

She glanced at Kellen's pale, expressionless face and knew it would simply be a matter of time before they would have to deal with the fallout.

As Kellen wiped a steak of blood from Tim's face, he opened his eyes. He blinked once, twice, and looked dazed. Confused. "Hey, Kel. What are you doing here? I thought you were grounded."

"I couldn't let you guys have all the fun," she teased and she lightly touched his face. "Tim, listen. I want you to focus on me. You got hurt, but you're going to be fine."

"Hurt?"

"That's right, but you don't need to worry about it. Dana and Gabe are getting you ready to move and then we're going to send you to Denver just to be on the safe side. But we have to work with them at the hospital, so try not to chase too many nurses. Okay?"

"Okay." He nodded weakly. "Kel? Is that why my head hurts?" His voice faded as his eyes closed.

Kellen raised her eyes to Dana, clearly trying to hold it together, pleading for reassurance.

"He regained consciousness." Dana answered the unspoken question. "He knew who you were. Those are both good signs."

The team lifted Tim onto a gurney, then transferred him to the helicopter. Life Flight had already been contacted and would meet them when they landed, then airlift Tim to Denver where a neurologist was on standby.

It all went beautifully. Like clockwork.

But Dana couldn't shake the feeling that Tim's shooting was just the tip of the iceberg.

❖

As the day waned, Kellen was surviving by a thread, trying to hold it together, at least for as long as it took to debrief the team.

"We heard a loud cracking sound—at a guess, it sounded like a rifle. I mean, we hear them often enough during hunting season, and that's what it sounded like. Tim dropped like a rock at almost the same moment," Gabe said. "But we couldn't tell what direction the shot came from. All we could do was try to deal with Tim's bleeding while waiting to get picked up, and hope in the meantime we weren't sitting there like ducks in a shooting gallery."

"Annie said the sheriff's office is already investigating and they've called the FBI. They'll have a forensics team come out and try to determine the trajectory," Jeff added. "But I'm not sure how that's going to help figure out who's responsible."

"I don't know either." Kellen exhaled softly, feeling bone tired but trying not to let it show.

"The sheriff said they're looking for something that might have a fingerprint or DNA they can use to identify whoever's behind this," Dana said. "Like an empty shell case or a cigarette butt."

"Well, until they do, we'll have to be extra vigilant and learn to put up with them being underfoot, because for us, it's going to be business as usual."

"What does that mean exactly?" Dana studied Kellen's face a moment.

"It means as of now, I'm back leading team one," Kellen said, annoyed that her pulse was a little quick, a little unsteady.

"Kellen? What are you talking about?" Dana's eyes widened at the remark. "You know you can't. Don't you realize your team is afraid? Not of you but for you? They don't want you getting killed because you give whoever's out there a chance to get to you. They want you alive. Damn it, we all want you alive, and I for one wouldn't mind if it was for a long time."

Without thinking it through, Kellen responded with heat. "Actually, what I can't do is sit back and watch this bastard pick off my team members one at a time while he waits for me to show up. I can't remain safe, hiding in my cabin or in my office, and let everyone else take all the risks. More than that, I won't do it. And if you don't understand that, you don't know me at all."

"Kel—"

With her attention laser-focused on Dana, Kellen heard Annie call her name as if from a distance. By then, she'd heard Dana's breath catch, had seen her features grow pale and pain flash in her usually vibrant eyes. She knew she'd gone over the line as her throat closed and it became difficult to swallow. "Damn. Damn. Damn. I'm sorry, Dana."

"It's all right."

"No it's not." Kellen felt a wash of regret and frustration. "I had no right to take a shot at you, but it seems you're a handy target right now."

Nibbling on her bottom lip, Dana eyed her warily. "Does that mean it's not part of the job description?"

Instantly grateful she hadn't caused irreparable harm, Kellen felt a ghost of a smile touch her lips. "Maybe, maybe not. Time will tell. Please, try to understand. Tim's not just a colleague, he's a friend. And he's lying in a hospital with a bullet wound to his head when we all know it should have been me. It's eating at me. But that's no reason for me to take it out on you."

"If it helps—"

"Ah, Dana," Kellen sighed. "Don't make offers I just might accept."

"Maybe, maybe not," Dana repeated and smiled. "We'll have to wait and see. For now, how about we take the team into town for some pizza and beer?"

Kellen studied her for a moment then looked away. "Sounds like a plan. Annie, why don't you get Lesley to put the writing down for the evening and join us? Then you, Dana, and Liz can round up whoever's not working."

"Aren't you coming with us?" Dana asked, a frown creasing her brow.

"Absolutely. I'll meet you in town in a bit. I need to feed Bogart and take him for a run. But first, I need to tell Cody and Ren what happened so they don't hear about it from someone else."

"Good idea." Dana looked at Annie then back to Kellen. "But you've got blood all over the bandages on your hands, so you might want to think about changing them before you see the girls."

"Damn." Kellen stared at her hands, covered in Tim's blood. "You're right, of course. Thanks for reminding me."

Chapter Fifteen

The music at Up the Creek seemed louder, and the energy felt a bit more frenetic than usual. Vacationers and locals filled most tables and kept the waitstaff moving in high gear. But it was perfect for getting everybody to forget what had happened to Tim, if only for a little while.

Several tables in the back had mysteriously been held for them and Dana had barely removed her jacket and tossed it on the back of her chair when pitchers of beer appeared at their table.

"Kellen called ahead," the server said. "The wings and pizza will be up momentarily."

"God, I love that girl," Annie said, while two members of the team started pouring beer into glasses and passing them down the line.

"The server? Should I be worried?"

Dana recognized the woman who'd just spoken from the photos on the back covers of her books, pleased that she was finally getting the chance to meet Lesley Marlow.

"Hell, no." Annie pulled Lesley down onto the love seat with her and gave her partner a quick kiss. "I'm talking about Kellen. She's always thinking ahead, doing all the little things to make sure everyone's taken care of."

"If you want my unsolicited opinion, I think it's a quid pro quo kind of thing," Dana said before turning to Lesley and extending her hand. "Dana Kingston. I'm a fan of your work."

Lesley's smile widened as she shook Dana's hand. "The new doctor I've heard so much about. A pleasure to meet you, and not just because you're a fan. I'm sorry we've not had a chance to meet before now, but I've been going slightly crazy trying to finish a book tour as well as finish the edits to my next book. I'm sure Annie has told you."

They continued chatting amiably as the food arrived and multiple hands immediately reached for their preference.

"You'd think they never eat," Annie said dryly, watching the food rapidly disappear while licking some teriyaki sauce off her thumb. "If Kellen doesn't get here soon, there'll be nothing left."

"Actually," Liz commented, "I saw her come in a minute ago. She's talking to the sexy redhead at the front."

Annie and Dana both looked up. "That's Michelle," Annie said. "She owns this place. Interested in an introduction?"

Liz took a longer look. "Maybe. One question first. Is there anything going on with her and Kellen that I should know about?"

"No. They dated once, but nothing came of it and now they're friends. Just friends. I would think it makes them both available, don't you think, Dana?"

Dana groaned, feeling the well-intentioned comment hit home. "Are you trying to match everyone up?"

"Always," Lesley said dryly. "Ever since we got together, it's like she can't help herself."

Annie shrugged. "I just want everyone to be as happy as I am. If this job has taught me anything, it's that life is unpredictable, and everyone should make the most of it while they can."

"I'll drink to that," Kellen said as someone handed her a beer. "Hey, Lesley. Glad you could make it. Is everyone doing okay?"

"Yes, now come and eat something before it's all gone."

Kellen looked at the remnants of pizza and wings and slowly shook her head. "Actually, I'm not very hungry."

Dana didn't like her answer. Nor her tone of voice. Kellen looked too pale, her eyes tired and flat. And she was holding her body stiffly, as if it was taking an act of sheer will to remain standing. "What is it, Kellen? Is something wrong? Is it Tim?"

"Actually, Tim's good. I talked to the hospital just before I got here. He was awake, his skull's not fractured, the neurological exam was fine, and the CT scan was normal. Balance, reflexes, memory, everything's fine. They're just going to keep him a couple of days to be sure."

"That's great news."

"Absolutely. He's got one hell of a headache and according to the doctor I spoke with he'll be dealing with post-concussion symptoms for a while. He's also not very happy they had to shave part of his head so they could stitch him, but hair'll grow back." Her voice faded and she paused as if uncertain what else to say. Or what else needed to be said.

"He'll be chasing nurses by tomorrow morning," someone said.

The comment made everyone at the table laugh and as they began sharing Tim stories, Dana tugged on Kellen's hand. "Will you tell me what's wrong?"

Kellen looked at her and shrugged. "I don't know. It's like everything has gotten out of sync all of a sudden and I can't quiet the noise in my head." She swallowed. "One millimeter, Dana. One millimeter to the left and he'd be dead."

Dana could hear the fear still lurking in Kellen's voice. "Try not to think about it."

"How am I supposed to do that?"

In the corner, someone dropped money in the jukebox and punched in the number for a ballad. Dana smiled, deliberately slow and sexy. "Come and dance with me. It'll get your mind off things."

"Ah, Dana—" Kellen seemed nonplussed for a second and a line formed between her eyebrows as she considered her options.

"Don't think. Just come and dance with me and, for a little while, try to forget about everything else." She held out her hand, pleased when Kellen finally took it and allowed herself to be led away from the table to the half-filled dance floor. A few members of the team looked up, smiled as they passed, and went back to their conversations.

❖

The music drifted over them as they got to the dance floor. With Dana settled in against her, Kellen wrapped her arms around her waist. Somehow she'd forgotten—forgotten how soft a woman's body could be. How warm and inviting.

The nearly foreign sensation should have made her pull back. She should have never compromised the safety of feeling nothing. But instead, she moved them in a tight turn, a move that brought one of Dana's legs between her thighs.

Almost immediately, a wave of heat washed over her, accompanied by a warning sound in her head. A litany she'd been repeating for a while. Or at least, that was how it seemed.

In spite of their disparate backgrounds—the wealthy East Coast doctor and the former runaway—they'd become friends. Possibly really good friends. She liked Dana. Not just her face and her body, but her sense of humor, her intelligence, her compassion. She enjoyed Dana's company and didn't want to do anything to jeopardize the relationship they'd developed. She needed to respect that, no matter how much her more primal instincts protested.

But more to the point, a person just needed to look at Dana to know she was made for better things. A long-term relationship. A lifetime commitment. While she was made for—just what the hell was she made for?

She licked her suddenly dry lips and heat rushed to her face when Dana slid her hands up her back, sending shivers racing through her. "Um…Dana?"

In the low light, Dana's eyes gleamed with mischief before she burrowed her lithe body closer and pressed her lips to Kellen's throat, licking the skin she found there with the tip of her tongue.

"Dana," Kellen whispered, trying to stop a whimper from escaping her throat. "God, you're so damn beautiful. And you're killing me."

"Really?" There was gentle, teasing humor in her voice. "Because I'd have to say you feel very much alive to me and I *am* a doctor. So trust me on this. But you do feel a little hot. Are you running a fever again?"

Yes. She spun Dana out to arm's length and then reeled her back in, buying enough time to take a deep breath. But all too soon, their bodies were once again lined up, breast to breast, hip to hip, causing full-body sensory overload as they swayed to the music. And when

Dana's hand slipped beneath Kellen's sweater and began moving in tantalizing circles on her back, it lit a fire deep inside her.

"I have a question," she murmured.

"Yes."

Kellen laughed. "But you haven't heard the question yet."

Dana tilted her head back, exposing the silky column of her throat as she stared back at her, her gaze intent. "It doesn't matter. The answer is yes."

The noise in the pub grew distant—the sultry blues music, the pool tables, the raucous laughter—then disappeared altogether as Kellen dropped her gaze to Dana's mouth. How many times had she wanted to taste that beautiful mouth? How many times had she wanted to feel those soft lips moving over her own? But she could also feel the lingering doubts, beckoning her to retreat, to throw up her walls of self-defense.

"Dana..." she tried weakly.

"Yes, Kellen. Don't you get it? It doesn't matter how many times or how many different ways you ask. My answer will still be yes."

Kellen blinked, taking a brief moment to align things in her mind. Only the moment didn't seem to help. Grateful for the shadows cast by the fire pit that would help hide some of what she was feeling, she managed to mutter, "'Kay."

Without saying another word, she drew Dana back to the group at the table and grabbed their coats. As she shrugged into her jacket, Kellen caught Annie's eyes. Saw her smile and mouth something that looked remarkably like *it's about time*. Then Dana reached for her hand again, their fingers entwined, and nothing else existed but the woman beside her. A woman who knew what she was and still wanted her.

The instant they stepped outside into the cold night air, Kellen stopped abruptly.

"Kellen," Dana questioned softly, brows narrowed in concern. "Is there a problem?"

Unable to speak, feeling a range of emotions too strong to deny, giving in to desire and longing, Kellen pulled Dana into a narrow alleyway between two buildings and pinned her against the wall.

Planting her hands, one at a time, on either side of Dana's head, she brought her closer, pleased when she saw Dana's eyes slowly close and her lips slowly part. And then she closed the remaining distance between their mouths, channeling everything into one singular activity. Focused solely on the amazing pleasure of kissing Dana.

Coaxing. Teasing. Hot. Possessive. Her thoughts scattered and she was enveloped by both Dana's and her own need. But her body had no trouble staying on track as they melded. Heat against heat. She drove her hands into Dana's hair, slanted her head for a better angle as her tongue slipped inside and she deepened the kiss. Pouring everything she had and everything she was feeling into the play of their mouths.

Wrapping her arms around Kellen's neck, Dana welcomed the wild dance of lips and tongue, returning every lick and taste until her body melted against the wall and only Kellen's strong arms were keeping her standing. She tasted need. Tasted desire. Tasted the barely concealed restraint.

When the kissing started to intensify, to turn into something far more involved than the simple press of lips and sweep of tongues, Kellen pushed back against Dana's shoulders, putting inches of space between them.

She looked at Kellen, at a loss to explain why the kiss had ended, while she willed some strength back into her legs. "Is something wrong?"

"I'm sorry," Kellen said, still breathing hard.

Dana frowned. "For kissing me?"

"God, no. You've had me so hot for so long, I'm barely hanging on right now. But that's no excuse for pulling you into an alley and—"

"I don't see anything wrong with where we are." Dana looked around and smiled. "In fact, another few seconds and I'd have started to rip your clothes off. Right here."

"Really?"

"Yes. You'll discover I'm remarkably low maintenance. But it is a little on the cold side, so for now, there's only one question you need to answer. Your cabin or mine?"

"Dana," Kellen whispered hoarsely, her eyes so dark they were nearly black. "I'm not—"

"Your cabin or mine, Kellen?"

Kellen closed her eyes and released a soft breath. "Mine. I want you in my cabin and in my bed. Does that make me too Neanderthal?"

"Actually, it sounds perfect." A laugh slipped out as Dana grabbed Kellen's jacket and pulled her closer. "I'm not going to hurt you."

"What if I hurt you?"

"That's a chance I'm willing to take."

Kellen cupped her face for an instant and gave her another kiss. This one sweet and much too brief, but it would have to be enough to hold her over as they walked in the dark and cold toward her Jeep.

The drive to Kellen's cabin was a blur. Dana was oblivious to everything except the pounding in her chest, the surge of arousal, and the liquid heat pooling deep inside her. So much so that she was nearly giddy with relief when they finally arrived.

Even as the front door closed behind them, they came together with greedy hands and hungry mouths. They shed jackets, tugged at sweaters, kicked off boots, and tried not to trip in the darkness.

"Bed," she managed to say between kisses.

They moved across the room without breaking the kiss, miraculously reaching the bedroom without falling. Kellen moved away from her long enough to pull the covers back from the neatly made bed. And then they landed on it together.

Eager to touch and be touched, Dana planted a kiss on Kellen's mouth. "Hold on a moment," she said, as she scrambled off the bed and out of her remaining clothes in record speed.

Finally naked, she turned back to the bed only to stop short. Kellen had shed her remaining clothes as well and was lying in the middle of the bed. Gloriously naked, desire burned in bright blue eyes. She gave a throaty laugh, held out her hand, and whispered, "Come here."

A thrill raced through Dana and her groin tightened.

She accepted Kellen's hand and allowed herself to be tugged onto the bed so that she ended on top of Kellen. Body to body. Skin to skin.

Straddling her hips, she leaned in, her breath hot on Kellen's neck. She gave a tentative lick to the tender skin she found there before moving to the underside of her jaw. And then she continued leaving a damp trail until their mouths met in a deep, soul-searing kiss that had their tongues touching, probing, and twisting together.

Breathing heavily, Dana finally tore her mouth away and pushed herself back. She felt more alive and charged than she'd ever experienced and she took her time, half mesmerized, drinking her fill of Kellen. From her half-closed eyes to her hot, swollen mouth to her toned, long, and lean body. Sleek and golden. Glorious.

Reaching out with a slightly shaking hand, Dana began gently to trace the contours of Kellen's collarbone, pausing while she used her thumb and forefinger to pinch and tease nipples into hard peaks. Closing her eyes, Kellen whimpered softly.

Driven by the sound, drawn closer still by the scent of Kellen's warm skin, and unable to further resist the allure of her small breasts, Dana captured an erect nipple with her mouth. She was rewarded by the unmistakable hitch in Kellen's breathing, as she continued on her provocative journey. She reveled in the feel of muscles moving beneath her hands as she slid down Kellen's chest and across her abs, moving lower, licking and placing barely there kisses.

Kellen watched breathlessly as Dana teased her, moving infinitesimally lower and lower, her hair flowing like silk against her heated skin. A part of her wanted it to go on forever. Another part wanted—

Oh God, yes. She felt the pressure of strong thumbs parting her, stretching her skin, then the welcome sensation of a flat, soft tongue. The contact was electric. She immediately drove her fingers through Dana's hair and arched her back, seeking to increase the pressure from that tantalizing tongue.

As Dana drove her closer and closer to the edge, Kellen held her tighter, trying to hold on, then flinched when Dana's finger tentatively started to slip inside. Dana's finger immediately retreated. But her mouth and tongue never slowed. Alternately licking, sucking, and biting the hot, hypersensitive flesh she found until Kellen's control began to slip away by degrees and her pulse was racing once again.

"God, Dana, if you're trying to make me go off like a firecracker, you're very close to succeeding."

Dana's laugh, hot and sexy, was nearly enough to send her over the edge. "Is that a bad thing?"

"No." She stared at her. Awed. Not only because of Dana's beauty, but because of her lack of pretense, and her eagerness to play. "Please. Don't make me beg."

"No problem…it seems we both want the same thing…"

In the next instant, Kellen threw her head back as acute waves of pleasure began rolling over her. An endless onslaught of pleasurable sensations stemming from Dana's relentless mouth that drove her higher and higher until she couldn't hear anything but the rush of blood through her ears, the sound of her own ragged breathing, and the scream trapped in her throat when Dana chose that moment to slide her tongue deep inside her.

She went over the edge. Willingly. Effortlessly. Hoarsely calling out Dana's name.

❖

For the second time in a few short days, Dana found herself laying in the darkness watching Kellen sleep. But for a change, she looked at peace. Happy. Sated.

And so she should be, Dana thought.

She remembered Kellen grinning as she crooked a finger. "Come here."

As she drew near, Kellen had cupped her face in her hands and leaned closer to kiss her. She had proceeded to cover her with soft kisses, gentle touches, and whispered words of longing. "I want to touch you. I want to make you feel like you made me feel."

"I want that too," Dana said against her mouth.

When Kellen's mouth took hers, it wasn't for anything other than to ignite. Heat and desire wrapped around her. Her breathing grew irregular as Kellen's lips trailed across her throat while her palms moved over her breasts, thumbs brushing over the already taut peaks. Returning to her mouth, she had nipped Dana's lower lip with her teeth, while her fingers started to inch downward, ghosting over her lower abdomen. And then she had kissed her again. Hungrily. Clearly letting everything she was feeling manifest in a dance of lips and tongue, while she slid three fingers into Dana, letting her ride her hand into a screaming orgasm.

As her breathing steadied, she considered staying exactly where she was. But then she heard Kellen's whisper, so soft she wasn't sure she'd heard the words correctly. "We're not nearly done yet. I've wanted to taste you since the first time I saw you."

Seconds later, she wasn't hearing anything.

Dana smiled as she replayed the night. Just thinking made her seek physical contact and she reached out, tracing an absent pattern over Kellen's back with the fingers of one hand. She paused for a moment and frowned when she encountered a small scar marring the satiny skin. But as she continued to touch, she found more of them. And in the dim light of early morning, she saw that they went all the way down her back, marring the perfection of her skin.

As she moved slowly from scar to scar, she suddenly realized Kellen was awake. She lay perfectly still while Dana's hand moved across her back. Not moving. Barely breathing.

Dana tried to think what could have caused all the scars. In a moment of clarity, she remembered Kellen saying her father had beaten her. And in a move driven by both instinct and need, she leaned closer still and brought her lips to the nearest scar. Leaving soft butterfly kisses, she moved from scar to scar until she'd kissed them all.

Several minutes passed before Kellen even moved, and when she did, she looked at her for a long silent moment. "Dana, I don't know what to say. This isn't easy for me."

"Tell me why. Surely other women have found you beautiful and wanted to be with you."

"Yes—but I didn't care what they thought."

CHAPTER SIXTEEN

They both remained silent for so long that Kellen wasn't certain if Dana had fallen asleep. She was nearing that point herself, ready to fall asleep, when Dana's voice washed over her. "You're okay with this, aren't you?"

She thought she knew, but needed to be sure. "With what happened tonight?"

Dana cleared her throat. "Yes…with tonight. And with us."

"I'm more than good. But I guess it's also fair to say we've got a conversation going unsaid between us," Kellen murmured. "But not now, if that's all right. Are you all right to wait?"

"It doesn't have to be now," Dana agreed. "I just want the chance to have it."

Without another word being said, they reached for each other, their lips coming together with a reawakened sense of passion. Hands, mouths, and tongues explored, tasted, aroused.

Seconds—or possibly minutes—later, they were pulled apart abruptly by the sound of whispered voices and Bogart barking. Quickly grabbing the edge of the bedding that had been kicked to one side, Kellen draped it over Dana and looked at the two girls standing in the doorway.

"Sorry, Kellen," Cody said, uncertainty flickering in her eyes. "Ren was having bad nightmares."

Kellen immediately understood and sent both girls a gentle smile. "And you thought you'd jump in bed with me until they go away?"

"Yeah, sorry." Ren nodded sheepishly. "I just need to be with my chosen family. You know it always helps when we come and join you. We just didn't know…Doc D would be here."

Kellen turned to Dana, an unspoken question in her eyes. "She means—"

"I know what chosen family means," Dana responded. Clearly trying not to laugh, she quickly added, "It's not a problem—if you wouldn't mind giving us a moment first?"

Kellen relaxed at Dana's calm response. "I think she means so we can get dressed. Could you give us a minute or two?"

Both girls nodded and stepped out of the room with Bogart on their heels.

"Do they do this often?"

"Not so much lately," Kellen acknowledged with a smile. "When they first came to me, it happened quite frequently. Both were prone to nightmares, but Ren's were by far the worse. Whenever it happened, they would come jump in bed with me and we'd cuddle. Does it bother you?"

"No, not at all." Dana laughed. "But your previous girlfriends must have loved it."

"Actually, this is the first time they've found someone in bed with me," Kellen said quietly. She got out of bed, picked their clothes up from the floor, then reached into the dresser for a couple of fresh T-shirts. As she turned around to toss one toward the bed, she realized Dana was watching her every move. "Is there a problem? Do you not want to stay?"

Dana shook her head as she caught the T-shirt one-handed. "There's no problem, and yes I want to stay. I'm just enjoying the view."

Kellen inexplicably felt herself blush. "Right. By the time I'm done with this body, I'll be nothing but a bundle of scar tissue." And that didn't account for the unseen ones, she thought.

"Stop it," Dana said, as she got out of the bed and pulled Kellen into her arms. "You've got an amazing body. Trust me, I'm a doctor, and I've spent years studying the human form. As for the scars, they just tell the story of where you've been, not who you are."

Two minutes later, Kellen, Dana, and two still-quite-fragile young women were cuddled on the bed amidst fits of giggles. There'd been no hesitation as Ren wrapped Dana in an octopus-like grip involving arms and legs.

Dana tightened her hold on the girl and laughed softly. "At least I understand why you've got a king-sized bed in here."

❖

The next few days were busy with an average of three callouts per day as better weather enticed more people to hit the trails. It meant she and Kellen didn't spend any time together except in passing, and it left Dana with far too much time to worry each time Kellen went out with the team.

At least the clinic was open, which meant she had plenty to do. But she was invariably tense until Kellen came back safe and sound and she could check her to make sure there were no new cuts that needed stitching or bruises needing to be iced.

Still, the stress was starting to wear. Especially on days like today, when it had grown dark, the temperature had dropped, and the team was still out searching for a lost hiker.

"She'll be back before you know it," Cody said reassuringly, her own nerves showing through in the grip she maintained on Ren's hand.

"You think so?"

"Absolutely. Kellen's the smartest person I know. Not in book learning, of course. That would be you. But when it comes to the woods and mountains, and finding her way, there's no one better."

Dana studied the two young women, their youthful faces and their old eyes. Not for the first time, she wondered who had hurt them and what each had endured, both before and during their time on the streets. Before Kellen came into their lives. "So you're telling me not to worry?"

"That's right," Ren responded. "Kellen always knows what to do. How to find water and food and shelter. How to track people in the forest and how to make sure she leaves no tracks for someone else to follow. And when she's in the forest, the wild animals protect her."

"What do you mean protect her?"

Ren shrugged. "The bears and wolf packs follow her, make sure she's safe. Keep anything bad away. I think she talks to them. And when she goes fishing, it's like the fish jump into her hands. She takes only what she needs for us and gives the rest to whoever's following—the bears or wolves. That's why you can trust that she'll always come back. The animals keep her safe."

Nothing she learned about Kellen surprised her anymore.

But in spite of their show of confidence, Dana could still hear traces of fear and uncertainty in both their voices. It seemed rather than visible scars, the damage they'd endured made itself known in different ways. Like an apprehension around people, something they all shared. Or Ren's drawings, which were at times dark and violent. Or in the increasing cycle of nightmares Ren and Kellen both had been experiencing of late.

"Doc?"

"Sorry, Ren, I drifted away for a moment," Dana answered softly. "The answer is yes. I trust Kellen will come back. I just worry that she'll get hurt."

"But then you can look after her, right? Stitch her up if she cuts herself?"

"I hope so—if she lets me. Do you have any idea how she got to be so smart about nature and survival?"

"Resorting to questioning the girls to get all the details about me?"

The low, sexy voice spoke softly from just behind her, sending wondrous chills racing down Dana's back. She turned around to see Kellen, smiling tiredly by the door. "Hey, you. Fancy meeting you here. Did everything go okay?"

"Yup. All the lost have been found and sent safely to their homes and families."

"I'm glad. And since you're back, maybe you'd like to answer my question."

"I'd be happy to," Kellen said and held out her hand. "Why don't you walk me back to my cabin so Bogart and I can both eat, and I'll share my secrets with you?"

She deliberated her answer for the second it took her to grasp Kellen's hand. They walked arm in arm with Ren and Cody until they reached the girls' cabin, where they wished them good night, before continuing hand in hand on their own, with Bogart bounding ahead.

❖

Kellen stretched out on the sofa with a bottle of water, deciding she really liked watching Dana cook in her kitchen. "I discovered libraries."

"Pardon?"

She could tell Dana was confused by her expression as she plated the eggs and brought them to the table. "You wanted to know how I got smart about things like edible plants and tracking and such. I discovered libraries."

"Will you tell me more?"

"Of course." Kellen ate some of the eggs and murmured her appreciation. "It was when I first found myself on the street. There were always people. Some were willing to share things about how to survive the street, places to go if you needed temporary help. But I never knew who I could trust—actually, I didn't trust anyone, which meant I'd never survive unless I quickly learned how to do things for myself. Unless I learned how to survive on my own. Does that make sense?"

"Yes."

"That was when I discovered libraries. The security guards, they weren't keen on homeless kids coming in, and if they caught us, they threw us out. Me and other kids like me. But I learned how to sneak by them and did so as often as I could. It gave me a place to stay warm, especially when it was bitterly cold outside, and at the same time, I could learn about things I'd never known before. Like how to build a snow cave, how to catch fish with my bare hands, and what kind of plants won't kill you or make you sick…which is really important when you're hungry."

Dana shuddered. "I hate the thought of you being a kid, hungry and alone on the streets. Trying to learn how to survive."

Kellen pushed her plate away and reached for Dana's hand. "Thank you for the omelet. It was exactly what I wanted and didn't even know it. As for the streets, I did more than learn how to survive. I made my way across the country, I saw amazing places I'd only read about, and I read everything I could get my hands on. I picked up odd jobs when I could, sold carvings when I couldn't."

Kellen paused when she saw tears glistening in Dana's eyes. Reaching over, she gently wiped the tears that had fallen with her thumb. "Don't, Dana. What I learned made me stronger. It enabled me to survive. I put myself through school living on the streets. I used what I learned to build a business that saves lives. And if I can pass on what I learned and help others, like Cody and Ren, then it will all have been worth it somehow, don't you think?"

Dana's jaw quivered slightly. "I think you're an amazing woman, Kellen Ryan. You're also exhausted, so why don't I put you to bed and let you sleep? I'll clean up and let myself out."

"I'd rather you leave the dishes until morning and stay the night with me. I've discovered I sleep better when I can hear your heart beating next to my ear. Would that be all right?"

"That would be perfect."

❖

Dana awoke with a start. For a moment, she lay still. Disoriented. Uncertain what had awoken her. And then Kellen screamed again, a sound filled with anguish and pain.

"Kellen, you're dreaming." Her words had no effect, and she was torn, uncertain what to do. Kellen had begun to thrash and the violence of her movements precluded Dana being able to get closer. It was then she saw Bogart, approaching Kellen from the other side. He licked her hand, nuzzled it, then remained still, muzzle in Kellen's open hand.

To Dana's amazement, Kellen's thrashing stilled. Her breathing slowed and then her hand twitched as she began to rub Bogart. "Thanks, Bogart," she murmured.

After giving the dog an affectionate head scratch, Kellen rolled over, her eyes widening the instant she remembered she wasn't alone in bed. "Sorry." Her voice was rough with sleep. "I should come with a warning to use at own risk. I didn't hurt you, did I?"

"No. I'm fine. Does Bogart always help you like that?"

"Yeah, I guess he does. It's like he knows."

"Amazing. Do you think you can sleep a bit longer?"

"I'm not sure. Sometimes, yes. Other times, it's not worth the effort."

Dana considered her, then extended her arm. "Why don't we give it a try? Get over here."

Surprisingly without argument, Kellen moved over and wrapped herself around Dana, who sighed contentedly. "Do you want to talk about it?"

"My nightmares?"

"Yes."

"There's no pattern. Sometimes I'm twelve again. Sometimes I'm back on the street, cold and hungry. Sometimes, I've just been shot. I can't hold on to the winch cable and I'm falling." Kellen shook her head and her voice faded. "Thank you for being here."

Dana lifted her head and placed a kiss on Kellen's temple. "You don't need to thank me. There's nowhere else I would rather be. Now tell me how I can help."

"That's easy." Kellen reached for her hand and linked their fingers together. "Just talk to me."

"About what?"

"You."

Dana remained still for a moment. "What about me?"

"Everything. Your favorite color, your favorite meal, your favorite way to spend a rainy afternoon."

"Oh, is that all?"

"No. I also want to know what you were like as a little girl and who gave you your first kiss. I want to know when and why you decided to become a doctor. And I really want to know how I got so lucky you ended up in Haven."

Dana's eyes widened. "You don't want much, do you?"

"Actually, I do"—Kellen smiled—"but this will make for a good start."

CHAPTER SEVENTEEN

A long run through the woods hadn't been enough to banish her demons.

Kellen sighed as she walked across the gym dressed in body-hugging workout gear and thin-soled climbing shoes. The group near the climbing wall parted as she approached, quickly absorbing her into their midst. Their welcome was like a balm after another sleepless night and she was grateful when no one commented on the matching set of shadows both she and Ren were wearing beneath their eyes.

Nighttime had become a time for thinking. For remembering. And for being haunted by what once was and what might have been. Sleeping? That was another matter altogether.

The one saving grace was Dana's presence. Because nights had also become a time for quiet conversations and getting to know the thoughts, dreams, and aspirations that had helped shape a complex, remarkable, and compassionate woman. Being warmed and humored by stories of her childhood. Learning facets of a life Kellen could only imagine. And simply just having her there.

"What seems to be the problem?" she asked.

Four people started to answer all at once before a single voice took over. The voice belonged to Jake, a just-turned-eighteen SAR volunteer who was first up every time a call for help went out. He'd been trying to impress her for some time and Kellen knew he'd been hoping to stick with the team on a full-time basis after the New Year.

"Sorry, Kel, but I'm starting to think it's hopeless. I just can't see any pattern on the climbing wall. Even if I'm working a simple route—the blue, the red, the yellow. It doesn't seem to matter how many times I try. I just can't get it."

"All right. Are you saying you want to give up?"

Jake's chin came up. "No. That's not what I want."

"Good answer." Kellen walked to the equipment cubicles and pulled out her harness, then buckled up and tightened without saying a word before walking back to the group. She noticed Dana and Annie had entered the gym but were staying well back, watching but not wanting to interrupt a training session.

"Pick a pitch, Jake."

Jake looked at her in apparent confusion. "You're going to climb with me?"

"No. I'm going to climb. You're going to be my eyes. Gabe will take the ropes." Without another word, she took out a piece of bright red fabric and pressed the material over her eyes before tying it into a knot.

"You're going to climb blind?"

"Remember what I said, Jake. You're going to be my eyes. What pitch, Jake? Pick one, take my hand, and guide me there."

Jake guided her until she was in front of a pitch, facing the wall. Stretching and taking a deep breath, Kellen put her arms out in front of her. "Talk to me, Jake. I can't do anything without you."

"L—left hand. Fingerhold at ten o'clock."

Kellen found the hold and slipped her fingers in. "On belay?"

"Belay on," Gabe responded as Jake called out the next hold.

"Right hand. One o'clock."

"Climbing." She found the hold, adjusted her weight, and waited for his next instruction.

"Left leg. Stretch about an inch and you'll find the hold."

He talked her through a dozen or so more holds while she skimmed her hands over each hold, feeling them, testing the surface, adjusting her grip, and continuing to climb while Gabe silently worked the rope. Finally, she stopped, signaled Gabe to bring her down, and removed the blindfold.

"Tell me what the lesson is, Jake."

"Lesson?"

"Yes, there's a lesson in everything. You just have to find it." She blew out a breath and pushed sweat-dampened hair behind her ears. "I couldn't have climbed the wall without you, Jake," she said softly.

"I saw the pattern," he said in a hushed voice.

"You certainly did." She gave his shoulder a reassuring squeeze and smiled when Gabe slapped him on the back. "Take twenty. When you come back, you get the blindfold. I want you to listen and feel. Don't overthink."

Once the team had dispersed, Kellen walked over to where Dana and Annie had been watching.

"That was amazing," Dana said.

"He's a good kid. He just needs to trust himself more, but he'll get there. In the meantime, I've added him to the team until Tim gets back. His mom's working two jobs and they can use the money." She paused and looked over to where Jake was standing with Gabe, deliriously happy with a wide grin still on his face. "What about you? I know Annie always refuses, but are you ever going to give the wall a try?"

Dana quickly shook her head. "No, thanks, I like my feet on the ground."

Kellen laughed. "So do I. It's just that sometimes the ground I'm on is at ninety degrees to the ground you're on." She noticed Annie's smile seemed strained. As she looked back and forth between the two women, her own smile slowly faded. "All right, who's going to tell me what's wrong?"

"Why don't we go to my office," Annie said. "We need to talk."

No good conversation ever started with the statement *We need to talk*, Dana thought. Not unexpectedly, Kellen's entire demeanor instantly changed. Her smile disappeared, her posture stiffened, and she walked without the loose-limbed grace Dana usually found so sexy.

Once they got to Annie's office, Kellen took a spot by the window, facing the mountains with a faintly wistful expression that indicated she wanted to be out there, on the jagged peaks above the tree line where it almost seemed possible to touch the sky. Or simply be anywhere but here.

"My father called," Annie began softly.

Kellen's back tensed, the only indication she gave that she was listening.

"You were right about Cody's mother. She never named a father on the girl's birth certificate, and there was no evidence to be found to indicate who her father might have been. Her mother was a groupie and ran away from home at sixteen to follow different bands around the country. That's where her addiction began. But it also means Cody's father could be any musician from any number of different bands."

The moment stretched, long and thin to the point of breaking, but Kellen gave no further indication she was listening. Dana felt Annie look her way and sent her a slight nod.

"Ren's situation is not quite as clear," Annie said as she continued. "Her mother died about two years after she ran away. The circumstances were considered suspicious at the time and there was speculation Ren's father might have had something to do with it. But the authorities could never make a case."

"Where is her father now?" Kellen asked.

"In jail—has been for the past eleven months—convicted of drug trafficking, assault, and kidnapping. He's a mean bastard, but being in jail precludes him from being directly responsible for the killings. It's always possible he hired someone else to do it, but it's considered unlikely. If it was Ren's father behind all of this—a hired hit—there would have been no reason to kill people outside our group. That brings us to your parents."

Ordinarily, Kellen could keep her expression blank. If Dana had learned anything about her, it was that her years on the street had taught Kellen to reveal nothing. It meant she could keep her eyes cool, her breathing steady.

But beneath the skin, it was a different story. She had never mastered indifference. She'd never learned to stop feeling. Never learned to stop hurting. Or to stop bleeding. It was part of what made her who she was, a complex woman doing her best to move beyond her past and live a life that would give her meaning. And as she finally turned around to face Dana and Annie, her eyes were awash with pain and her face was an emotional wasteland.

"My father's people have been able to ascertain your parents can't be held directly responsible. They were both at showings in different parts of the country at the time at least two of the killings happened. But as with Ren's father, it doesn't preclude your parents from hiring someone to carry out their wishes. They can certainly afford it."

Kellen closed her eyes. "To what end? My father beat and raped me. My mother's reaction on discovering what he'd done was to take me to a city I'd never been before and simply discard me. She never even looked back. They never came after me, never tried to look for me or find me."

Dana hated the heartbreaking pain in her voice. "We can't tell you why, Kellen. There's no possible answer that would begin to make sense of what your father did. What both your parents did."

"I know that," Kellen said, her voice dead quiet. "I stopped looking for logic years ago and I guess it doesn't really matter. He wanted me. I'd seen it in his eyes too many times when I'd been forced to pose for him and his friends. But it doesn't explain a need to find me now, after all these years. Or eliminate me, let alone kill those other people."

"You're right, but what you need to know is that eighteen months ago, a small law firm in Connecticut contacted your parents. It seems your paternal grandmother left you a small trust that kicked in on your thirtieth birthday."

"A trust fund?"

Annie nodded. "It was for two-and-a-half million dollars. You need to understand, it's not about the money. According to my father, your parents are quite wealthy in their own right. But the trust fund started people asking questions about a daughter who disappeared—ran away from home, according to the story—shortly after she turned twelve. And the law firm advised your parents that they'd hired a private investigator to try to find you."

If possible, Kellen paled even more. "Jesus. They've been looking for me for eighteen months?"

"Kellen, it'll be all right. I promise. Yes, it's possible your parents will try to find you before the lawyer's investigator does. They're not going to want you telling people what happened to you. What your father did. But it won't just be your word," Annie said. "My father's lawyers have filed to get copies of the medical records from when you were hospitalized in Chicago."

Dana's concern increased as she watched Kellen's eyes shadow. "Kellen, you need to see you're not alone this time. We're here for you and we won't let anything happen to you. Please believe me."

Kellen slowly shook her head as if she was trying to clear it and struggled to take a deep breath. "I'm sorry. I need to get some air. And I have to talk to the girls. Would you mind if we finished this later?"

Kellen thought of the deep sympathy she was certain she'd seen in both Annie's and Dana's expressions. Sympathy and what looked to be a heartfelt wish to share her pain and take it away.

She wrestled with conflicting emotions. And then she began to run. Physically. Mentally. Emotionally. With good reason. Every time she thought she was distancing herself from her past, she felt it clawing back at her. Only this time, the instinct that had enabled her to survive on the street was back in full force. Telling her to run.

She stopped only once on her way to her cabin. Just long enough to speak to Cody and Ren and issue terse instructions. She then ran the rest of the way, struggling to breathe against the rising panic in her chest.

It took her less than five minutes. She grabbed a couple of sleeping bags and pillows, made a thermos of coffee, and grabbed a bag of food and a bowl for Bogart. Turning in a slow circle, she looked at everything she'd gathered to make the cabin a home. She closed her eyes briefly, aware of a pain deep in her chest as she committed the images to memory. Then she walked to the front closet, took down her backpack, and walked out the door.

Cody and Ren stared at her wide-eyed, but they didn't say anything as they helped her pack what little they were taking into the Jeep. Quietly, they got into the backseat, leaving the front passenger seat for Bogart. Kellen could see tears in their eyes. But neither one said anything as she put the Jeep in gear and drove away.

They would need to talk. They would need to have a chosen family meeting and make decisions. But she was too emotionally vulnerable right now. She would first need to put some distance between them and the one place people would eventually look for her. The place that had been her home for the last ten years.

After some time on the road, she reached for the radio, scanned until some music filled the Jeep. It would help on what would be a long and tiresome drive. And much better than the twenty-four-hour talk show where people called in to rant about politics and life in general. With care, she reached for the thermos and started to pour herself some coffee, barely taking her eyes off the road. Murmured thanks when Ren took the thermos from her and finished filling her travel mug.

She drove with her left hand, sipping coffee and listening to the radio until her eyes burned and her throat ached from holding back the scream that wanted release. But she kept her eyes on the road— both ahead and behind them—and drove long into the evening.

Dana stared at the Mickey Mouse clock on the wall in Annie's office, slowly counting off the minutes since Kellen had left the room to get some air. It was taking too long and she couldn't shake the feeling things were about to get worse. Much worse.

"Kellen made that clock for me," Annie said. "She and Cody put it together as a project and then Ren painted it. They gave it to me for my fortieth birthday. Something about Mickey making the passage of time seem like fun."

"Somehow, that sounds like something the three of them would do." Dana tried to laugh but couldn't get the sound past the knot that had formed in her throat.

She was worried about Kellen. She was worried about how she was coping and hated seeing the situation tear her apart. She also hated not being able to do anything to help.

The longer she thought about it, the more she felt her heart rate accelerate. And then, just as her anxiety threatened to bubble over, she realized the truth. "Oh God, Annie. I think she's going to run."

"Please, no. Don't say that. Don't even think it." Annie jumped to her feet. "She wouldn't. She promised my father—"

In a heartbeat, heedless of the cold and the fresh snow that had started to fall, Dana and Annie ran out of the office building, not bothering to even grab coats, as they headed for Kellen's cabin.

The first ominous sign was the lack of life at the cabin Cody and Ren shared. By then, Dana could already see that Kellen's Jeep was missing from its usual spot beside the last cabin. But nothing was clearer than the instant she stepped into the cabin and looked around.

It was neat the way Kellen liked it to be. But there was no sign of life. The coffeemaker sat empty, waiting to be used, and Bogart wasn't there to greet her. As she turned, she saw the front closet door had been left partially open, and she saw the backpack was no longer in its familiar place on the top shelf.

With a sinking heart, she knew what it meant.

Kellen was gone.

It was nearly midnight before Kellen next pulled off the highway. After getting gas and letting Bogart run a bit, she noticed the coffee shop was still open, a bright oasis in the endless darkness. She mulled it over, then woke the girls up and pointed. "Fresh brew?"

Five minutes later, a tired woman, two sleepy girls, and a dog were seated near the door, drinking bad coffee and contemplating the vagaries of life on the road once again. A life Kellen had believed she'd left behind. Not only for herself, but for Cody and Ren and Bogart.

She'd made them all a home. And now it seemed she was deciding for all of them. Deciding they needed to leave the sanctuary they'd found in Haven. Determining they needed to run.

That was not how it was supposed to work in chosen families.

She caught Ren looking at her and tried to smile.

"Kel, could we have a chosen family meeting?"

She looked at Ren, heard the jagged ache in her voice, and saw a pain in her eyes she wanted to chase away. She turned to Cody and saw her nod in agreement. "Of course. Now?"

Both girls nodded. "We know what you said," Ren began. "That Cody would be safe no matter what—"

"But Ren's not going anywhere without me," Cody interrupted. "We love each other. We're a team. And we, the three of us, we're supposed to be a family. A chosen family. We're supposed to make decisions like a family."

"So why aren't we doing that this time?" Ren asked plaintively. "And if we have to run, why aren't we taking Doc D? She should be here with us. With you. Instead, she's back at the cabin alone. She'll be sad knowing we've all gone."

When had these two young women grown up, Kellen wondered. Sometimes it seemed like it was only days ago that she'd picked them up in Seattle. Painfully thin, hungry, brutalized by life on the streets and barely communicating. And now look at them. Confident. Speaking up. And painfully right. Damn, it was no wonder she loved them.

"You're right," she acknowledged after a long moment. "I've handled this all wrong and I'm sorry."

"It's all right," Ren said. "You got scared when they said your birth father was looking for you. I know how that feels. But we can still fix this, can't we? We can still decide like a family?"

Kellen nodded as she closed her eyes. "Of course we can."

"I vote to go back to Haven with the two of you," Cody said. "We made a family there. We worked, we helped find people who were lost or hurt, and we had friends there. It was the first and only real home I've ever had and I don't want to lose it."

"Same goes for me," Ren added when it was her turn to speak. "I know I'll still be scared there, at least for a little while. Until Annie's dad and the police catch the person who hurt you last year. And stop your birth father—and mine—from getting anywhere near us. But there are people in Haven who can help us. People like Doc D, and Annie and her dad. And the people on the team like Gabe and Sam and Tim and Jake. And Bogart. In fact, I was thinking maybe we could get another puppy so we can start training her, and Bogart can have a friend."

As her words stopped, the silence poured in, and for an endless moment, all Kellen could hear was the sound of her own breathing. All she could feel was the wild pounding of her heart in her chest. She knew she didn't want to run again. Didn't want to live in a state that muted every color. She wanted to feel, and see, and taste life. She wanted a chance—

"I guess we're going back to Haven." She opened her eyes and stared at the two girls who meant so much to her. Reaching into her pocket, she took out enough money to cover their three coffees plus a good tip for the tired-looking waitress. She then stood up and shrugged into her jacket, watching while the girls did the same. "A puppy?"

CHAPTER EIGHTEEN

After Annie left, Dana wandered aimlessly around the cabin, lost in thought. She stared in awe at a number of carvings Kellen had finished, saw other works still in progress. Felt much the same as she looked upon some paintings that were clearly Ren's work. Evidence of incredible talent in two lives abandoned suddenly and unexpectedly.

It didn't seem right.

But then nothing seemed right. The hours that had elapsed since Kellen had taken off dragged by and still she was unable to do anything but watch the clock and wonder how far from Haven Kellen and the girls had gotten.

Were they safe? Would they drive through the night? Would Kellen prefer the illusory safety of darkness and take her chances with the winding mountain roads?

The thought frightened her. She knew between Ren's nightmares and Kellen's own, it had been too long since Kellen had gotten a decent night's sleep. She'd been visibly exhausted for the last week even as she gamely responded to callouts. And she was certainly in no condition to be driving all night, let alone making life-altering decisions.

Making decisions that don't include you, isn't that what you mean?

For a moment, Dana was pulled back to the life she'd left behind in Boston, a life where all decisions were made for her. It had been inconceivable that she would refuse to follow the path her father had laid out for her, starting with Harvard medical and ultimately taking a place at his side in his practice.

The expectation had always been that she would mirror her parents' values, opinions, and wishes. And for a long time, Dana had allowed herself to be shaped and molded into the perfect child her parents had wanted. She had excelled in her studies, and if there had been moments when she'd longed for something more, she'd suppressed them.

And felt smothered by it all.

Her first true act of rebellion had led her to New York. But while her time there challenged her professionally and sharpened her medical skills, it had left no time for anything else. And if anything, it confirmed what she'd long known. That she wanted a life for herself quite different from that of her parents.

She wanted a life that, yes, included a career that was satisfying and fulfilling. But she also wanted a life that included laughter and friendships and love. Much like the life she'd started to build in Haven. Before Kellen made the decision to run.

Annie had looked at her with compassion-filled eyes and hadn't wanted to leave her. But Dana had told her she'd be fine. She wanted to be alone, to think about what had happened. She knew one thing for certain. *I'm going to wait for her.* What else could she do? Because if nothing else, she was convinced Kellen would be back.

Maybe she needed to believe it, but it was the only answer that made sense. Kellen had poured her heart and soul into Alpine Search and Rescue and into making a home for the girls. Once she had a chance to distance herself from the fear brought about by knowing her father was looking for her and a stranger was trying to kill her, she would come back to the one place—the only place—she felt safe. Haven.

Releasing a sigh, Dana found a pair of Kellen's pajama bottoms and a T-shirt, changed into them, and lit a fire before laying on Kellen's king-sized bed. It was a bed they'd shared often lately, but as she pulled the duvet over her body, it brought no warmth. Only a penetrating chill as a trace of Kellen's scent wafted in the air.

Epiphanies, it seemed, could happen at any time.

Nothing had prepared her. Nothing could have. Everything in Dana went painfully still as memories slashed through her. She tried to move. Couldn't. Tried to breathe. Couldn't. She glanced at the clock, saw the hour pushing deep into the night, and closed her eyes as her emotions threatened to overtake her. Leaving her struggling with the bittersweetness of the moment, Kellen's name burning in her throat.

Oh my God, I'm in love with her.

She was—there could be no denying it. She was deeply in love. The kind of love that inspired poets. That inspired thoughts of forever.

And she was terrified to her core.

She knew now the first bolt of lightning had hit her while sitting on the side of a mountain road with a flat tire. Just as she knew she and Kellen belonged together. There was no question in her mind that Kellen was right for her. She just didn't know if she was right for Kellen.

That fear left her vulnerable. Exposed and raw. Certain she'd just opened herself up to the potential for a lifetime of near-debilitating pain. Because when all was said and done, there was one question she couldn't answer.

What if she didn't come back?

Closing her eyes again, absorbing Kellen's scent, she replayed the sound of Kellen's voice, over and over again, as she whispered words to her while making love. Words that made her heart pound wildly, her breath catch in her throat, and need course through her body. She groaned and a shiver worked its way through her when she remembered the heat of Kellen's mouth, the taste of her.

Oh God. At this rate, she would be crazy by morning.

Or maybe she already was.

Just before six, just after she'd built the fire up once again and gone back to bed, Dana was positive she heard the sound of the cabin's front door open, then close with a barely discernable click. She held herself perfectly still and called herself every kind of fool possible, realizing how rash she'd been when she'd chosen to stay in

Kellen's cabin, alone, while Kellen's father, a private investigator, and an unknown killer continued to hunt for her.

Held immobile by fear, a scream formed only to be caught in her throat the instant she saw who was standing at the bedroom door. No ghost, no phantom, no illusion.

Her hair was tangled around her face as if she'd run her hands through it one too many times. Her eyes were huge and shadowed and she looked exhausted.

But Dana had never seen anyone more beautiful. Relief swept through her so hard it made her tremble. Her eyes filled with tears and her hands came up to cover her mouth and hold in the sob that wanted to escape.

"There's a coffee shop along the highway about six hours from here. It's on the route to Salt Lake City," Kellen said. "Have you ever been?"

"No, I can't say that I have," Dana whispered, unable to say more. The tears were closing in on her. Clogging her throat and searing her eyes.

"Well, it's there. I know because I was there just a few hours ago when I stopped for gas. And the girls and I, we had a long overdue chosen family meeting. It turned out no one wanted to say good-bye to what we'd started here in Haven. We all recognize the risk, the danger inherent in our decision. But it seems we all want a chance to see this through. To see how things can turn out when you don't have to run before the end arrives."

"Does that mean you're back to stay?"

Kellen swallowed nervously. She'd faced a lot of things in her relatively short life. Everything from snowstorms and floodwaters to street gangs to well-intentioned social workers. None of them had caused fear like what was now stirring inside her. But she knew this was no time to retreat.

"I never really left. Not in here." She touched her hand to her chest where her heart was beating hard and fast. "But it doesn't change the facts. I know my birth father is out there somewhere. I understand he wants to find me before the private investigator hired by my grandmother's lawyer finds me. If my father…if he finds me first, I don't know what he'll do, but I can't imagine any happy outcome from that reunion."

"Kellen, there are things we can do."

"Please. I need to say this. I need to know you understand."

"All right."

"Thank you." Kellen took a deep breath and tried to steady her racing pulse. "Other than my birth father, I know there's someone else out there who wants to kill me. I don't know who he is or why he wants me dead. He just does. I also know I'm screwed up."

"No, Kellen—"

"It's all right, Dana. I know what I am. You can't spend half your life being invisible and living between the cracks and not be a bit messed up. So I don't know if it makes me stupid or crazy that I think things might turn out differently this time."

Outside, the wind whispered against the windows. Inside, the fire crackled, adding warmth to the chill in the air and casting shadows in the cabin.

"What are you trying to tell me?" Dana asked.

"I'm saying I can think of a thousand reasons why it wouldn't be a good idea for you to get involved with me," she said through the tightness in her throat. "And I can only think of one reason why you would even want to try."

"What's that?"

"Because I think there's something real between us. Something special. We shouldn't fit, Dana, but we do." Kellen pushed through a sudden surge of uncertainty. "I don't believe people get a lot of opportunities at something like this, and I, for one, would like the chance to see what it might look like if we tried. I don't want to lose this chance."

Dana's lips curved into a slow languorous smile as she got out of bed and walked toward her. "Is that so?"

For the first time, Kellen realized Dana was wearing *her* pajama bottoms, *her* T-shirt. Then she couldn't think of anything beyond the warmth emanating from Dana's body as she drew near. "Yes."

"Good." Dana's voice was still whisper soft but suddenly edged with steel and her body vibrated with challenge. "Then in the future, don't try to make decisions for me, okay?"

Kellen nodded wordlessly.

"And just so we're clear, the only reason for me not to get involved with you is because you don't want me."

"Not want you?"

Dana effectively cut off anything else she might have said, momentarily pressing two fingers against her lips. "I'm very much aware the paths each of us followed to where we find ourselves today are wildly different. I know you've seen and experienced things I can't even begin to imagine. I'm not that naive."

"I never thought you were."

"Good. As long as we understand each other."

They stared at each other, unblinking. And then ever so slowly, Dana extended her hand. Kellen met the intensity in her gaze, afraid to make another mistake. Afraid to misread what she was seeing. An offer to help carry whatever burdens Kellen had been shouldering alone until now.

Taking Dana's hand, she drew her closer until they were a breath apart. "You never miss something more than when you believe you've lost it. Damn, I missed you."

"I'm glad because I missed you too."

The first hesitant kiss briefly gave way to something stronger as Dana's lips parted to meet hers.

Once she moved past the shock of having Kellen in her arms once again, Dana was consumed by a desire to tell her how she felt. To tell her she loved her. She knew her desire was based in part on an irrational fear Kellen might disappear again, without ever knowing how she felt about her. But she also knew it was too soon.

She knew Kellen felt something for her. She'd said as much. But Dana didn't want to come on too strong and frighten her at a time when she was struggling to handle everything already on her plate. Like trying to protect the girls. And trying to stay alive.

Saying *I love you* would complicate things needlessly. There would be a better time.

Hesitantly, with fingers trembling so badly she could barely control them, Dana stroked Kellen's cheek as she inhaled deeply. Kellen's scent always called to mind a forest at midnight, dark and secret and sensual. "Damn, that perfume you're wearing should be declared illegal," she murmured.

"I'm not wearing any perfume."

It mattered not, Dana mused. Her scent was still intoxicating and she wanted to bury her hands in Kellen's hair and kiss her. Wasn't that what this moment called for? The better question might be, how far was she willing to take this moment?

They remained standing, swaying precariously as Dana tightened her hold. She felt some of the tension that had surrounded Kellen since she'd appeared at the bedroom door begin to dissipate. But there were lines visible around her mouth and shadows under her eyes and she realized Kellen was looking at her through a haze of exhaustion.

"Let's go to bed, Kellen. Neither of us has slept in far too long and you look like a gentle breeze could knock you down. We can talk later, figure out what we need to do to keep you and Ren safe and protected, and take it from there. We'll get through this—you, me, the girls—and we'll all come out stronger on the other side. You just need to believe me."

Kellen gave her a crooked smile and nodded tiredly. "I believe you."

A few short minutes later, Kellen was sprawled facedown on the bed. Her dark hair fanned out across a pillow and covered most of her face, but the steady rise and fall of her back indicated she had fallen asleep. Dana stroked Kellen's hair and wished she could take away the pain of the past.

She couldn't, of course. All she could do was be there for her. Help her through the nightmares that haunted her. Help her find the peace she so richly deserved.

As she gazed at her in quiet contemplation, Dana saw a woman of strength and conviction, passion and raw courage. Kellen never hesitated when it came to the people who were important to her. Never faltered. She also put it on the line for strangers—those lost or injured in nearby forests and mountains. But she seldom let others see her vulnerability, a fragility that stirred something deep within Dana.

She knew this latest turn of events made no sense within the context of what had once been a carefully planned and ordered life. But then again, Dana reminded herself, she had deliberately chosen to leave the life and plans her parents had made for her. She'd only compounded it by accepting the position here in Haven.

She had wanted something different. Had hoped on some level that the move to the Colorado Rockies might enable her to find not only professional challenge and satisfaction, but just maybe the one person she could share her life with. And in spite of their vastly different backgrounds and the ever-present danger currently surrounding her, she was sure she had found that person in Kellen.

She knew one thing for certain. She'd never been in love before. While it had been a long, long time since she'd been involved with another woman, nothing she had ever experienced came close to how she was now feeling. She had never felt anything this strong. Never experienced the intensity and the sheer wonder. The inevitability.

This was what she'd longed for. Dreamed of. Whatever was happening between them, it *was* different. It felt different. It felt right.

How ironic. In the past, she'd never been quite certain how much the women she'd dated were with her because of her name and who her family was. Never certain if it was because being with her could further their own ambitions. But now, if she was certain of anything, it was that Kellen didn't give a damn about any of that and could come up with a thousand different reasons why they shouldn't get involved.

She watched her for a long moment. Just watched her. Everything else faded until there was only her. Always her. Kellen.

Slipping lower on the bed, Dana wrapped her arm around Kellen's waist and joined her in sleep.

Chapter Nineteen

By late afternoon, life at Haven had slipped back to normal. As if the late-night drive through the mountains had been for pleasure rather than driven by a fundamental need to survive. It might be a new normal, Kellen thought wryly, but it was still filled with heightened vigilance, constant awareness. Ever watchful and alert. On second thought, maybe not that different after all.

She sat in her office, finishing the changes to the training curriculum that would be used with the next group of students. She reviewed the work schedules, checked the training schedule for the new group of volunteers, and followed up on the maintenance report for one of the helicopters.

All perfectly ordinary. As if less than twenty-four hours earlier, she hadn't been ready to walk away from it all. As if she hadn't taken the first step to yet another name and another life.

Closing her eyes against the hazy sun, she sifted through countless thoughts. Possibilities and probabilities. Working to connect the dots with lines that didn't make sense.

"Are you taking a catnap?"

Opening her eyes, she saw Dana and Annie standing at the doorway. Looking at her with concern. Amusement. Affection.

"I was just thinking," she responded slowly. "Something occurred to me and I'm just trying to make sense of it."

Dana met her gaze. "What's the thought? Care to share? Maybe we can help."

"The shooter. He can't be someone hired by my birth father."

"Why not?" Annie asked.

"Because he would have had no need to kill all those other people. Or shoot Tim. He would know where I am. Who I am. He could have taken me out at any time, quite easily."

Kellen saw the effect her words had on the two women. She saw both grow pale. Saw Dana chew her bottom lip. She hated that her words had the power to hurt them. Make them fearful. But she had to push on. She needed their help if she was going to follow her current line of thinking and be able to determine the identity of the shooter.

"That's not to say my birth father's not looking for me. He has every reason to want to find me. I can't disregard the possibility he'll want to silence me before the truth of what he did comes out. He will still need to be dealt with, but that's for later. After we find the shooter."

"My father will be able to help you with that," Annie said.

Kellen smiled. "Believe it or not, I'm counting on his help."

"We'll all help," Dana said on a broken breath. "What about Ren's father?"

The fear in her voice wrapped itself around Kellen's heart. "Maybe it's just my gut, but I don't think it's him either, for much the same reason. If he'd hired someone to get me out of Ren's life, or to grab Ren, there would have been no need to hide or distract by killing anyone else."

"If it's not someone hired by your father or Ren's father, then who is after you?" Dana challenged. "Who's been killing members of SAR teams around the country?"

Kellen heard Dana's frustration and tried to keep her own from turning into anger. "I don't know yet, that's why I need your help. Whoever it is, the motivation is tangled in search and rescue. I was the first. According to the FBI, he moved on and now he's circling back to finish what he started. I don't know about you, but that tells me whatever set him off, it started with me. Something I did or something I didn't do."

"Something you did? Are you crazy?" Annie's voice wavered, but her eyes were clear and angry. "I've been with you from the very beginning and if anyone should know something, it's me. In all the time I've known you, you've done nothing wrong except maybe take too many risks with yourself. But it was always about getting people home to their loved ones. What else do you think you could have done?"

Kellen sighed and pushed a hand through her hair. "I'm not saying I did anything wrong. I'm saying maybe it's not about what I did or didn't do, but what came afterward."

"What does that mean?"

"We know the FBI's been looking at people who lost someone—a family member, a friend, a loved one—someone a SAR team failed to rescue. They've also looked at people who wanted to become a member of a SAR team and failed to make the cut."

Dana's eyes narrowed. "But the FBI has found no one that fits. At least not so far. What are you thinking?"

"What if the person we're looking for lost someone who worked on a SAR team? It wouldn't even have to be here in the US. For the last ten years, we've been training people who go on to take jobs on SAR teams around the globe. We all know what we do is dangerous. What if one of them got killed on the job after I trained them? What if the shooter blames me for the death of their loved one?"

As Kellen's words hung suspended in the air, Dana and Annie turned simultaneously and stared at her. In turn, she offered them both a wan smile that died before it reached her eyes.

"Is that what your gut is telling you?" Dana asked.

"Yes."

"That's good enough for me. How can we help?"

"Thank you for not thinking I'm crazy." Kellen released a long and weary sigh. "We need...I'm thinking we need to access the main database and see if we can compile a list of everyone we've trained."

"That's easy enough to do," Annie said. "But how are we supposed to track them from there?"

Dana watched Kellen shift uncomfortably and tried to process what she was seeing. "What's going on in that head of yours? I know you've got something in mind, something you think we won't like, so you might as well tell us."

Kellen leaned her head back and turned to look out the window. "I thought maybe we could give Calvin Grant a call. I'm not particularly fond of them, but it seems to me the FBI could look into all our former students much faster than we could, even if we knew where to start. They could see if any of them got seriously hurt, or killed, after completing their training."

For a moment, no one said anything. And then Dana started to laugh. "Oh, my God. I can't believe what I'm hearing. You, of all people, want to reach out to the FBI? This is too perfect. You're a genius."

"You're too kind," Kellen muttered dryly, but then shrugged good-naturedly.

"Actually, I'm not, but I'm glad you think so." She was rewarded when Kellen lifted her head and Dana was suddenly captured by her smile, consumed with wanting to touch her, and as their gazes met and held, she thought she saw something flicker in Kellen's eyes.

Whatever it was, Dana felt it, as clearly as if the contact had been electric, before Kellen blinked and looked away. Suddenly remembering they weren't alone, she turned around to find Annie looking from her face to Kellen's and then back again, a smile on her lips.

"Since it's too late in the day to contact Grant," Annie said, "why don't you two call it a night? Both of you look like you could use some rest. We can start fresh in the morning."

Simple relief washed over Dana and she could feel the tension in her muscles slowly release. "That's a great idea. Kellen, why don't you go get the girls? I'll meet you at your cabin with a pot of vegetarian chili I've got going in the slow cooker. Do you want to join us, Annie? I'm pretty sure I made plenty."

Annie appeared to deliberate then shook her head. "Thanks, but I have a date with a hot tub and an even hotter writer. You kids run along and have fun…and Kellen?" Annie held out both arms in open invitation.

Kellen stepped into Annie's arms without hesitation. From where Dana stood, the hug looked comforting and tender, exactly what Kellen needed, and for a moment it appeared as if Kellen couldn't let go.

"I'm glad you decided to stick it out here with us," Annie told her. "I'll call my father in the morning and see what can be done to head off both the private investigator and your father. After that, I'll take Dana with me to work on the grand opening for the clinic and leave you to deal with Calvin Grant."

Kellen's laugh was dry. "Thanks for making the tough call for me. I would have never been able to decide between working on plans for the gala—which I happen to despise—and spending face time with my favorite FBI agent. How can I ever thank you?"

Annie chuckled. "Having you back is thanks enough. In the meantime, call me if you need anything. Promise?"

"I will."

When she stepped out of Annie's arms, Kellen turned toward Dana and extended her hand, her eyes revealing far more than she probably intended to. "Come on. Why don't we go get the girls together? They can help carry the pot of chili and whatever else you need to bring."

Dana felt the husky timbre of Kellen's voice as it wound through her and didn't hesitate. An instant later, Kellen's calloused fingers were intertwined with her own.

❖

Dinner went much better than expected.

Kellen had been nervous, knowing neither Cody nor Ren was very good when it came to experimenting with unfamiliar foods. She didn't often push them beyond their comfort zone, and she had learned through personal experience that both could be brutally frank if they didn't like something.

She understood. Their time living on the street, like hers, had left an indelible mark and their tastes ran to simple, even after all this time away from the alleys and culverts. Grilled cheese, soup, and fruit salad were staples. Vegetarian pizza from Up the Creek was a treat. And apples. Ren loved apples.

If that was what made them happy, Kellen would happily oblige. The two girls were what counted. They were her family, and she would do anything to protect them and keep them safe and happy. It also made it imperative they get along well with Dana, because Dana was rapidly consuming all her thoughts.

It turned out she needn't have worried. As they took their first tentative tastes from the bowls of chili Dana had served, their delight was quickly apparent. Almost as strong as their reaction when Kellen and Dana had appeared at their door hand in hand. In fact, Kellen was starting to think both girls just might have tiny crushes on the beautiful doctor. Not that she could blame them.

Since Dana had made dinner, Kellen insisted she relax with the girls while she cleaned up. She enjoyed watching the three of them build a fire and cuddle on the couch with Bogart lying at their feet. The girls told Dana more about Haven, about summer visitors who came for hiking and camping, about kayaking on the river, and how Kellen had taught them to fish without hooks and rods, just using their hands.

Dana sounded intrigued and Cody and Ren immediately offered to teach her. They also peppered her with questions about her life, her family, and studying to become a doctor.

"My parents wouldn't let me consider anything else but Harvard. It was where my father went to school and if it was good enough for Davis Kingston..." Dana shrugged.

"Your birth father's a doctor?" Cody asked. "Is that why you became a doctor?"

"Yes, my father's a doctor, but that's not why I became one too. I always knew from the time I was a little girl that I wanted to help people."

Ren's smile widened. "You mean like Kellen?"

Dana grinned. "Yes, I guess something like Kellen, except I like my feet on the ground when I do it."

Listening to the ongoing conversation had been an interesting experience, Kellen thought and smiled, because she realized she was learning things she hadn't known before. She had just finished putting everything away when she heard Ren ask Dana if she would answer a more personal question.

She wasn't surprised when Dana said yes. Turning around, she held her breath as she waited for Ren's question, wondering what it could possibly be.

But nothing could have prepared her when she heard Ren ask, "Do you love Kellen?"

❖

Dana was stunned.

Of all the questions Ren might have asked, that was not one she could have ever imagined. But answering it right suddenly became critical.

She heard the innocence in Ren's question, an innocence that had miraculously survived whatever the girl had experienced in her past. And she saw hope burning brightly in her eyes as she waited for an answer.

Dana knew Kellen had heard Ren's question. She stood frozen in place, her eyes widened in shock.

And then she remembered Annie asking her if she knew Kellen and the girls came as a package deal.

If she failed to answer Ren's question honestly, all of them—Kellen, Ren, and Cody—would see through her attempt to prevaricate. And that could destroy any chance they might have, as clearly as if she said no.

Acting purely on instinct, she closed her eyes and held out her hand toward Kellen. Hoping more than anything she would take it because she could think of no alternative and there was no turning back.

Five seconds became ten then became twenty. An initial thread of worry increased and Dana's heart began to accelerate under a very real fear she had overplayed her hand. Waves of mortification washed over her and she wished she was anywhere but here. *What the hell was I thinking?*

Suddenly she felt the warmth of Kellen's hand holding hers, followed by the gentle press of Kellen's lips against her own. She felt lightheaded, heard the unmistakable hitch in her breathing, and as she pulled away and opened her eyes, she saw Kellen's incredible blue eyes staring back at her.

She struggled to find her voice and whispered, "Yes."

Chapter Twenty

Calvin Grant quietly shook his head as he stared at the stack of computer printouts on the desk. "I have to admit, you are the last person I ever expected to hear from."

Kellen shrugged. Grant might not have expected her call, but she was aware he'd been staying close nonetheless, having taken a room in a local hotel. Clearly he had chosen to stay close enough to respond, but far enough away not to raise the ire of Senator Parker.

She started to take a sip of her coffee, but quickly set the mug back down when she realized her hand was shaking. "As long as we can work together and find out who's behind the shooting before anyone else gets hurt, I don't really care what you think of me."

Grant sent a long, slow gaze in her direction. "I don't dislike you, Kellen. Hell, if you want to know the truth, I actually admire you and what you've managed to do given where you started. Maybe when this is over, we can sit down and talk, over a beer."

"Yeah, maybe," she answered slowly. "For now, tell me what you need and let's get it done."

For the next few hours, they worked with a young tech Grant brought in to set up a computer system, replete with access to FBI and State Department files. "How long do you think this might take," Kellen asked, sitting back and rubbing her temples.

"It's hard to say. It's not that the list you've got is that long. It's that the people on the list could have gone anywhere in the world after they left you. If our guy's American, we should be able to access some kind of death certificate or obit. But you also train quite a number of people from elsewhere. Chile and Australia, for example. Tracking them will be more difficult."

"Impossible?"

"Nothing's impossible."

"I'm not sure how you do what you do," Kellen admitted, "so I had no idea when I called you if what I was suggesting was possible."

"It's more than possible. It just won't necessarily be quick and easy. But it's a hell of an idea, and I've a feeling we'll find our shooter here."

Kellen raised an eyebrow. "Do you rely on gut instinct a lot in your job?"

Grant laughed. "I know it's not very scientific, but in a lot of cases, gut instinct will often lead the way faster than technology. You don't believe in following your gut?"

"On the contrary. You're talking my language now."

"Good. Because right now my gut is telling me you've got a killer headache. Why don't you take something for it and call it a day?"

Kellen considered his suggestion and knew he was right. "All right, as long as there's nothing else I can do."

"There is one thing."

Damn it, she thought. Just as she was beginning get comfortable with him. "What might that be?" she asked, her voice holding a frosty edge.

"It's something I want you to consider, that's all."

"Go on."

"We both know our shooter's here. You feel it as much as I do if not more. So I'd like to suggest adding a couple of sharpshooters to your teams each time they go out, so we can be better prepared when he does show. Because he will. You know that, don't you?"

Kellen nodded slowly.

"They're trained. They shouldn't have any problem keeping up with your teams, and who knows, they might even help. But you don't need to decide now—"

"Will your sharpshooters be able to protect my people?"

Grant's face softened. "I can't guarantee anything, Kellen. What I can tell you is they'll do their damn best to finish this before anyone else gets hurt."

"Okay."

❖

It was early evening before Dana was ready to head to her cabin. The hours had somehow flown by and she was exhausted.

The clinic had been busy with a rash of minor injuries and people from neighboring counties had taken to dropping by, wanting to check things out, get acquainted, ask for advice, or make appointments. After the chaos she'd left behind in the ER in New York, it felt amazing.

The two family medicine doctors who had come on board were fitting in and working well together and she had worked out a schedule with Liz and Annie that would ensure emergency coverage at all times. The rest of the time would be allocated for scheduled appointments, walk-ins, and callouts.

Happy with how things were going, she'd left Liz to continue overseeing things in the clinic and spent the remainder of the day working on the endless planning involved in arranging the gala. Key donors would be in attendance, including Senator and Mrs. Parker. But the guest list also included nearby resort owners and community leaders from several neighboring towns, all of whom were routinely served by Alpine and would benefit from the clinic's presence.

At least Annie seemed pleased with the progress they'd made, though the task list had seemed daunting when the day began.

Dana stopped by Kellen's office on the way out, planning on seeing what she wanted to do about dinner, and was surprised to find it dark.

"She left early. Maybe a couple of hours ago," Gabe said. "I talked to her for a bit when she came by looking for something to help with a headache. She looked a bit rough."

"I'll check on her," Dana offered quickly. "Her cabin's next to mine, so I'm heading in that direction anyway, and if she hasn't eaten, I can make her something."

Gabe gave a quick smile. "You take good care of our girl, Doc. And if you need any help, you let me know."

"I will." Before leaving, she grabbed her medical bag, just in case. She then made her way through the darkness toward Kellen's cabin, the night air reviving her.

She knocked softly on the door, growing concerned when she heard Bogart on the other side of the door, but there was no sign of Kellen. After another knock, she pushed the door open and let Bogart lick her hand as she slipped out of her boots.

"Kellen?"

A sound coming from the living room drew her to the sofa where Kellen was curled on her side, her face pale. Normally she hummed with energy, as though she were plugged in to some cosmic power source. Not today. Today she was tight, not vibrant.

"Talk to me, Kellen. Tell me what's wrong. Let me help."

"It's just a headache," she answered quietly, as if the sound of her own voice made the pain worse. "I can't seem to shake it."

"Gabe said you'd been looking for something to help alleviate it. What have you taken so far?"

"Nothing."

"You didn't take anything at all? How come?"

Kellen gave her a wry smile. "The meds leave me feeling disconnected. And I...I realized I need to stay aware."

Dana understood. "All right. No pills. What you really need is sleep." She weighed her options then turned back to Kellen. "Do you think you can make it to your bed if I help you?"

"If you're afraid I'll get sick on you, don't worry. I've nothing left inside—except this headache."

"Oh Lord," Dana murmured. Before Kellen could respond, Dana got her onto her feet, pausing long enough to let her regain her equilibrium when she started to sway. "Okay?"

Kellen nodded. Moving slowly, she allowed Dana to lead her to her bed, where she quickly collapsed, stretching out on her back while Dana settled beside her.

When she brought her thumbs to Kellen's temples and began kneading gently in slow circles, Kellen released a low moan. Dana smiled and kept the soothing motion up until she felt the tension ease from Kellen's muscles as she relaxed under her touch. Until Kellen's slow and steady breathing deepened and told Dana she was asleep. Smiling, Dana lay down beside her and closed her own eyes, letting Kellen's scent and warmth envelop her.

❖

For the first time she could remember, several different and distinct sensations brought Kellen out of her nightmare. One was the familiar touch of Bogart's nose against her hand. The others were an amalgam. The warmth of the body spooned against her back, the hand gently stroking her, the soft voice whispering soothing words. And the scent. The scent that was Dana.

"It's okay, I'm awake," she said, her voice raspy and still sleep filled.

Dana's hand didn't stop stroking her arm. "How are you feeling? How's the headache?"

"It's good. Clearly, you have a magic touch. Thank you."

"You're welcome. But I think you mostly needed to sleep. You've pushed yourself ragged, Kellen. You need to slow down and let others help you now."

"I am." Kellen knew her reply was defensive and tried to tone it down, without a great deal of success. "I spent yesterday working with Special Agent Grant combing through records of people I got to know. People I trained. If that's not accepting help, I don't know what is."

She felt Dana's gaze and wondered what she saw.

"Is that what triggered the headache?"

"No. Yes. Ah hell, Dana, I don't know. As I looked at the old files of former students, I couldn't stop thinking. These are people I cared about and one of them is more than likely dead—who knows, maybe more than one. And whoever they left behind is grieving so badly he can't think straight. He's hurting. In pain. And it's making him strike out."

"I know, love," Dana said. "But you can't own responsibility for it. And you need to play it safe. The shooter may be grieving, but he's still a killer, no matter how you look at it."

Kellen nodded. "I know. It's why I agreed to let Grant place a couple of sharpshooters on my teams during callouts."

"You did?" She sounded surprised.

"Yeah. Grant said there're no guarantees. He can't promise someone won't get hurt, but I knew I had to try and prevent what happened to Tim from happening again. If you don't learn from past mistakes, the pain of them is pointless. So I knew I had to do something."

Dana sighed. "You do know you didn't make a mistake when Tim got hurt, don't you?"

"Sure I did. I knew he was out there. We all did. And I let you and Annie ground me, believing if I wasn't available, the shooter wouldn't do anything. I was wrong and I didn't do anything to protect my people."

"If that's the case, then we all share the blame, Kellen. You, me, Annie, the FBI. We were all wrong. What's important is that Tim will be fine. Before you know it, he'll be back on your team, teasing you and driving you crazy."

"I hope so. Tim's one of the good guys, and if you ever tell him I said so, I'll deny it, but I miss him." Kellen briefly closed her eyes. "Right now, what I need more than anything is coffee."

"Would you like me to make it while you rest a little longer?"

Kellen laughed and realized it felt good. "No offense, but I've had your coffee. How about I make it and take a quick shower? By the time I'm out, the coffee will be ready and I'll bring you some in bed."

"I've a better idea," Dana countered. "How about you make the coffee and hop into the shower. I'll let Bogart out and then join you in the shower in a few minutes."

"I like how you think, Doc," Kellen said as she slipped out of bed.

Chapter Twenty-one

It was late afternoon when a call came in about a couple of lost snowboarders. The caller indicated the pair had been exploring a remote region when they'd last communicated with their families, admitting they were lost and wet and digging a snow cave for protection.

Snowboarding, particularly in back country, was an inherently dangerous sport. Given the high avalanche danger and limited daylight, Kellen immediately put together a small team to start the search, while reserving most members for a full-scale search the next day.

"I'm available. I know I've not done a night search before, but I'd like to help."

Kellen turned to find Jake standing there, squaring his shoulders as he looked to her for a response. She met his gaze. "The area we're going to is notorious—the conditions change very quickly. Are you prepared to walk all night, while the temperatures dip below zero? Or spend the night out in the freezing cold and bed down with the victims if we find them?"

Jake didn't hesitate. "Yes."

"Good answer." Conceding with a nod, Kellen's lips tugged into a half-smile as color burned across Jake's cheekbones. "Go get your gear together. You're with me."

On a bright winter's day, the location they were searching was inviting, luring hikers and extreme-sports enthusiasts to its untouched trails, the sunshine sometimes whispering a false sense of security. But Kellen knew from experience it could change in an instant. The clouds would quickly roll in, the snow would start to fall, the winds would pick up, and even the best outdoorsmen could find themselves caught out.

Even so, the appeal remained—the challenge of tough terrain and the thrill of virgin snow. She knew it well.

Progress was slow, and as darkness descended, temperatures on the mountain plummeted below zero. The good news was the snowboarders had been equipped with transceivers and the search team had begun sporadically picking up signals. But the mountainous landscape meant the signal bounced off the uneven geography, producing many inaccurate readings.

After countless false starts, they finally picked up a solid electronic signal. As the crow flew, they were less than a mile away. But due to the steep terrain, it took several hours for the team to circle around to the location.

The deep, fresh snow was soft and slowed their progress, with searchers, including Grant's sharpshooters, trading off to break trail. The wind continuously pounded them and they were cold and tired. But still they pushed on, persevering until at last they reached the lost snowboarders and shifted gears from search mode to assessing the victims and administering first aid.

Kneeling by the first man, Kellen had difficulty getting him to answer questions. He could barely tell them his name, finally managing to tell them it was Don. But he was unsure of the date and began intermittently sobbing, thanking them profusely, and trying to tell them what happened all at the same time. More worrisome, she could see he wasn't shivering, which told her he was likely so hypothermic his body had lost the ability to warm itself.

"Frostbite on his hands and feet," Gabe murmured.

Kellen nodded and continued talking to Don. Reassuring him while working side by side with Gabe, putting heat packs in his armpits and groin area, then wrapping him in blankets. She knew he would need to be airlifted out, and as she moved to kneel by the second victim, she began considering the best location for a landing zone.

The other rescued snowboarder was so elated he immediately began to talk Jake's ear off, showing no sign of slowing down. One of a rescuer's most important activities during missions was to manage other people's emotions. Kellen could tell the man was simply overcome with relief at having been rescued and was pleased as she watched how Jake handled him, listening and providing reassurance.

She made eye contact with her trainee, just long enough for her to silently tell him he was doing great. Jake stared at her a few seconds longer then broke into a wide grin.

Then Kellen heard the bullet, the crack echoing all around her. The searing burn followed a second later. She jerked and dropped to the ground at the same instant she heard a cry of pain coming from Jake. Turning her head, she could see blood staining the snow near him.

"Jake—how bad are you hit?"

She heard Jake groan before he answered. "My arm...I think it went through my arm. Jesus, Kel. It hurts like a son of a bitch."

She heard the pain in his voice and smothered her own inside her rage. But there was no time to do anything as three successive shots quickly followed, striking the ground inches from her head.

This time, she heard the FBI sharpshooters fire back.

She felt blood drip from her neck, but knowing there was nothing she could do, she closed her eyes to wait. It was either that or stare up at the hypnotically falling snow. Been there, done that. Not again.

The day had proven relentless and hectic, and it was long after dark before Dana realized Kellen had gone on a callout.

"They're looking for a pair of snowboarders whose families last heard from them early this morning," Annie told her.

Dana frowned. "When did the team head out?"

"Early this afternoon, just after the call came in. Truthfully, no one's really expecting them back before tomorrow morning. The area they're searching is pretty remote. Kellen arranged it so that if they haven't found them by morning, we'll send a second team out to resume the search."

Processing the information, Dana tried to push her concerns out of her mind. But she had little success. It would be cold on the mountain and the forecast called for heavy snow at higher elevations, which would make the search area even more treacherous. Especially at night.

Her mind immediately created a jumble of scenarios for her consideration. And if those weren't bad enough, she couldn't forget the shooter was still out there.

"If it makes you feel better, when the team went out, two FBI agents went with them." Annie shook her head, clearly surprised by the move. "Who would have thought?"

"Kellen told me about that," Dana confessed. "She said she'll do anything she can to protect everyone on her team. Even if it means working with Grant and having FBI sharpshooters on her teams."

"I always knew she was a smart woman." A spark of humor crept into Annie's eyes as she leaned closer and pulled Dana into a tight embrace. "And you need to believe she'll be fine. Because she's on a mission, she'll already be hyperalert, focused on finding the two snowboarders. She's also a superb tracker and knows the terrain—these woods and mountains—like no one else I know. So she'll be aware of anything that doesn't look right or feel right. The FBI can take care of the rest. Have faith in her."

Dana rested her head against Annie's shoulder and just breathed. "I do have faith in Kellen. It's just that I have this feeling I can't shake. He's out there, Annie. And it's Kellen he wants."

They waited together until it was clear the team wasn't coming back that night. Dana offered to put Annie up in her cabin.

"And where will you sleep, as if I don't know?"

Dana felt a hot blush spread across her face. "Does it bother you?"

"That you've been spending your nights with Kellen? On the contrary," Annie said, "I couldn't be more pleased, for both of you. Has she told you how she feels?"

"No. I believe…I know she cares. She has so much heart, so much emotion. But it's like every time it comes close to the surface, it scares her and she shuts it all off."

"It shouldn't surprise anyone, given how she grew up. But you can see how she feels every time she looks at you. We've all seen it. Be patient, Dana. Give her time."

Time. It passed inexorably, relentlessly, slowly. She dreamed of snowshoeing and skiing with Kellen. Of sitting by the fire reading while Kellen worked on a carving. The dreams left her aching and needy and finally chased her from her bed.

After a long hot shower and a quick coffee, she made her way back to the clinic only to find it a hive of activity. She looked for Liz to find answers. "Have they found the snowboarders?"

"Yes. I understand one is in pretty rough shape, but thankfully, they should both make it."

She knew immediately there was something else. She could hear it in Liz's tone, see it in the serious, professional look that came over her face, and in the stiffness of her stance. "There's more, isn't there. Something you're not telling me. What is it?"

"There was another incident involving the team. Another shooting. Sam went out at first light and is bringing in the injured along with the snowboarders. Two of them."

Dana went very still, her eyes half-closed. Hearing the words but unable to decipher them. "How badly is she hurt?"

Liz's eyes were filled with compassion. "I'm sorry, Dana. I wish I could tell you more but I just don't know. I didn't get a lot of details. But I don't think either of them is badly hurt."

She thought Liz was holding back, leaving something out. But she didn't know how to press her into telling her everything. All she could do was wait.

Awash in pain, Kellen's head pounded, trying but failing to keep rhythm with the sound of voices and the noise of the helicopter rotor beating the air. She gritted her teeth, shivered, and listened to Gabe talking on the radio.

But through the din, she could still hear it. The echo of the bullet that creased her neck sending shards of pain shooting through her before drilling through Jake's upper arm as they crouched over one of the snowboarders.

Another scar, she thought and wanted to laugh. She probably would have, except her head hurt too much now that the adrenaline had faded. So she concentrated on listening to Gabe talking to dispatch.

"We've got a male, thirty-two. Name is Don McVeigh. Hypothermic, dehydrated, and has frostbite on his fingers and toes. We've administered IV fluids, cranked the chopper's heat, have heat packs in his armpits and groin, and have him wrapped in blankets. We've managed to get him shivering again, but he'll need to go to Denver for a couple of days—they can check his kidney function and treat the frostbite."

"Good job. What about the other snowboarder?"

Dana's voice sounded tinny and echoed over the radio, but it was still immediately recognizable and made Kellen smile hazily. What did that say about her? God, she had it bad.

Gabe laughed. "Sorry, Doc. I didn't realize it was you on the other end. Don's buddy is twenty-eight. Name's Frank Dillon. He's mostly scraped and bruised, goose egg on his forehead, slightly disoriented, a touch of frostbite on his feet."

"Roger, team one. We'll have Life Flight standing by when you land and will notify their families."

"Thanks, Doc. You might also want to have a couple of sewing kits ready. But nothing too serious."

There was a slight pause before Dana's voice came back. "Roger, team one."

Gabe signed off and turned to look at Kellen, picking up her wrist and checking her pulse again. "Are you hanging in? Because I've got to tell you, you look like shit."

Kellen turned her head to scowl at Gabe and immediately felt dizzy with reaction. "Did Tim ask you to take his place here at comedy central?"

"As a matter of fact," Gabe responded with a smile. "Seriously, Kel. Your face is white as a damn ghost, your pulse isn't great, and you're cold and shaking. Talk to me. How are you feeling?"

"Like I've been shot," Kellen said and grimaced. "*Again*, damn it. How am I supposed to feel?"

"I know. I'm sorry."

"No, I'm sorry, Gabe. I shouldn't be taking it out on you. It's just that it makes no sense. How is it I lived on the street for years and never came close to getting shot? And now, twice, in a little over a year—?" She could feel herself fading and tried to pull herself back, struggling to stay awake. "Have you checked on Jake?"

"Yeah. He's sleeping like a baby. Bullet went straight through. Looks like it did minimal damage all the way around, if you don't count the dead first-aid kit."

Kellen surprised herself and a weak smile curved her lips. "Is that where the other bullets ended up?"

"Yes." Gabe laughed. "And there's more good news. One of the agents says they found some blood that's not yours or Jake's. The two FBI guys think maybe they winged the shooter when they fired back."

"Is that a good thing?" she murmured, uncertain how she should feel.

"Yeah. It's a very good thing. At the very least, it should slow the bastard down while Grant and his boys try to figure out who he is."

"Maybe. But if he got that close to us, tell me why he didn't just kill me. He's proven how good a shot he is. Why am I still alive?"

"I don't know, Kel." Gabe checked her pulse again and stroked her hair. "We've an ETA of about fifteen minutes or so. Why don't you close your eyes and rest until we land?"

Kellen nodded and winced but ignored the pull on her neck as her eyes closed and her head lolled.

Chapter Twenty-two

As soon as the helicopter landed, Dana went to meet it and began to coordinate the transfer of the gurneys holding the two snowboarders. She quickly checked their vital signs and IVs, and relayed their medical status to the Life Flight crew who were prepared to take over.

It was only after she heard the thumping beat and saw the Life Flight helicopter take off over the treetops that she allowed herself to look for Kellen. Thankfully, it didn't take long. She found her leaning against Sam, watching intently as Gabe helped a bloodied Jake down and handed him over to Liz and one of the doctors, who quickly ushered him into the clinic.

Dana took an uninterrupted moment to study the strain and exhaustion evident on Kellen's face, to take in her torn and bloodied jacket, and the dark red stain leaking through the bandage visible on her neck. She continued to stare, frozen in place, shuddering when Kellen turned and met her gaze.

Kellen made it across the short distance separating them and gathered her close. "Hey, you," she whispered. "It's okay. Jake's going to be fine. I'm fine."

She could feel Kellen's hands as they came up and framed her face, then felt the fleeting, silky soft touch of her lips. Lighting a fire inside her and numbing her mind of everything except Kellen. But only for an instant. As she drew back, she narrowed her eyes and studied her intently.

"How much?" she asked. Her voice shook with repressed energy. "How much of the blood on you is yours?"

"Only a bit. Honestly, most of it belongs to Jake. I promise."

Dana shuddered again, then reached for Kellen's hand and led her to the clinic and into one of the exam rooms without saying another word. Helping her out of her jacket and tattered sweater, she removed the bloodied bandages and examined the deep gash along her neck. "I can't remember if I've asked you before. Any known allergies to medications?"

"No."

Working in silence, Dana concentrated on treating the wound, not stopping until it had been closed by a neat row of stitches and covered with fresh bandages.

She had just finished when Annie poked her head around the curtain. "So? How's our girl?"

"Stitched and bandaged," Dana answered, managing to get the words out before her throat closed and her eyes filled with tears. Life really was a game of inches, she thought. An inch to the left and the bullet would have missed her completely. An inch to the right—

"Annie," Kellen said, "my sweater's trashed and my jacket's not much better. Do you think you could get me something to wear?" As soon as Annie disappeared from view, she got up, pulled the curtain closed, and drew Dana into her arms. "Talk to me. Tell me what's going on inside that head of yours. Please, don't shut me out."

Dana burrowed into the security Kellen's arms offered. She felt the steady beat of Kellen's heart and the strong arms that held her where she knew she was safe. Where she knew, if she let herself, she could fall apart. "I'm not shutting you out. Not really. But it scares me to realize how close he got to you again, in spite of having those two sharpshooters along for the ride."

"Dana—"

"No, Kellen. Even you have to admit the situation is going from bad to worse. It's like he's toying with you. A game of cat and mouse. Trying to show you he can get you at any time, no matter what you do." Dana swallowed. "And I'm scared. Damn it, I've just found you and I don't want to lose you. But this bastard's doing his best to kill you."

"Maybe. But we're not going to let him, are we?"

Dana shook her head. "No. But I've no idea how the hell we stop him."

"I don't know either," Kellen admitted, exhaling a ragged breath. "Something doesn't feel right, but I'm hurting, I'm tired, I've lost a bit of blood, so I'm not thinking straight. I just know I need to figure it out because I won't live in fear. I had enough of that when I was growing up, living on the street. I won't go back there."

"And I don't want you to. But I don't know what I can do. How can I help?"

A mere breath away, Kellen spoke softly. "Just be with me. With you I can be me, without worrying about who that is."

Dana's eyes widened and Kellen realized that was probably the closest she had come to telling her how she felt. But she also sensed more than knew that Dana didn't want to talk about how she was feeling anymore. Her emotions were too raw, the wounds still too fresh.

Leaning closer, Kellen whispered, "As soon as Annie brings me something to wear, why don't we go back to my cabin? The girls will need to see I'm all right, Bogart will need to be fed, and you, Doctor, look like you need to rest after all this."

"Are you going to rest with me?"

"Where else would I be?" Dana's skin was soft, the feel of her breath warm. Kellen kissed the top of her head and held her close a little while longer.

Hours later, Dana lay sleeping, her left arm tucked under Cody, her right holding Ren close. Standing in the shadows, Kellen dragged a hand through her hair. She was bone tired, her head ached, and her stomach growled, reminding her too many hours had passed since she'd last eaten.

But she had no real interest in food. Nor could she pull herself away from where she stood. Watching the three most important people in her life sleeping soundly in her bed.

The feel of Bogart's nose against her hand reminded her that others still relied on her for their needs. "Sorry, Bogart. Don't know what's wrong with me."

After putting food and fresh water out for him, she put on her boots and grabbed a jacket, so she could take him out as soon as he was finished eating.

Short minutes later, she was enjoying the affirming sting of cold air. Watching puffs of vapor form as Bogart ran down the laneway and back, returning to her side each time with the brightly colored ball she'd thrown. Panting, tail wagging, waiting for her to throw it again. All perfectly ordinary. Lighthearted and innocent.

Until Bogart alerted.

Kellen went very still. The wind blew her hair in her face, but she didn't try to stop it or push it back. She didn't move at all because she felt the presence of a predator, somewhere nearby.

In that fleeting instant, she also saw a movement. Someone coming along the lane toward her. A hand raised in greeting. A shadow that morphed into Calvin Grant while Bogart continued to look at the woods to her right.

She thought about it—for less than a second. And then she stopped thinking. She simply acted. She felt herself move toward him, knew her boots were crunching ice and snow, felt the wind whipping her hair. Then everything faded as she lunged, hitting Grant in his midsection, taking him down hard and leaving them both desperately short of breath. An instant later, a bullet whistled mere inches above their heads.

"Jesus, that was too close," Grant muttered in her ear as he regained his breath. "Whatever you do, Ryan, don't move."

"Not moving." She couldn't have moved if she'd wanted to. The world had become gray and out of focus.

Keying his body mic, Grant called out reinforcements. Kellen listened as he gave them his present location, advised them he was not alone, and indicated roughly where the shot had come from.

Kellen remained where she was, lying on top of Grant. Acutely conscious of the pounding of her heart, while Bogart remained protectively beside her. Too visible, she thought, and patted the snow beside her until he lay at her side.

It felt like an eternity passed before one of the FBI sharpshooters returned. "You're safe to move," he said. "We know where he was, but he's long gone. All I can tell you right now is he left behind a shell casing and some blood. Vasquez, Roberts, and Singer are following his trail, but they're not optimistic about finding him. It's like we're chasing a ghost."

He reached a large hand and helped Kellen to her feet, then gently touched her neck and stared at his fingertips. "That's blood. You're hurt."

Kellen felt Grant and the sharpshooter staring at her as she touched her neck, felt the wetness there, and only now started to feel the pain. "It's not new," she said. "It's from my last encounter with the bastard, from this morning. I must have popped a couple of stitches."

"Frankly, I don't care when it happened. We need to get you some medical attention," Grant said. He started to pull her in the direction of the clinic, but Kellen resisted.

"It's okay. Dana—Dr. Kingston—is at my cabin and it's closer." She pulled her hand back only to sway beneath a wave of dizziness. Grant steadied her, and between the two FBI agents, they helped her back to the cabin, with Bogart following close behind. As she walked, she couldn't help but wonder if Dana and the girls had heard the shot and had been frightened. And how annoyed Dana was going to be that she was bleeding again.

Dana opened the front door before Kellen and the two FBI agents made it up the steps. Her heart had been pounding wildly since the crack of a single rifle shot had shattered the stillness of the evening.

Cody and Ren had wanted to immediately go out and find Kellen, and as much as Dana wholeheartedly concurred with the sentiment, her first responsibility was to keep the girls safe, and it had taken everything she had to convince them to stay with her. Inside Kellen's cabin, waiting for her to return.

She had to return. That was the only outcome Dana could conceive because Kellen not coming back to her was simply not possible.

And now here she was. Covered in snow and blood. Being helped by Calvin Grant and one of the steely eyed FBI sharpshooters, while Bogart followed her every move.

"Oh God, what have you done?"

"It's nothing, Dana. I just popped some of the stitches when I tackled Special Agent Grant."

Dana looked toward the tall heavyset agent and back to Kellen. "You tackled *him*? Jesus, Kellen. Are you crazy? He looks like he should be playing pro football."

It was Grant who finally spoke. "I don't know how she knew he was there. I do know she likely saved my life. If she'd been a second or two slower in bringing me down, the shot you heard would have taken me out."

"Bogart alerted," Kellen said wearily. "When I saw you coming toward me, I don't know why, but I knew he'd go after you, not me. Maybe this shooter is trying to terrorize me by picking off those around me. And I don't want anyone else hurt on my account."

As Grant stared at her, his expression softened. "Whatever the reason, thank you."

The urge to hold Kellen in her arms and never let go almost toppled Dana. Instead, she reached for Kellen's hand and squeezed. She then pulled her to the kitchen and sat her at the table while Ren fetched her medical bag and Cody stoked the fire.

As she carefully removed Kellen's coat and sweater, and cut off the bloodied bandage from her neck, she felt her throat tighten. The images of Kellen hurt and bleeding that had haunted her since hearing the echo of the gunshot returned and almost unraveled her composure.

Kellen reached for her, held her hand for a moment. "I'm right in front of you. Real, solid, and very much alive."

Disregarding the two FBI agents in the room, Dana pressed her lips to Kellen's temple. "What is it with you and the girls? Are you all mind readers? Ren gets my medical bag without my asking. Cody stokes the fire before you start to shiver. And now you reassure me everything's all right without my saying a word."

"It's what happens when you care about each other, I guess. Part of being a chosen family."

Dana nodded, and with a strong sense of déjà vu, she cut off the bloodied bandage on Kellen's neck and once again began the process of cleaning and stitching the bullet wound. Except she really had been there before. Just a few hours ago.

She wondered if she would ever achieve the kind of connection the girls and Kellen seemed to share. A connection she'd previously not understood and now wanted more than anything.

"You already do," Kellen said. "You just don't know it yet." She gestured to the FBI agent. "What about you, Special Agent Grant," Kellen asked, aware the agent's eyes missed nothing. "What was it that brought you out this fine evening and nearly got you killed?"

Grant gave her a sharp look and she suddenly realized his presence this evening wasn't just because of the pending case.

"One of these days, you're going to call me something other than my title, which no one else manages to say quite so derisively. But if you must know, I heard you'd been hurt this morning and I wanted to check and see how you were doing."

"Really?" Kellen bit back a grin. "Keep that up and someone's going to suspect you actually like me."

"They'd be right. Damn. Never thought I'd see the day, but I do like you, Kellen Ryan. Even if you are going to be the death of my reputation." Grant laughed. "Now it's time to sleep. We've still got a shooter out there and if I've learned anything over the years, it's never to miss an opportunity to sleep. You never know when you'll get another."

When Grant and his silent sidekick left, Kellen remained at the table lost in thought until Dana approached.

"How did you know he was there?"

"Like I said. Bogart alerted."

"Kellen—"

"I just felt something was wrong. I felt it in my gut."

"You trust your gut, don't you? Has it ever let you down?"

"Only once." Kellen fell silent, absently rubbing Bogart's ears. "My parents...I never saw that coming. But then, maybe I didn't develop my gut until I had spent some time on the street. It's a wonderful teacher, the street. It teaches you lessons in ways you never, ever forget."

"Is that why you keep that backpack in the front closet?" Dana stared at the closed wooden door as if it was holding back a dark monster. Or perhaps she had already come to regret her question.

"Kel?" Ren approached her quietly. "Do you want me and Cody to go so the two of you can talk?"

She shook her head, flinching slightly as the new stitches pulled. "No need. We're family." Getting up, she walked to the closet and retrieved the backpack. And then she gave it to Dana. "Have at it," she said. "I've nothing to hide from you."

❖

Dana stared at the backpack, her heart pounding and her head spinning with uncertainty. She wanted to ask Kellen more questions, to make sure this was really all right. To make sure looking didn't imply a lack of trust. Then she realized letting her see was Kellen's act of trust. Her gift. And then she pushed all hesitation aside, opened the backpack, and spilled its contents on the table.

She found herself at a complete loss for words.

In among the jeans, T-shirts, boxers, and socks, was a thick stack of twenty dollar bills, a number of credit cards, and three passports, along with a variety of legal documents. Dana could see birth certificates, university diplomas—

Picking up the closest passport, she opened it and found herself staring at a photo of a blue-eyed woman with short, spiked blond hair. From Montreal, Canada. She looked different, but there was no question the woman in the picture was Kellen.

"I speak, read, and write French. Quite fluently. So does Ren, for that matter."

Nodding uncertainly, Dana put the passport down and picked up a second. This time the Russian-born American citizen had short dark hair and dark, nearly black eyes.

"Contact lenses. And yes, I'm equally fluent in Russian. German as well," she added with a touch of humor.

The last passport had yet another slightly different version of Kellen. Closer to her current reality, except it had a different name and identified her place of birth as Louisiana.

Dana held it in her hand, stared at the photograph. "Is this where you're from originally?"

Her question brought a faint smile to Kellen's face. "Why do you ask?"

"I'm not sure." Dana shrugged. "I guess because you have a trace of an accent I've always wondered about."

"That's funny, because you're not the first person to think that. And New Orleans happens to be one of my favorite places. But no. I wasn't born there."

"Um, okay. But can I ask how—" She indicated the passports, uncertain how to frame her question.

"When you live on the street, you meet all kinds of people. And if you're willing to pay, you can get top quality for whatever you want. Good enough to pass any customs or border check."

"Oh." Reaching over, Dana tucked a few stray strands of hair behind Kellen's ear. "And if I asked, would you tell me where you were really born?"

Kellen grasped Dana's hand and brought it to her lips, placing a gentle kiss on her fingers. "Of course. I was born in New York."

Dana lowered her eyes and nodded, even as she tried to understand and absorb everything she'd seen and heard over the last few minutes. That she and Kellen were lovers was not in question. But Dana was uncertain how or when she'd given Kellen reason to trust her with so much. So completely.

"I didn't need a reason," Kellen whispered. "I just knew—from the first time I saw you."

"You're reading my mind again. Do you suppose it's something I'll eventually learn?"

Kellen dazzled her with a smile. "Who knows? In time, I'd say anything's possible." And then she tipped Dana's head back and claimed her with a kiss that ignited her senses.

CHAPTER TWENTY-THREE

Under normal circumstances, Kellen would have started her day with a workout of some kind. A run, time in the gym, or some laps in the pool. Anything to get out some of the frustration flowing in her veins. Anything to calm her less than steady nerves.

Except things were far from normal. Nor had they been for quite some time.

The FBI insisted she couldn't go running through the woods until further notice. Not until they caught the man seemingly intent on killing her. And the woman in her bed, a woman who was consuming all her waking thoughts and dreams, had warned her to stay away from the gym and the pool, because she had no interest in stitching the bullet wound in her neck a third time. She was also restricted from going on any callouts other than avalanches.

So instead, the new normal had her spending a good part of the day in Annie's office. Finalizing the seemingly endless plans for the grand opening of the medical clinic. The event had been intended as a celebration, involving financial backers and the local communities that would benefit from the clinic. But now, security measures had taken on a life of their own.

The lack of escape avenues available to her had Kellen tied up in knots, leaving her feeling grateful when a telephone call from Harrison Parker interrupted the ongoing discussion. Special Agent Grant stepped out of the room and Kellen put the senator's call on speakerphone, enabling Dana and Annie to participate in the conversation.

Except the senator wasn't calling about the opening. He made that perfectly clear as he quickly got to the heart of the matter.

"I've spoken to your grandmother's lawyer, Kellen. He's agreed to call off his investigator if I can provide him with a blood sample that can be used for DNA testing to prove who you are. He's also agreed he doesn't need to know *where* you are if my lawyers act on your behalf and handle the bequest."

"I can handle the blood sample," Dana said.

"I figured as much," Harrison said. "Kellen? You do understand it's a mere formality, don't you? Anyone who's ever seen you and knows who your father is—well, there should be no doubt. Feature for feature, you are the very image of your father. As for strength of character, we can all be grateful you turned out like neither of your parents."

"Thank you, Senator."

"You're very welcome." There was a noticeable pause before Harrison spoke again. "You should also know I ran into your parents at a showing in DC a couple of days ago."

Kellen tried to push back an immediate reaction as her heart began to jackhammer and she felt an unwelcome weakness in her knees. "I see."

"No, I don't think you do. At least not yet." His voice was remarkably gentle. "I made it a point to speak with them. I hope you don't mind, but I let them know I was speaking to them on your behalf. I told them you are alive and well and under my protection, and that I plan to keep you that way. And then I showed them a sample of some documents and photographs I obtained from a hospital in Chicago, relating to an eleven- or twelve-year-old Jane Doe who'd been savagely beaten and raped almost twenty years ago."

"Oh God." Kellen's eyes burned and the edges of her vision grayed. Her legs started to fold and she staggered, reaching for anything to keep herself upright before dropping to her knees. But she could still hear the senator.

"You saved my daughter's life, Kellen. In the years since that time, you allowed me to get to know you. Enough that you've become like a second daughter to me. I consider you family and I protect my own. So I told them if they ever come near you or try to hurt you again in any way, the documents I have will be made public. I don't care about statutes of limitation. I guarantee they will both be destroyed in the court of public opinion. Do you understand what I'm saying?"

Kellen tried to speak, tried to respond, but she couldn't get any words out. All she could think was that a man she respected and admired had seen the photographs. Read the reports. He knew everything her father had done to her. The knowledge rolled around in her mind until a wave of nausea threatened to bring her down.

As if from a distance, she heard the senator continue speaking to Annie and Dana. She thought she heard him ask them to make sure she was all right and that she should call him later. Once she'd had a chance to absorb what he'd told her.

Before the senator hung up, Kellen was on her feet and out the door. That she left her jacket behind didn't matter. She didn't feel the bite of the cold air. She didn't feel anything except conflicting emotions.

The horror that photographs and documents revealing the extent of what had been done to her were now public knowledge. Preserved for eternity. And the sheer wonder that someone had stood up to her parents on her behalf.

She ran past Grant's security team without stopping. But all it had taken was one look at her face and they had allowed her to pass. She even managed to make it into her cabin before being wretchedly and violently sick. After which she dragged herself into the shower, turned on the hot water, covered her face with her hands, and tried to get warm as she wept for the first time in a very long time.

Dana found her there thirty minutes later, still fully dressed in jeans and a long-sleeved T-shirt. Sitting in the shower with her face pressed against her knees, shivering under a stream of scalding hot water.

If only she'd known. But then again, Dana knew she couldn't have gotten to Kellen any sooner, because she'd had to deal with Cody and Ren. Both girls had seen Kellen run by and had been frightened. Kellen had been crying. And nothing made Kellen cry. Not ever.

So she'd talked to them. Soothed and calmed them. Explained that Annie's father had taken steps to protect Kellen from her father, and that Kellen had been overcome by his act of kindness. His unbelievable generosity. But most of all, she assured them Kellen would be okay. Hopefully more than okay.

She barely had time to second-guess her own words when she found her. Dana turned off the water, got Kellen to her feet, and somehow helped her out of her sodden clothes. Kellen's eyes were bloodshot and glassy with shock and she remained docile as a lamb, standing mutely while Dana dried her and got her into pajama bottoms and a fresh T-shirt. And then she allowed Dana to tuck her into bed without protest.

After picking up Kellen's wet clothes, she left Bogart to watch over her and walked out to the kitchen. Annie was there, sitting at the table holding a bottle of wine, while Cody and Ren were at the stove making soup and sandwiches.

"Our hearts were all in the right place, but the girls are being much more practical than I was," Annie said as she opened the wine bottle. "Soup is probably about all Kel will be able to handle when she gets up. But I thought I'd bring some wine, just in case."

"Well, if Kellen's not interested in the wine, I certainly am."

"Me too." Annie filled two glasses before asking, "How is she?"

"Overwhelmed, I think." Dana wet her throat with the wine.

Annie nodded. "She has enough to deal with right now. I don't know what to do for her, what to say. I don't know how to help her, and I hate the thought that my father has somehow made things worse."

"What your father did was probably the single most incredible thing anyone has ever done for Kellen," Dana said. "But at the same time, I think she felt humiliated to think he saw the photographs and read the reports detailing what her father did to her."

"That's not—"

"She knows that wasn't the senator's intent." Dana reached out and held Annie's hand while Cody set soup bowls in front of them. "Or she will once she's calmer and feeling a bit better."

"I hope so."

"I know so. But with everything else she's been going through, with Tim getting hurt and the shooter getting so close, I don't think she can deal with any more."

"You'd be right."

Dana turned at the sound of Kellen's voice and saw her. Standing barefoot in the shadows, her damp, tangled hair haloing a pale face and accenting dark, tired eyes. "Hey, you. How come you're up? I had hoped maybe you'd sleep for a bit."

"My head." Kellen shrugged uncomfortably. "I couldn't get it to shut down. And I thought—I realized—I guess I didn't want to be alone." Before she could say another word, Ren was across the room and in her arms, almost knocking them both over.

"I love you, Kellen. Are you all right now?"

Dana felt her throat tighten as she watched Kellen hold Ren tight and run her hand through the girl's silky hair. "I love you too, Ren. Don't ever doubt that. And I'm fine. Just fine."

"Cody and I made soup and sandwiches, and Annie brought wine."

Approaching the table with her arm still draped around Ren's shoulders, Kellen smiled tentatively. "My stomach's not feeling too friendly at the moment, so I'm pretty sure I'm not up to wine. And though the soup smells wonderful, I think I'll pass and maybe just have some juice."

"I'll get it for you."

While Ren went to the fridge for the juice, Kellen looked at Dana and Annie, her face tinged with something akin to embarrassment. "I'm sorry about what happened earlier. I think everything got the better of me. I'll give the senator a call later and apologize."

"He'd like to hear from you," Annie said. "But don't ever feel you need to apologize for being human."

"Human?" Kellen dropped into a chair and let out a long breath. With a slightly bemused smile, she added, "I guess that means I'm not superwoman anymore."

Dana got up and wrapped her arms around Kellen. "I wouldn't be too sure about that."

"Please," Cody said as Ren put the juice in front of Kellen and sat back down. "There are impressionable children present."

Ren laughed, and for at least a moment the world felt normal.

Mine. The thought—or feeling—had occurred to Dana the last time she and Kellen had made love. It now returned full force, except this time she realized the love she felt included Ren and Cody.

Life was curious, she mused. When she'd first come to Haven, she'd been looking to escape her family and find a place far removed from where she'd grown up. She'd been looking for a place she'd fit in. A place she could call home.

She'd found all of that. But somehow, in finding Haven, she'd also found herself a family.

❖

"You haven't eaten," Dana said after everyone had left. "And you really could use a meal. Why don't you let me make you something? It doesn't have to be much. Some soup, maybe, or even just some toast."

Kellen shook her head. "No thanks, maybe later. There's something else I want first."

"Name it and it's yours. What can I get you?"

"You." Kellen put her hands on Dana's face and kissed her. Long and slow and deep. She slid her fingers through silky blond hair as Dana's arms came around her. Took comfort and tried to give some in return. "You make me feel strong and whole. Like my past doesn't matter to you. Like I can do anything, walk down any path, and you'll be there with me. Standing beside me."

"I am." Dana kissed her brow, her lips, her throat. "I will be. For as long as you want me to be."

"What if I don't want to let you go?"

Dana eased back so that their eyes met. "I'd say that would be perfect."

With the fire stoked and Bogart settled for the night, they walked into the bedroom, undressed, and slid onto the bed. Facing each other, they touched. Explored. As if it was their first time coming together. Tender, loving hands. Slow caresses. Quiet whispers. Unhurried passion. A gentle rise and an intimacy that came from the heart and touched the soul.

Kellen knew she'd never be as good or as comfortable with words as Dana was. But in this, in completely surrendering herself to her lover, she hoped she was saying more to Dana than words ever could.

❖

Kellen looked every bit as tired as Dana felt the next morning. She found her in the kitchen, hair still wet from a shower, leaning against the counter drinking coffee.

Kellen smiled when Dana approached, but her eyes were deeply shadowed, proof if needed of yet another restless night. Dana could see it even if Kellen refused to admit it. And when Dana touched her back, the set of her muscles confirmed she was tired and tense at the same time.

Maybe when this was all done, what Kellen needed was a few weeks of skiing and laughing and loving to take away the shadows behind her smile. Dana planned to make it so.

"Why don't you go back to bed and get some sleep?" Dana suggested.

Rubbing a hand over her face, Kellen gamely put on a brave front. "It's a nice thought, especially if you were to join me."

She inched closer and kissed Dana, softly at first and then with increasing enthusiasm. Dana responded with a muffled sound of pleasure, deep in her throat. The sound was involuntary, uncalculated. But she noticed it seemed to further ignite Kellen's passion.

At the next opportunity, she tipped her head back and looked at Kellen. "Tell me, do you like women who are…vocally demonstrative?"

Kellen laughed softly and traced a knuckle along Dana's jaw. "If you're vocal, then I like that. If you're not, then I'm fine with that too. What I like is you—in my arms and in my bed."

"Hell of a good answer," Dana murmured as she slipped her hands under Kellen's sweater so she could touch the skin that lay just beneath. Kellen smiled in a way that said she liked it as much as Dana did.

She reached for Kellen's hand and was about to lead her back into the bedroom when she heard a soft knock on the door.

Kellen groaned. "Damn."

Dana seconded her sentiment. She kept her arms wrapped around Kellen's waist and held on a moment longer. She felt uneasy but could see that while Bogart looked toward the door, he didn't alert. It told her the knock might be an ill-timed interruption, but they would not find a foe on the other side of the door.

She opened the door, acknowledged Grant, and then waved him inside while Kellen poured an extra cup of coffee and set it on the table for him.

Grant paused long enough to take a grateful swallow. "You were right when you thought the shooter might be connected to someone you'd trained in the past. We've identified him. His name is Douglas Broussard."

Kellen turned and looked out the window, a thoughtful expression on her face. "I trained someone by the name of Tommy Lee Broussard about three years ago," she said. "He hailed from some out-of-the-way parish in Louisiana, down by the Gulf. Any relation?"

"The shooter's his father."

"Damn." Kellen closed her eyes. "That means Tommy Lee's—"

"Dead. Yes. He died about a year and a half ago. Killed in an avalanche in southern Chile. Did you know him well?"

"Yes. He was really something, a natural," Kellen said softly. "Fearless but never foolish. Great instincts. I wanted to hire him after the first time I worked a callout with him. He knew it too, but he begged me not to say the words. He'd spent his whole life in a small backwater town, and he wanted to travel, see something of the world before settling down. And he knew if I offered him a job, he'd take it and possibly regret later that he never had a chance to explore. He asked me to give him time, three years to get the travel bug out of his system, and then, if I was still interested, he'd gladly come on board. We both knew I'd still be interested."

"I'm so sorry," Dana murmured and put her hand on Kellen's shoulder, offering what solace and support she could with her touch.

"Tommy Lee had two older brothers," Grant said. "Declan and Nathan Broussard run a pair of fishing boats. It's what Broussard senior expected of all three boys, and according to Declan, his father took Tommy Lee's death hard. Surprising because strained would be a safe characterization of Broussard's relationship with Tommy Lee. Regardless, he blames you for filling his boy's head with thoughts of seeing the world."

"I—"

"It doesn't have to be the truth," Dana said. "It's what the man chose as a way of rationalizing what happened. It made it easier for him to deal with his son's death."

Grant nodded. "Douglas Broussard grew up hard, in and around the Louisiana swamps. He got out briefly and did a stint in the army, which turned him into a sharpshooter. After he got home, he began using his newfound skills to bring in extra income, mostly hunting alligators, sometimes running contraband."

"Do they have any idea where he is?"

Grant shook his head. "According to his sons, he disappeared about a month before the first shooting happened and hasn't been home since, although he's maintained sporadic contact with both boys. The only thing they know for sure is he plans to see this through all the way. He has no intention of going home again."

"Oh, Jesus." Dana murmured. "What happens now?"

CHAPTER TWENTY-FOUR

There was a storm brewing. Kellen could feel it in her bones, smell it in the wind, and sense it in the tension in the air.

She sat on the front step of her cabin, Bogart by her feet, and stared out into the growing darkness. Shadows slipped and fell, pushing and pulling at her from all directions. But they didn't change the one incontrovertible fact echoing in her head.

Douglas Broussard was out there somewhere.

The truth cut through her, bringing with it a penetrating chill. She'd felt his presence before. The only difference was then he had been an unknown presence. Now she knew who he was. She could put a face to the specter shadowing her life.

The FBI had made it clear they were prepared to wait him out. They said he was hurt and, sooner or later, he'd be unable to continue the game of cat and mouse he was currently playing with her. He would act more rashly and make a mistake. And when he did, they'd be ready.

But Kellen didn't want to think about the endless possibilities that lay between sooner and later. Because she knew Broussard would do whatever he needed, including hurt people who were important to her. Anything that meant driving her out from behind a phalanx of FBI protection, if only for a second or two.

According to Grant, he was that good. He wouldn't need much more than an instant to take her out. She shuddered and wondered if that was meant to somehow reassure and comfort her. *It will be over quickly.*

The FBI had brought Harrison Parker into the discussion, bringing him up to date and advising him against attending the clinic's grand opening. True to form, the senator refused to even consider it. Said both he and his wife would be there. For Annie and for Kellen. Even though everyone agreed if Broussard wanted to make a statement, the gala and the number of public figures present would give him a perfect platform.

Which left her exactly where?

Thinking about what was coming and wondering what, if anything, she could do to alter the course of events. Kellen didn't want to put anyone else at risk. But she also believed she'd been punished enough for some transgression or wrongdoing she hadn't even committed.

And the cost had been high. Her childhood. Her parents. She'd been left with only memories of horror, ugliness, and betrayals. Remnants of broken dreams. How could she now—

"You must be freezing, sitting out here by yourself. Are you okay?" Dana's voice wrapped itself around her just before she felt warm hands on her shoulders.

"Just tired." She started to deflect, then stopped herself. After so many years when there'd been no one, she had never learned how to open herself up. How to share. But the opportunity to make a course correction was lost as her phone rang.

"My son is dead."

Kellen remained where she was, apprehension running through her, and she wondered how close he was. Was he nearby? She was numbed by the realization he could have her squarely in the crosshairs of his rifle.

"I know Tommy Lee's dead, Mr. Broussard. I'm sorry. He was a good man."

"Don't tell me you're sorry," he replied, his voice brimming with unrelieved grief. "You might as well have killed him yourself, filling the boy's head with thoughts of traveling to godforsaken places and becoming some kind of hero. It's your fault he got himself killed."

"Mr. Broussard—"

"Don't bother. There's nothing you can say that will make me change my mind. I'm just calling to tell you that you'll pay through everything and everyone you love. You will know a hurt so deep you won't want to go on. By the time I'm done, you'll be begging me to kill you. That's a promise."

He hung up as if the conversation was finished, leaving Kellen holding the phone to her ear a few seconds longer. She knew she should call Grant. But not yet. Not yet.

❖

Dana watched her for a long moment, not bothering to be subtle about it. Kellen's face was still and pale. And when she looked into her eyes, for an instant it was as if Kellen allowed her in, and she could see something dark and anxious and heavy.

"That was him."

Kellen nodded slowly.

"What did he say to you, Kellen?" When Kellen remained silent, she tried again. "Tell me what I can do to help."

"Just be with me."

The quiet words whispered through her. Touched her in ways and in places she'd never been touched before Kellen entered her life. She didn't understand how it had happened any more than she understood the quickening that burned through her every time Kellen was near.

Uncertain what to do, she did the only thing that occurred to her. She sat on the front step beside Kellen, wrapped her arm around her, and drew her closer. And then she waited for Kellen to talk about whatever a killer had just said to her.

"This place—Broussard is threatening this place and everyone in it. Everyone who means anything to me."

"He's trying to get to you," Dana said. "He wants to frighten you."

"He succeeded." The emotion was evident in her voice. "And if you leave—"

"What?" Dana turned Kellen's face toward her until their gazes met and locked. "Why would I leave? What's going on?"

"I was thinking—"

"Thinking too much is more like it."

"That may be." She shrugged and looked away. "But it occurs to me if you stay here, if you're anywhere near me, for as long as Broussard is out there trying to hurt me, it puts you at risk. So I'll understand if you leave, if you choose to go someplace else, someplace safe. In fact, that might be the smartest thing to do. But then I'd no longer fit in your life. This is the only place I've ever fit. Either way, I stand to lose you."

Her voice stopped Dana cold. It was filled with pain and pleading and hope. And Dana knew she had to formulate her response carefully. Thoughtfully. Without putting any more pressure on—*fuck it*.

"Kellen, that's just crazy," she said calmly. "I'm not going anywhere. What's more, I have no intention of going anywhere in the foreseeable future. Not without you, unless it's a beach somewhere we can skinny-dip and make love under the stars. So you might as well get used to the idea."

"Promise?" As soon as the word escaped her, Kellen shook her head. "No, I'm sorry. Please don't answer that. I'm not being fair and it's not realistic."

Dana lifted a hand and smoothed a silky dark strand of hair from Kellen's face, tucking it behind her ear. She knew with everything going on around them, it would be crazy to even think of making a promise right now.

"I promise," she said. "And just so we're clear, you may not think so, but you fit just fine with me. It also doesn't matter where we are, although I'm really hoping it's here, because I really like it here. What's more, you like it here and the girls like it here."

Dana glanced at the sky, at the dark storm clouds rolling in. She reached over and took Kellen's hand and pulled her to her feet. "Let's go inside. The storm's coming in faster than they predicted and I, for one, would like to watch it while curled up on the sofa in front of the fire. With you. But right now, it would be like holding an ice cube. Once you're warm again, while we still have cell service, we'll find Grant and tell him about Broussard's call."

She thought Kellen might argue with her. But it seemed the call from Broussard had taken the fight out of her. At least for tonight. "Okay."

Kellen glanced out the window as she refilled her coffee cup. The wind had died down and was no longer howling like a wounded beast. But the front edge of the storm had already dropped over a foot of fresh snow and the weather service was predicting more snow and gale-force winds were still to come.

In the meantime, white shrouded everything familiar and Kellen felt completely disoriented. *Symbolic of my life?* Maybe so, because for the first time in her life, she had no idea what to do. No viable options. All she had were her instincts, and she was afraid they were all wrong, at least as far as Dana was concerned.

She tried to imagine returning to a life without Dana, and the bleakness of the prospect shook her. She then tried to think about all the things she couldn't control and nearly laughed. Because at the moment, that seemed to apply to everything in her life. Including the escalating discussion between Dana and Grant.

"Why can't you track his cell phone?" Dana asked.

"If he calls again, we can try. But you can't expect too much," Grant said.

"You're saying it won't help."

He looked at the ceiling for a long minute and finally relented as he turned back to Dana. "Let me try to explain. The most common method of locating a cell phone is through the use of triangulation. Since phones connect to multiple towers, signal strength is analyzed and the distance from each tower is estimated. The more towers a phone is connected to, the better the estimation."

"But—"

"But it takes time and all it will end up telling us is what general part of the forest he was in when he called, not what tree he was hiding behind."

"Well, damn." Dana blew out a hard breath. "Then what do you propose to do?"

Grant turned to Kellen as if seeking her intervention. She responded with a gentle shake of her head. There was no way she was getting in front of a clearly agitated Dana Kingston. Actually, she wanted to get out of the cabin.

Maybe she could take Bogart out, stop by the clinic to make sure everyone was all right, and then bring the girls back to her cabin for the night. Neither Cody nor Ren did well with storms, and with Broussard's whereabouts unknown, she wanted to keep them close.

As soon as Kellen grabbed her boots, Bogart went to the door, tail wagging enthusiastically, which had Dana looking up. "Going somewhere?"

"Rain or snow, Bogart still needs to go out. Then I thought I'd check on the folks at the clinic before bringing the girls back."

"Why don't I go with you as far as the girls' cabin?" Dana stood, signaling an end to her conversation with Grant. "I can spend some time with them until you get back."

"That would be nice. Storms tend to scare them both. Just one question, though." The corner of Kellen's mouth lifted. "When was the last time you were on snowshoes?" Dana's eyes told Kellen all she needed to know. "That's what I thought. Don't worry about it. We'll take it slow."

CHAPTER TWENTY-FIVE

As the blizzard settled in and buried the region under new snow, state emergency coordinators advised everyone to stay inside and avoid all travel, especially in the backcountry.

Not that the warning was needed. Nothing was moving. Deep drifts had made the roads impassable and power outages were being reported throughout all the nearby counties.

Something about the howling winds and snow piling up at a rapid rate reminded Dana of long-forgotten childhood winters in Boston, when storms had paralyzed the city. In those days, she'd failed to see a problem. Now she watched with growing concern.

The clinic was equipped with standby generators, so they'd be operational in the event of a power outage, and since most of the staff was on hand, bunking in the student dorms until the storm blew over, they were well-situated to deal with emergencies.

But she knew a lot of people in and around Haven weren't as lucky.

So she wasn't surprised when the state police radioed and asked if Kellen and her teams could provide assistance and temporary shelter to some of the people the extended power outage had left in the cold. Nor was she surprised when Kellen immediately agreed.

"We can move the girls into my cabin," she suggested. "I have more than enough firewood, and even the cabins that are still being renovated will serve. At a minimum, they'll provide warmth and shelter, and we can provide food."

Annie nodded. "And once those are all in use, and the dorms, there's always the gym. I'm sure we can come up with enough sleeping bags to see us through."

Dana watched with a combination of pride and fear as Kellen gathered her team and they prepared to head out on snowmobiles in near constant whiteout conditions. Kellen paired them up and ensured everyone had a radio to communicate, not only with each other, but with Annie and Dana in the clinic.

Dana bit her lip, worried about Kellen working under dangerous conditions. Worried she would take too many chances if it meant helping someone. But she knew this was who Kellen truly was. The first one out the door, ready to help.

She suspected Kellen's time on the street had helped shape and strengthen this particular aspect of her nature. Remembering all those times she had needed help and no one had been there for her no doubt fueled and drove her to ensure no one else went through what she had on her own. Dana even admired the trait, but she feared where it might lead.

For what seemed a long time, although it might have been measured in seconds, she stood silently watching as Kellen prepared to leave, waiting until the last moment before she reached for Kellen's hand. "Please be careful. And please don't do anything heroic or crazy out there. I know you're doing what's necessary, but it's not just the weather I'm worried about. It frightens me because I know Broussard is still out there."

"With the near-zero visibility, Broussard won't be able to see the broad side of a barn, let alone be able to hit it," Kellen said with a wry smile, but she left her hand in Dana's. "So please don't worry. In fact, if he's smart, he's holed up somewhere he can safely ride out the storm."

"God, I hope so."

Kellen drew her closer. "As for what we're doing, it's all in a day's work, so have faith. We won't take unnecessary chances, and we'll be back with plenty of houseguests before you know it. In the meantime, maybe you could do me a favor?"

"Anything."

"Can you keep an eye on the girls? Especially Ren."

Dana looked at her sharply. "Why? Is something wrong?"

Kellen shook her head. "Neither of them deals well with crowds. Ren just has a harder time. It'll help if you keep Bogart with her. He'll help to keep her calm and grounded in the present."

"Like he does with you," Dana murmured. "How long do you think she'll need? How long did it take you to come to terms with what your parents did to you and what you experienced on the street?"

Tension visibly washed over Kellen's face and Dana silently cursed herself. *How could I have asked that?* But by then it was too late.

"Twenty years and counting," Kellen answered roughly.

Just before she headed out, Kellen heard Liz call out to her. Pausing in the act of slipping on a helmet over her full-face ski mask, she turned and waited.

"Maybe while you're rescuing people, you could try to convince Michelle this is a better place than Up the Creek to ride out the storm," Liz said.

"Michelle Barret?" Kellen looked at Liz for a long moment then nodded and managed a soft laugh. "About time—she's a terrific lady. Let me see what I can do for you."

"You do that." Liz grinned. "And be careful out there. It looks positively brutal."

Brutal turned out to be putting it mildly.

It was colder than expected and progress was painfully slow. The high winds, coupled with treacherous drifting snows, had left cars buried and roadways blocked, which would make it harder for plows and utility trucks to get through once the storm system passed. In the meantime, visibility was so bad it hampered rescue efforts and left the teams unable to see more than a foot in front of them.

But their focus remained reaching people and places otherwise inaccessible and rescuing anyone in emergency situations. People who needed medical care, food, or whose homes were without heat. Some had also been without water since the power had gone out.

Everyone worked tirelessly, and with each trip back to the clinic, those who'd been rescued brought what food staples they could carry. Kellen noticed Dana, Liz, and one of the other doctors had set up a triage area, checking the health of each person brought in and assigning them beds, while Annie, Cody and Ren, and several volunteers gathered the food and offered hot soup, sandwiches, and coffee.

But there was no relief in sight. Hazardous conditions and deteriorating weather complicated the rescue of both locals and stranded motorists which continued throughout the day and well into the night.

After another run back to the clinic with a special passenger for Liz, Kellen accepted a coffee and stood off to one side, closing her eyes and wondering if it was possible to fall asleep standing up. She figured she might find out if she could stand there for just another couple of minutes…

"You should probably have something to eat with that coffee," Dana said softly, deliciously warm body heat emanating from her as she wrapped her arms around Kellen's waist. "Why don't I get you a sandwich while you go sit in my office for a few minutes?"

Although she wasn't particularly hungry, Kellen nodded, recognizing on some level it had been hours since she had last eaten, and if nothing else, she needed to replenish the calories she was burning.

She made her way to the quiet office, struggling to work the zipper on her jacket with cold and unresponsive hands before finally managing to peel it off just as Dana returned. She gratefully ate the thick cheese sandwich Dana brought her, downed two cups of hot coffee, and felt infinitely more human.

"You should try to rest for a while before you go out again," Dana told her. "You're running on fumes and you're more likely to get hurt if you keep going like this."

"Actually, I'm good," she said. "The food and caffeine did the trick and we still have a stretch of homes to check on. In fact, I should go." She leaned closer for a brief, tantalizing moment and kissed Dana full on the mouth. A short, gentle kiss that nonetheless sent a flash of heat and desire that burned deep inside her.

Dana looked at her, speechless and startled, and Kellen had the pleasure of watching her eyes darken with need.

"Do me a favor and hold that thought until I get back."

❖

Dana spent the better part of the next few hours dealing with everything from mild frostbite to a heart attack one man had suffered while trying to shovel his way out of his home. Through the chaos, she tried to keep an eye on Cody and Ren, aware that as time passed, both girls had grown more quiet and withdrawn.

She had promised Kellen she'd keep an eye on the girls, so during a much needed break, she grabbed a couple of coffees and brought them over to where Ren was sitting, absently stroking Bogart. "If I remember correctly, you take your coffee with lots of milk."

Nodding and murmuring thanks, Ren took a few hesitant sips before looking at Dana. "Do you think Kellen's okay out there?"

"Yes. She'll be cold and tired by the time she gets back, but she'll be fine. Not only is she doing what she loves, it just so happens she's the best at what she does. Is that what's troubling you?"

Ren looked down at the coffee cup in her hands before she shook her head. "No. I just don't do well when there are too many people around. It scares me and reminds me of before."

Dana wasn't certain whether she meant when she lived on the street or what came before that, at home with an abusive father. Probably a bit of both. But she left the question unasked. "Would you prefer I leave you alone?"

"No." Though she still appeared to be uneasy, at least Ren was watching her with more interest than trepidation now. "You're different."

"What do you mean?"

"She means you don't look down on Kellen or Ren and me because we lived on the street," Cody said quietly as she sat on the floor beside them. "Even though you came from a real home with parents who actually cared about you."

Cared about her? In spite of their inability to be demonstrative and openly show affection, in their own way, Dana knew her parents cared and wanted what was best for her. The only real issue between them was a fundamental disagreement about what constituted the best for her.

But she knew neither Ren nor Cody had experienced anything remotely close to parental love. "That doesn't make me any better than you," she said. "You know that, don't you?"

"Maybe. But a lot of other people, they think they're better than us, or think we did something to deserve where we ended up." Cody shrugged and drew Ren closer to her. "You're not like that. We also think it's kind of nice that you don't seem to mind Ren and me being around all the time."

"That's because I don't mind."

Cody mulled that over, clearly trying to make up her mind whether she was going to buy it. "And you don't seem to mind that we climb into bed with you and Kellen when we get scared."

"I don't mind that either. In fact, I kind of like it."

Cody swallowed, looked at Ren, then back again. "And you don't laugh at us because there's so much we don't know and need to learn. Or mind that Ren and Kellen have so many nightmares. Or that Ren starts to draw and forgets to eat or sleep or show up for work. Or that Kellen needs to go off and be by herself every now and then."

Dana nodded thoughtfully. "You're right. I don't mind any of that. Do you know why?"

"Because you love Kellen."

"That's true, but it's only part of the story. What else?" she asked, aware both girls were studying her.

It was Ren who answered this time. "Because maybe you think we're not so bad." Her tone was guardedly hopeful.

Dana smiled. "Not bad. Try again."

This time, the vulnerability on Ren's face as she stared at her cut straight to Dana's heart and she had to force herself to keep still. "Because maybe you love us too?"

"That's the right answer," Dana said softly, and the answering smile on Ren's face brought tears to her eyes. An instant later she was pinned to the floor as the two girls hurled themselves into her arms, embracing her with the most amazing hugs she'd ever received.

They remained in a tight huddle and Dana didn't realize she'd dozed off until the squawk of a nearby radio intruded. She opened her eyes and saw Liz approach.

"Sorry to disturb you, but Gabe's on his way in with Meg Waters and her slightly ahead of schedule newborn baby girl."

Dana stared at Liz, not certain she had heard correctly. "She wasn't due for another couple of weeks. Is everything okay?"

"So I'm told. According to Gabe, he and Kellen delivered a healthy baby on Meg's kitchen floor about forty-five minutes ago." Liz shrugged. "I'm guessing it wasn't exactly the home birth Meg had planned, but Gabe said it was a textbook delivery and mom and baby are both doing well."

"All things considered, that's wonderful." Dana gave a quick smile of relief and got to her feet. "Is Kellen coming in with them?"

"Um...no."

"Liz? Is there a problem?"

Liz shrugged helplessly. "Meg's kid sister Josie moved in with her recently and when Meg started to go into labor, in the middle of a storm with the power out, Josie went out to try to get help. Kellen's out searching for her."

Dana had met Josie on a couple of occasions. She pictured her now, a slightly built, shy fifteen-year-old, then glanced out the nearest window and confirmed for herself nothing had changed in the last half hour. The heavy snow falling showed no sign of abating and the winds were continuously swirling it around, making visibility almost nonexistent. She tried to imagine Josie walking through waist-deep snow, and shuddered.

"Don't worry, Dana," Cody said quietly. "If anyone can find her, it'll be Kellen."

Dana nodded and got to her feet, mentally already going through what they would need to care for a newborn. And trying not to dwell on Kellen, out in the unrelenting storm, looking for a lost fifteen-year-old.

❖

Endless swirling drifts, snow-covered trees, and fallen branches. It all looked the same. Time trickled by and she was feeling increasingly numb from the cold, but she refused to allow the pain in her body to win.

When the lights from the clinic finally appeared, they became a beacon and the only thing Kellen allowed herself to focus on, trying not to lose them in the endless white. She gritted her teeth and pressed on harder, but in spite of her best effort, reaching them took longer than she anticipated.

She'd known she was in trouble from the moment she climbed out of her insulated snowmobile suit and put it on Josie in an effort to get the girl warm. The relentless wind had immediately reached for her. Surrounded her. So cold it hurt, leaving her wet to the bone and freezing cold.

But there had been no choice as far as she could see. Josie Waters was only fifteen years old. Too young to die trying to save her older sister and newborn niece.

With an effort far out of proportion to the task, she brought her snowmobile to a stop near the clinic's front door. But once she arrived, she could do no more. The adrenaline rush she'd experienced when she first found Josie had long since worn off and she had nothing left.

She wanted to curl up in a ball, she wanted to get warm, but her body wouldn't cooperate. She couldn't remember how to lift her leg, didn't know how to help get Josie inside, and the pain she'd staved off through sheer will now hit her with a vengeance.

Struggling to maintain her equilibrium, she all but fell over. But she sensed several people running toward her. Removing Josie from the back of the sled. Talking to her, then lifting her and bringing her inside.

Time ceased to matter. She was aware her jacket and boots had been removed, her frozen jeans and thermal long johns were cut off, and she was hooked to an IV with warm saline. A heartbeat later, she was wrapped in a soft, warm blanket.

Faintly disoriented, Kellen was aware of people moving around her, someone taking her temperature while someone else held a warm, sweet liquid to her lips and encouraged her to take a sip. She tried her best to put her game face on, but chills were racking her and her teeth were chattering.

The drink was pulled back, and then a different set of hands took over. Soft, warm fingers wiped her face before placing something in her mouth. She'd know those fingers, that gentle touch anywhere, just as she knew the scent and taste of the chocolate melting in her mouth. She struggled to bring her world back into focus.

And then she saw Dana's face. Her beautiful, worried face. Hovering over Kellen as if she'd dreamed her. As if she'd wanted and needed her so badly at this moment that she had caused her to materialize.

Kellen blinked.

And Dana was still there.

Dana's hand was shaking slightly as she brushed wet hair away from her face and stared at Kellen, as if memorizing each of her features. Dana then drew her close to the heart of her, where Kellen knew she'd be safe.

"How're you doing, sweetheart?"

"F-fine. Not so cold."

"You're going to be fine. No sign of frostbite, so we're going to warm you up nice and slow. Okay?"

"'Kay."

"As soon as you're warmer and up to it, there are a number of people waiting to talk to you," Dana murmured softly. "Cody and Ren need to see you're really all right. Josie wants to thank you for saving her life. And Meg wants to let you know she's naming her new baby after you."

"If you want to warm me up quickly, skin to skin usually works the best," she said hoarsely, and one corner of her mouth tipped up in her best effort to smile.

Amused bafflement transitioned to a soft smile before Dana pressed her lips to Kellen's forehead. "Have another piece of chocolate and then we'll see about letting all your admirers in to see you. After that, we'll talk about skin to skin."

Kellen felt a latent spark of sexual heat spread through her chest, and a flame ignited deep in her core, heating up her blood. "Are you going to just make promises, or do you plan to deliver anytime soon?"

Dana laughed, slipped another piece of chocolate between Kellen's lips, then kissed her on the mouth.

CHAPTER TWENTY-SIX

The storm system stalled and battered the region for nearly forty-eight hours, before it finally relinquished its hold and moved on. In its wake, the weather turned clear and the sun returned.

Everyone pitched in to clear the streets, digging out buried cars and making way for the plows to come through. The utility trucks followed and worked to restore power. And slowly, the community returned to some semblance of normal.

Once Dana released her from the clinic, Kellen went home and had a long hot shower, then dressed in sweats, wrapped herself in a blanket, and for what seemed like forever, sat in front of the fire, still trying to get warm. A miracle according to Annie. Cody and Ren stayed by her side, helping to look after Bogart and simply keeping her company.

The following morning, Dana left her sleeping when she got up, turned the coffeemaker on, and headed for a shower. But on her return, she saw the bed empty and found the three of them—Kellen, Cody, and Ren—standing in the cold on the front deck, steaming coffees in hand, sharing the birth of a new day. The connection between them was tangible, and Dana was hesitant to intrude.

Cody saw her first, standing just inside the doorway, and motioned for her to come out on the deck with them. But it seemed a special moment, like a bonding ritual, and she didn't want to disturb them.

Then Kellen turned and reached for her hand, drawing her out onto the deck to stand beside them. She didn't say anything. No one did. They simply watched the dawn spread over the mountaintops in silent communion.

Afterward, Cody and Ren went back inside, leaving Dana with Kellen alone on the deck. "You should go in," Dana finally said. "It's still much too cold."

"Soon, but not yet. It feels too good being out here."

They remained side by side for a few minutes longer, Kellen's hand caressing the back of Dana's neck in a gentle random pattern before she drew her closer and kissed her. Softly. Sweetly. "Okay. Let's go in."

Dana nodded. "You just want more coffee, don't you?" Her heart warmed as Kellen laughed. A beautiful sound.

"You know me too well," Kellen said.

"Not yet," Dana responded, "but I will."

Several heartbeats went by without Kellen saying anything, but then she softly sighed. "Will you still want me when you know all my secrets?"

"I can't imagine a time when I won't want you. Is that going to be a problem for you?"

Kellen smiled. "No, it's not a problem. Let's go find that coffee before the girls drink it all."

❖

When her cell phone began to vibrate, Kellen's chest stilled.

She already knew who was going to be on the other end of the call. They all knew. The three smiling women around her looked up simultaneously and their expressions mirrored each other, smiles fading, expressions becoming fearful. Worried. For her.

Once again, he wasted no time. "Do you know why I'm a happy man, Ryan?"

Kellen turned away from the others. It didn't matter that he hadn't identified himself. She'd know his voice anywhere. "No, Mr. Broussard. I have no idea why you're happy."

"I'm happy to know you survived the storm," he said with a laugh. "I can't have no damn storm taking you out. That pleasure belongs to me alone. It was all I could think about these past few days."

"I'm glad to hear you survived the storm as well, Mr. Broussard. But winter weather in the mountains can be unpredictable. Mother Nature can be wicked and can turn on you in a flash. You may not be so lucky next time. Don't you think it's time you went home?"

"You and I both know that's not going to happen."

"What about your sons? What about Declan and Nathan? They're worried about you."

There was a momentary silence, as if he was weighing his answer. "This isn't about them. This is about my youngest boy, and he's dead. Because of you."

Kellen squeezed her eyes shut, desperate to remain calm. Desperate to find a way to reach a grieving father. "I'm sorry for your loss, Mr. Broussard. Truly I am. Has it not occurred to you that even if you kill me, Tommy Lee will still be dead?"

"I'm not stupid, girl. I know that. But when I'm face to face with my boy, I'll have the satisfaction of knowing I avenged his death. You'll be dead as well. At my hands. I want you to think on that because you won't have much longer to wait."

He rang off without another word.

When the call ended Kellen remained still, her knuckles white as she strained to hold the phone steady. She tried to slow her heart rate. Tried to gather her composure. Tried not to absorb any more of Broussard's anger and pain than she already had, afraid if she did she wasn't going to make it through this.

When she felt a hand touch her arm, she jumped and spun around.

"It's okay, love. It's just me," Dana said. "What did he say?"

"More of the same." Kellen shrugged tiredly. "He said he's glad I survived the storm so he can kill me."

"That's twisted," Cody said as she drew Ren closer.

Kellen nodded. "He won't stop. He's really quite mad, you know, and I don't want anyone else getting hurt. So I'm going to ask that none of you go anywhere alone, that you don't stray far from a safe place, and that you look out for each other. Watch each other's back."

"That goes for you too," Dana said.

"It goes for all of us." There was nothing else to say and Kellen was left wanting nothing more than to get lost in the comfort of Dana's arms. In the feel of her. In the heat and strength of her. Telling her in silence what she continued to struggle to say in words.

As if reading her mind, Dana put her arms around her, reaffirming the bond that had been forged in spite of everything.

❖

When they left the cabin a short time later, they didn't get far before they ran into Grant and several of his team, looking to meet with Kellen. A reminder, if one was needed, that with the storm over, their focus had returned to finding Broussard.

Dana accompanied them as far as Kellen's office before continuing on her own to the clinic. There were a few patients scheduled, but that didn't account for the number of people in the waiting room.

The walk-ins turned out to be mostly strains and sprains from people trying to move beyond the storm's aftermath, and for the next few hours, she was happy to lose herself in the familiar routine.

It was well after six before Dana came up for air, glad there was only one more patient waiting. Her smile widened when she saw it was Meg Waters, bringing in Josie, and young Kelly. It seemed everyone had heard the story by now, and most conversations today seemed to revolve around Kellen and Gabe delivering the baby on Meg's kitchen floor.

"I know we don't have an appointment, but Josie said she had to come," Meg said. "I don't know if she's having problems with her hands and she's not telling me, so I thought it was better to bring her in. Maybe she'll talk to you."

"It's not a problem." Dana turned and smiled at the girl. "Follow me, and we'll take a look at how you're doing."

She took Josie into an examination room, gently removed the gauze wrapped around her hands, and checked the frostbite, the only visible remainder of the girl's frightening experience during the storm. "How do your hands feel?"

The girl wriggled her hands a little. "They feel a little stiff."

Dana smiled. "That's to be expected. They'll take a while to heal, but I don't expect there to be any permanent damage."

"Is Kellen going to be all right too?"

"Absolutely."

"Good." Josie seemed pleased with the answer. "She's not here, is she?"

One brow lifted. "Kellen? No, I'm afraid not. Did you need to see her?"

Josie stared at the floor for a moment. "I remember she kept talking to me while she was digging me out of the snow. She wouldn't let me do anything—"

"That's because when someone has hypothermia, like you did, moving too much causes the cold blood from your arms and legs to move toward your heart and that can be bad," Dana explained.

"That's what Kellen said. She also said if I stayed awake and talked to her, she'd take me fishing once summer's here. Is it true she catches fish with just her hands? No rod or reel? No hooks?"

Dana smiled at the girl's enthusiasm. "It's true. She's already taught Cody and Ren to do it and she's promised to teach me as well. Maybe we can all go together."

"That would be great," Josie said as Dana led her back from the treatment room. "Um…can I ask one more thing?"

"Of course."

"Is it true what people say?"

"What's that, Josie?"

"That Kellen used to be homeless? That she used to live on the street?"

Oh shit. Dana stiffened and her smile froze into place before fading. She heard Meg hiss at Josie. Saw the girl hang her head and stare at the floor.

She realized it was the first time she found herself confronted with the question, something Kellen and the girls had no doubt experienced far too many times. And the possibility Meg and Josie somehow thought less of Kellen because she'd lived on the street made her both angry and sad. But she also knew she needed to respond appropriately. In a way that would hopefully help the girl understand.

"Does it bother you to know Kellen lived on the street?"

Josie stared at her newly bandaged hands for a moment and finally shook her head.

"Then why did you ask the question, Josie? What is it you want to know?"

The girl chewed on her bottom lip to the point Meg started to intervene, but Dana shook her head and Meg remained silent.

"Before," Josie began haltingly. "Before our parents finally agreed to let me leave and come live with Meg, I had thought of running away. I figured I'd be able to handle it. Then after I got lost in the storm the other day, I realized I wouldn't have survived. But I've heard people talk about Kellen. About how she's the best tracker and if someone's lost, they better hope it's Kellen that goes out looking for them. So I guess I just wondered how she learned so much and got to be so smart."

She wasn't looking down on Kellen, Dana realized, as relief flooded through her. What she had was a mild case of hero worship. Or possibly a first crush. She was on the verge of responding to Josie's question when she felt a warm and familiar hand squeeze her shoulder.

"Living on the street doesn't make you smart, Josie," Kellen said gently. "It's hard and rough and dangerous, and you're cold and wet and hungry a lot of the time."

Josie studied her through narrowed eyes. "Then how'd you get to be so smart?"

"I don't know that I am, but whatever I know, I learned by studying and reading books. Every kind of book I could get my hands on. Especially books about nature and how to survive in the wild. About plants that are good to eat and how to build shelters."

"And how to fish without a fishing rod?" Josie added.

"Yes," Kellen smiled. "Even how to fish with just my hands, which taught me an even more important skill. Patience."

"Why patience?"

"It takes an incredible amount of patience to stand perfectly still in a river or stream until dinner swims your way."

"So you're saying I should read books and study?"

"Exactly. And the next time I take Cody and Ren into the woods for a real-life lesson, perhaps Meg will let you join us."

Josie's eyes widened and her smile could have lit up the room. "That would be so—oh God, Meggie? Can I go with them? Please?"

"As long as you promise not to cause trouble and to do everything Kellen tells you to do." Several seconds passed and then Meg spoke again. "Kellen, I hope you weren't upset by Josie's question. She didn't mean any harm. You're all she's talked about since you saved her. And just so you know, I knew...I've known for a long time you'd lived on the street."

"And to think you still named that beautiful baby girl after me," Kellen said with a grin.

"Damn right I did," Meg replied. "When I look at everything you've accomplished, and everything you're doing for our community, it makes me proud to name my baby after you. So thank you. Thanks for saving all of us."

Maybe not just one case of hero worship, Dana thought wryly, wrapping her arms around Kellen after the others left. "Are you done for the day?"

"Grant and his boys are finished with me for the moment, if that's what you're asking. With all this fresh snow, they want to take a chopper up tomorrow and see if they can spot anything that may indicate where Broussard is hiding."

"What else did they want to talk to you about? You were gone a long time and you seem, I don't know, on edge, I guess. Tense."

Kellen shrugged. "They also wanted to discuss security for the grand opening. They seem to think because I know both the clinic and Haven better than most and by nature am always looking for escape routes, that I might be able to help them. With things like lines of sight and where to post sharpshooters."

"Oh, shit." Dana looked at her more closely, looking for signs of fresh damage. "Are you okay with all of this?"

"It wasn't exactly a comfortable conversation, but it involves everything and everyone I care about, so yeah, I guess I'm willing to try anything."

"Anything?"

The change was instant. Kellen responded with a devastating smile, having clearly not misunderstood Dana's tone. "Tell me what you need, and I'll do my best."

"I just want you," Dana said softy. "Let's go home so I can have my way with you."

Kellen couldn't remember getting back to the cabin and lighting a fire, let alone getting out of her clothes. All she had was a vivid, visceral recollection of Dana unzipping her own jeans, letting them fall to the floor, and stepping out of them before pulling her sweater off and standing in front of her. Naked and perfect.

The glow from the fire provided just enough light for Kellen to see the gold flecks in Dana's eyes as she caressed her. She could feel her body respond to Dana's touch in a way it hadn't responded to another woman. Ever. She'd never felt so alive.

She reached for Dana's hand and drew her onto the bed where she could adore her with her hands and mouth. She was surprised by how much she needed her. Something she hadn't been able to admit to herself. Until now.

It was crazy. Incomprehensible. But her entire life had changed since she'd met Dana.

"I want you, Dana," she murmured. "More than I've ever wanted anyone in my life." Her kiss this time wasn't gentle. It was hard and demanding.

She couldn't get enough of her. Couldn't touch her enough. Couldn't taste her enough. Couldn't kiss or lick her enough. Couldn't do anything fast enough or deep enough or long enough.

Not enough for Dana either, apparently, because she cleverly turned the tables, rolling Kellen onto her back and straddling her hips.

Heart pounding, breath ragged, body trembling with pent up longing, she sensed Dana's need to take control. So she gave it to her and hoped she showed her this wasn't just about a physical connection.

She'd never felt closer to anyone in her life. And this was about telling her without words what a miracle she was in her life. About how she couldn't imagine anyone else in the world that would ever come close to meaning as much to her as Dana did.

She lay beneath her, forced her hands to stay still, and watched her move in the flickering candlelight that bathed her in gold. She groaned when Dana ground her pelvis against hers. Sighed as she felt the heat and wetness between her thighs. Stopped breathing when Dana planted her palms on the bed on either side of her shoulders and kissed her. Open mouth seeking, hot and hungry, while her tongue was sweeping and bold.

When her amazing mouth moved lower, nipping and kissing her jaw and her throat, flicking the tip of a pebbled nipple with her tongue before lightly biting, Kellen writhed and let her know how much she loved it.

An instant later, Dana's mouth and hands were everywhere. Feverish. Arousing. Demanding. Moving lower, she briefly slipped a finger inside Kellen and then her tongue replaced her finger, stroking her, her mouth open and feasting, while her hands cupped Kellen's buttocks, holding her in place.

A feral groan escaped Kellen. "God, I love when you do that to me." She arched her back, pressing her head against the bed and her pelvis against Dana's mouth, asking for more. Demanding more.

She was insatiable. Determined to lose herself in Dana and equally determined to bring Dana with her.

She heard a low keening sound in the stillness of the room and recognized it as her voice. Her unarticulated moans of passion. But further sounds became strangled in her throat as Dana sent her free-falling over the edge.

She was dimly aware of Dana's arms tightening around her, holding her as the next wave hit. Then she felt the sudden rigidity and trembling in Dana's body as she joined her in release. Kellen welcomed her with her arms, her body, her heart, and her soul. With the last of her strength she called out Dana's name. And then everything receded into a velvety blackness.

❖

Sated and floating on a soft cloud of lassitude, Dana lay on her back, waiting for her breathing to return to normal and the world to slip back onto its axis.

She assumed Kellen had fallen asleep. Her body was still. Her eyes were closed. And her face was surprisingly tranquil with a small, almost dreamy smile, while her silky dark hair was damp with sweat and plastered against her forehead.

Watching her, Dana felt something tighten in her chest. She loved her passion. Loved her taste. Loved the strangled, desperate sounds she made and how she called out her name when they made love. Loved her—beyond anything she might have imagined.

She lay motionless, transfixed, as a deep, heavy heat coiled through her. Did she still want her? God, yes.

She could feel the aching need building once again. But she couldn't stop staring at the picture Kellen made lying there. Her lips were swollen from Dana's kisses. Her skin was flushed from her touch. Her breathing was slow and deep. Slowly, carefully, she rose on one elbow, leaned over, and gently kissed her forehead, then tenderly kissed Kellen's lips, lightly tasting them.

"I love you," she whispered.

She had just settled back on the bed facing Kellen and closed her eyes when she felt Kellen shift beside her. Felt her warmth draw nearer, followed by the pleasure of her lips as they skimmed along her jaw, while her hands roamed the length of her back and down to her hips. Dana made a humming sound of approval and offered her mouth as they shifted on the bed, a tangle of limbs.

Kellen's taste, hot and wild, infused her mouth and stirred her as it always did, made her want more than she'd known there was to have. She opened for her, both invitation and demand. In response, Kellen's tongue dipped, tasted, savored, while her long, skilled fingers began arousing her mercilessly until she was mad for more.

Incapable of thought, Dana attempted to pull her closer still. Kellen immediately stilled, then took Dana's hands and placed them over her head. "Don't move," she murmured.

It was unquestionably an order, but unable to refuse Kellen anything, Dana did as asked. And then Kellen opened her even more and took it all. Lingering in all the tender places, the hidden places, the secret places. Her hands caressing Dana as her mouth tasted, hovered, tasted again. Unraveling her in a loving that was both passionate and tender.

"Do you want me, Dana?" Kellen's voice was smoky, intimate. Demanding an answer.

"Yes," she whispered. There could be no other answer. "Oh God, yes."

"How?" Kellen murmured as she continued to stroke hot, delicate skin. "Gentle? Hard? Fast? Slow? Tell me what you want, Dana."

"All of the above. I want you—in every way possible."

An instant later, Dana was unable to do anything but feel, as she was captured by the searing demands of Kellen's mouth and the world came apart around her. Kellen tasted her lips, feasted on the hollow of her throat, and on her breasts. Eyes open, wild and blind with a hunger she didn't fully understand, Dana felt consumed as Kellen lingered, touched, tasted, and caressed, learning and memorizing the very pulse of life beating within Dana as she slowly moved down her body.

Nearly drowning in waves of pleasure, Dana writhed while Kellen moved in calculated slowness. Never wavering, she continued to explore. Taking, demanding, giving, worshipping. Desperate for release, Dana gasped for air. And then Kellen drove her over the top on a wave of rapture and she came until she couldn't even draw a breath to whisper Kellen's name.

Urgency mellowed into tenderness.

Kellen reached out a strong arm and drew her closer. Caressed her before putting her hand under her chin and kissing her slowly. Gently. Thoroughly. And then she softly murmured, "I love you too."

Chapter Twenty-seven

D awn was still an hour away.
In the soft light, Kellen focused on tuning out the familiar sound of the helicopter's rotor as Sam lifted off, taking a couple of FBI agents with her. She watched the chopper briefly hold at one hundred feet and then begin the search pattern Grant had mapped out, knowing that in addition to providing the spotters with a bird's-eye view, they'd be using the three new cameras the FBI had installed: two standard cameras equipped with powerful zoom lenses, and a thermal-imaging camera, which would enable them to detect heat signatures.

This was not how she'd wanted today to start. But then she'd all but forgotten she'd agreed to do this—to be out tramping through the woods in the chilly pre-dawn air with Grant instead of being cuddled under a duvet, making love with a beautiful woman. What was worse, although Bogart wasn't alerting, apprehension prickled along her skin and it felt as if even the forest was holding its breath.

Kellen suppressed her impatience and remained motionless in the shadows a minute longer. Finally, the helicopter moved on and the silence returned.

Slowly she allowed her gaze to move around, looking for signs in the shadows. She hunched down lower and concentrated, tried to detect anything out of the ordinary, any visible disturbance indicating someone had come this way. Scrapes, broken branches, or marks of any kind.

But it was hard to still her mind when the skin between her shoulder blades itched as if Broussard had painted a target on her. She could feel him, like a wolf stalking his prey. He was close, but not close enough. Not yet.

She retraced her steps, examined the ground again, looking at the snow more closely. Time seemed to slow down and finally she detected what she'd been looking for. What she'd known she'd eventually find. Faint shadowed shapes leading into the bowels of the forest, marking someone's passage. "He's been here—sometime after last night's snowfall."

Grant came up and stood beside her, staring at the snow-covered ground. "I don't see anything. How can you tell?"

Kellen pointed to a spot. "The snow here's been disturbed where he brushed it to cover the tracks left behind by his snow shoes. It has to be Broussard. With your sharpshooters maintaining watch along the path, only someone with his skill could have gotten this close and not given himself away. And if it was anyone else, they wouldn't have bothered covering their tracks."

Grant didn't say anything but drew his weapon, sweeping it around in a wide arc.

She frowned. "What the hell, Grant?"

"What's wrong?"

"Would this be a bad time for me to tell you I'm not a big fan of having guns that close to me?" Aware he was weighing her words, Kellen remained still and waited.

He stared at her for a few seconds, then slowly shook his head. "You're something else, you really are. Do I need to remind you there's a man out here somewhere who wants to kill you? And do I have to remind you the reason I'm here is because it's my job to protect you? That I promised Senator Parker I'd look after you?"

Angry, feeling cornered by life, something tightened in Kellen's chest. She knew there were things from her time on the street that would never leave her. Not completely. Like her innate distrust of authority.

Grant's words had her squaring her shoulders, folding her arms across her chest, and lifting her chin as she turned to face him. "I can look after myself."

"Kellen," he responded softly, "I don't doubt that. In fact, if anyone can, my money's on you. But this guy Broussard? He's damn good. He's proven it time and time again by having already killed too many people, and he's made it clear he's coming after you. You're the only target that really matters to him now. The rest were practice so he could come back and correct his failure."

She licked her lips. "Are you trying to frighten me?"

"No…well, maybe. Maybe I want you scared enough that you won't take any unnecessary chances. Mostly I'm just trying to lay out the facts for you to see. And those facts include me telling you I'm not letting Broussard come close to you. Not on my watch."

His words reminded Kellen of something she had learned a long time ago. Life wasn't fair or unfair. It was simply surprising.

Sometimes, like her parents, the surprises could be breathtakingly cruel. Other times, like being with Dana, they could be simply breathtaking. As for having a federal agent protecting a former homeless kid? She didn't know the answer to that just yet, but as she watched Grant, the corners of her lips twitched. "You're telling me I have to put up with your gun, aren't you?"

"You got it in one." Grant smiled faintly. "If it helps, I'll try to keep it out of sight as much as possible when you're around. But if Broussard's nearby, I want an opportunity to level the playing field. So it's going to be visible."

"Then I guess I shouldn't bother to remind you he uses a high-powered rifle"—it took all Kellen had to keep her grin to a minimum—"and if he has us in his sights, we're both dead and there's nothing you and that little gun you're holding can do about it."

Grant stared at the gun in his hand a moment longer, then started to laugh. "Well, hell," he said and conceded the point.

"Actually," Kellen murmured thoughtfully, "that begs a different question. The odds are high Broussard has us in his sights at this very moment. So tell me, Special Agent Grant, why are we being played with? Why doesn't he finish me off here and now in a single merciful stroke?"

"I asked that very question last night when I was talking to the behavioral analysts in Quantico. They're not sure, but they think maybe he wants to make one final grand gesture."

"You mean during the clinic celebration, don't you? With all those politicians and dignitaries on hand."

Grant nodded. "We're down to the wire. And the experts have concluded your little celebration will undoubtedly bring Broussard out so he can finish what he started."

Kellen thought about that for a minute or two. "Do your experts think he'll hurt anyone else? Or just me?"

"They aren't sure."

"That's not a very good answer. What do your years of experience—what does your gut instinct tell you?"

Grant sighed. "I'm sorry, Kellen. I honestly don't know."

"Then why don't we let him find me? And in doing so, make sure no one else is close enough to get hurt?"

"Kellen…"

They stared at each other in silent contemplation. And then, without saying another word, Grant put his weapon back in its holster and they resumed checking the perimeter of the property.

While Kellen knew they were both looking for signs that might tell them where Broussard had been and where he could be hiding, she understood Grant was also looking for potential placements for his team. Places that would afford the best lines of sight on every approach that led to the clinic. They just needed to be ready for him.

They needed to be ready for anything.

Thinking about that made Kellen realize something else. Nearly twenty years ago, her father had made her a victim. At the time, she'd been too young, too inexperienced, too trusting to prevent what had happened. None of those words could be used to describe her anymore. This time around, she wasn't about to let Broussard or anyone else make her a victim, which meant she had to push back fear and be ready and willing to do whatever it took to bring this nightmare to a close.

She wanted—no, she *needed* to move forward again.

That knowledge left her with a heady sensation of being freed from a cage. Able to move in a breathtakingly beautiful direction with a woman who didn't care where she had been or who she had been in the past. She simply loved her for who she was.

Closing her eyes, she took a deep breath and retreated, as she did when in crisis, to a quiet place inside her where she could listen to her heart and know what to do. Surprisingly, it didn't take long. "Um…Grant?"

❖

Dana leaned against the kitchen counter, took her first sip of coffee, and grimaced.

This was not how she'd imagined the day beginning. But after spending the night spooned against Kellen, holding her tight and relishing her words of love, she'd awoken to find herself alone in bed. And if that wasn't bad enough, she'd found the sheets cool to the touch, telling her Kellen had been gone for quite some time.

She'd tried but couldn't fall back to sleep with the bed beside her painfully empty. For a few sweet moments, she tried floating on a memory that made her forget everything else.

Tell me what you want, Dana.

I want you—in every way possible.

But then she blinked and Kellen was still gone.

She had a vague recollection of hearing someone knocking on the front door. Or at least she thought she did. She could even picture Kellen getting up to check while she had drifted back to sleep, fully expecting Kellen to come back to bed.

Clearly, that hadn't been the case.

Releasing a sigh, Dana closed her eyes, not certain what had happened, even more uncertain about what would happen next. But as she listened to the silence, she could only hope something other than fear had driven Kellen from her bed.

One thing at a time.

She opened her eyes and rolled from the bed. She took a deep breath, inhaling the seductive pull of their mixed scents—her own and Kellen's—before leaving them behind. Forced to contend with a coffeemaker that seemed to cooperate with only Kellen's programming, she swore softly after taking another sip of what she'd produced and dumped the contents from her cup into the sink.

Stripping out of her pajamas, Dana headed for a hot shower and tried to rub a combination of tension and fatigue from her neck before going back into the bedroom and getting dressed for the day. All the while pondering both the wonder and absurdity of life.

Last night, Kellen had said she loved her.

It hadn't come as a surprise. In her heart, Dana had known for some time how Kellen felt about her. It showed in her every look and every touch. She just didn't realize how much she had wanted to hear the words until that moment. And hearing them…hearing her say the words for the first time, that had meant everything. It also made it so much more difficult to accept she was nowhere to be found this morning.

The challenge was that she could be anywhere.

She could be taking Bogart for a run…or debriefing a team after a callout…or dealing with Grant and the FBI's security plans for the celebration…or terrified by what she'd revealed and gone walkabout.

The last possibility left Dana shaken. Could that be what happened?

She had long ago accepted Kellen came with issues that made her own pale by comparison. Kellen was uncomfortable in crowds, was frequently haunted by nightmares, and remained fearful of her past—and her parents—catching up to her. Hell, Dana didn't even know her birth name.

But the truth was she didn't care. Because somewhere between leaving New York and now, she'd found exactly what she had always hoped to find. An intelligent, passionate, and loving woman with whom she could talk, laugh and cry, and share her life. A place where she could sink permanent roots. A job that satisfied her professionally. And a chosen family to call her own.

She was in love with Kellen and had resolved to give her the time and space she needed to come to terms with having someone—having Dana—in her life.

Perhaps she had given her too much room.

Determined to deal with the situation directly, she left the cabin. She first checked on the clinic, but Liz had everything under control. Her next stop was the office by way of the gym. Kellen was nowhere to be seen, but last-minute preparations for the gala were clearly well in hand.

Annie looked up and smiled as Dana entered the office before her expression slowly gave way to one of concern. "What's wrong? What's happened?"

Dana shook her head. "I don't know. Nothing...everything." She shrugged and pressed forward. "Have you seen Kellen?"

Annie's eyes narrowed and she studied her more closely. "I believe she's still combing the woods with Grant and his team, finalizing placements for all those FBI sharpshooters he's brought in. At least that's where she was when I sent Cody out with coffee for them about twenty minutes ago. Why? What's the girl done?"

Dana let out a long breath. "She told me she loved me."

Clearly confused, Annie leaned back in her chair. "That's wonderful, sweetie. I happen to know you feel the same way, so forgive me if I don't understand. What's wrong?"

"Loving her is easy, Annie. Losing her terrifies me." Her throat had tightened and she found it hard to swallow. "I woke up alone this morning, after the most amazing night of my life. It scared me more than I thought possible. It made me wonder if it had all been a dream. Or worse, that Kellen panicked when she realized what she said and took off."

"No dream. And definitely no panic."

The husky voice had her whirling around. Kellen stood at the door, and Dana saw a kind of elemental wariness in the depths of her eyes. "No?"

Kellen shook her head. "No. Just an obligation that slipped my mind." She approached Dana slowly. "I forgot I'd promised Grant I'd help him with a couple of things this morning. Or maybe I got so preoccupied with other more important matters that I forgot, until he showed up at the cabin. But the things he needed my help with, they're all done now."

Dana swayed slightly, lulled by the low voice. "Finished? Really?"

"Really. Except for this." Kellen reached for Dana, threaded her fingers through her hair, and brought her face closer. They stared at each other and long seconds passed without a single sound. "I love you, Dana Kingston," she whispered just as their lips touched.

CHAPTER TWENTY-EIGHT

Hundreds of tiny white lights glittered like stars on the tall dark pines, casting a soft glow on the footpath and marking the way to the clinic, while soft music filled the evening air.

As Kellen made her way from room to room, people greeted her with smiles. Ignoring the rapid pounding in her chest, she licked her lips, politely paused to exchange a few words, and was happy to defer any acclaim for the success of the clinic to Dana and Annie.

She knew they had worked tirelessly, not only to pull this evening together, but to make the clinic something far more than it would have been had she been left to her own devices. Something truly special for the whole community. And if it meant forcing herself out of her comfort zone and mingling for one evening, then that's what she would do.

The turnout had been tremendous. The silent auction was a huge success and would go a long way toward funding some much-needed equipment. And everyone seemed happy to join in the celebration. Standing off to one side talking with her parents and Leslie, Annie waved and beamed in her direction. With the speeches over, Annie could now relax, and it was clear she was thrilled.

Rightfully so.

Gabe walked by and put a plate of hors d'oeuvre in her hand, but Kellen's appetite had vanished long before people had started arriving. She held the plate long enough to keep others at bay, then at the earliest opportunity, handed it off to one of the servers Michelle had provided, choosing to hold an untouched glass of champagne instead.

It still didn't come easy to her, this being surrounded by so many people, no matter how many she actually knew or how motivated she was. She tugged at the collar of the black turtleneck Dana had asked her to wear—*because I like how you look in it*—and tried to recollect a time when being in a crowd had energized her. But if it ever existed, that moment was buried deep in the past, as irretrievable as her childhood.

It was futile to mourn what could not be changed. She could, however, change the present, and as the clock ticked off another hour of being surrounded by too many people, swallowing became more difficult, her heart beat much too fast, and she needed to take a moment for herself. She needed to step outside and find a place where she could breathe once again.

"Are you looking to make your escape?" a delicious soft voice whispered in her ear.

Kellen turned and felt a flood of warmth fill her as her eyes connected with Dana's. In spite of the lighthearted comment, she saw Dana's eyes were dark, saw concern in them, and it bothered her. She saw the lines of tension around Dana's mouth, knew it was because of her, and felt even worse. But there was nothing she could do.

"Have I become so transparent?"

Dana laughed softly. It was a sweet sound, and with it, some of the tension in her face faded. But not the concern. "Ordinarily, I would say no. But tonight you do have a certain deer-caught-in-headlights look about you."

"I'm sorry—"

"Don't," Dana said, pressing her fingers against Kellen's lips. "I know how much this is costing you, and don't ever feel you have to apologize for being who you are."

Kellen kissed the tips of her fingers. "Thank you."

"Any time, love. But try to remember if Broussard is going to make his move, tonight's the perfect time for it. All the FBI agents I keep tripping over say so, which means if you're going to go outside, you need to let Grant know and take a couple of his guys with you."

Unwilling to give Broussard more control of her life than he'd already wrested from her, Kellen shook her head. "How about I take you instead?"

"How about we do both," Dana said, suggesting compromise as she reached for Kellen's hand.

Kellen marveled at the ease with which Dana slipped through the crowd and captured a glass of champagne from a passing server, while at the same time signaling their intent to Grant across the room. Grant responded with a quick nod of understanding, and an instant later one of his agents slipped through the doors just ahead of them.

Kellen no longer cared, because while night had descended and there were still too many people standing near the entrance, the air was crisp and clean as she stepped outside. And as she gazed up at the moon, a thin silver sickle, the din slowly receded, the tension deep inside her loosened, and she began to decompress.

"Thank you," she murmured as she began to breathe more easily. "This is exactly what I needed."

"You're welcome." Dana smiled. "Have I told you how hot you look tonight?"

Kellen felt herself blush. "All that matters is that you're happy."

"Very, although it's difficult to keep my hands to myself. Do you think you can survive another couple of hours or do you need to sneak away?"

Slowly, Kellen shook her head. "No, I'll stick it out. But I was thinking—maybe on Sunday we could take a drive into Denver."

"Sure, if that's what you want. What's in Denver?"

"Susan, Bogart's vet, has an eight- or ten-week-old rescue pup. A border collie. Only thing wrong is she's underweight, and I was thinking the girls—"

Dana smiled and lightly brushed her lips against Kellen's. "I think that's a wonderful idea. In the meantime, will you at least let me get you something to help with that headache?"

Kellen was aware yet another person was coming up the path toward them, and sighed. "I will if it gets any worse."

And then her heart began to beat faster.

The person approaching was a big man, dressed to fit in with the occasion in a tuxedo and a dark cashmere coat. Clean shaven, his dark hair clipped short and touched by gray at the temples. Surrounded by numerous men dressed similarly, he was unremarkable and would have aroused no suspicion, had anyone thought to compare him to any of the photos the FBI had distributed.

But his resemblance to Tommy Lee Broussard was unmistakable.

❖

Dana watched the stranger as he slowly reached the bottom of the front steps to the clinic, hands in his coat pockets. He didn't say anything. He simply remained silent as he looked up and watched Kellen. Calm and patient and quiet.

She couldn't say she recognized him. But as she felt Kellen stiffen beside her, Dana released a muffled sound of shock and she suddenly knew who he was.

Douglas Broussard. The man who had sworn to kill Kellen.

Dana was too surprised to say or do anything. And then it was too late.

"Hello, Kellen Ryan." His voice was flat. "I've wanted to meet you face-to-face for some time now."

Kellen didn't respond, but Dana saw her flex her fingers, watched her burying all her emotions in that one gesture. Turning back, she saw Broussard's stance. Saw the dead, empty look in his eyes. It was the look of someone who had nothing left to lose. Somebody who didn't have to think anymore.

Too frightened to even blink her eyes, Dana wondered where Grant and his sharpshooters were. She wondered how Broussard had gotten this close and why he was still standing, mere feet away from Kellen. She wondered if this was really happening.

An instant later, she stopped wondering. Stopped thinking. Stopped breathing.

In that moment, Broussard pulled his coat open and everything else going on slid into the background as she saw he'd strapped a dozen or more cylinders to his chest.

Dear God, she thought, as her fingernails pressed into her palms and she swallowed reflexively. Pipe bombs?

"This is a compression switch in my left hand. A dead man's switch," he said, clearly addressing Kellen. Once again, he sounded calm. Like ice water ran through his veins. Like he wasn't wearing death.

"Show me how bright you are, Ryan, and tell those FBI sharpshooters protecting you to back off. If one of them thinks he wants to take me out, I suggest they think again. If I release this, at a minimum, you and I go. Your girlfriend beside you goes with us. But that won't be all. I'm certain I've got enough explosives packed in here that quite a bit of this clinic and a lot of people inside will go as well."

Dana stared at him. Well past frightened now, she moved into a surreal stage, where nothing really registered anymore. Nothing mattered except—

"Please," she said, hands out, palms up. "Mr. Broussard, you don't want to do this." She'd witnessed enough working in emergency departments to know what harm people could do to people. But those other times and other situations hadn't threatened the only woman she would ever love all the way to her soul.

The silence stretched. Thinned. Snapped.

❖

Kellen didn't think she had enough energy left to feel frightened.

She had a past so dark that at times it could still make her flinch, but her mind struggled to make sense of what her eyes were seeing—a man in a tuxedo, wearing a suicide vest, was threatening to destroy everything that meant something to her.

The only time she could remember feeling this disassociated was the day her father had come home in an out-of-control rage and began beating her. It happened shortly after he'd knocked her to the floor. Even as she'd tasted blood in her mouth, he'd pulled out a knife and sliced open her bright yellow T-shirt—

Kellen shuddered and forced herself to think of the present, not the corrosive past.

One thing she knew for certain. This situation, rightly or wrongly, had started with her when she'd trained Tommy Lee. And now she needed to finish it. She owed that much to the people who had unknowingly already played a part in this drama and paid for it with their lives, all because she had failed to die when Broussard first tried to exact his revenge.

She couldn't afford to make a mistake. Not here. Not now. Not when everyone and everything she cared for was at risk, starting with the woman beside her whom she loved more than she'd ever thought possible. Cody and Ren were also nearby. As were Annie and Leslie. Senator Parker and his wife. Liz and Michelle. Gabe, and the other members of her team. This was her *family* Broussard was threatening and he had to be stopped. She needed to stop him.

She drew in a breath and turned her full attention to the man standing at the bottom of the steps. As her eyes locked with his, her breathing hard, emotions roiling, chills rippled over her skin in primal recognition of the truth, and Kellen accepted that whatever was going to happen would happen.

But if she was going down, she would go down fighting. In spite of all the curves she'd been thrown, life had only scarred her. It had never managed to break her will to live. Not Kellen Ryan. And that was who she was.

She slowly eased forward until she was positioned between Broussard and Dana.

"Stop right there." Broussard raised his right hand and Kellen found herself staring at a gun.

"All right." She did as she was told, knowing she didn't have any other option, and her world in that instant narrowed to one goal—not getting killed. She shivered from the cold, felt a flicker of energy surge back into her system, and recognized it for what it was. Adrenaline. She didn't think it would hurt, and it might just help her get through the next few minutes.

"Do you know I've thought about this moment a thousand times in the past year? I've thought about killing you a thousand different ways."

The pleasure in his voice stripped all the moisture from her throat, leaving behind a desert. "I imagine you have." She bit her lip. "So what are you waiting for? Why don't you go ahead and shoot me and be done with it, if that's what you want?"

She heard Dana's shocked hiss, knew she couldn't afford to be distracted. She reached, grabbed Dana's arm, and squeezed. But she kept her gaze fixed on Broussard, watched as his features tightened.

"Are you saying you want to die?"

She saw something in his changing expression and realized she'd surprised him. "No, not at all. But you might as well shoot me, because I'm not about to let you walk into this building filled with people I care about and set off your bombs, no matter what."

He laughed then. A harsh, rasping sound. "You know you can't stop me."

She considered that for a minute. "Maybe, maybe not. But maybe you can help me understand. Is it because *you* want to die? Like your son? That you can't survive knowing he died even though he was doing something he believed in and loved?"

For a second or two, Broussard seemed to waver, to lose focus. Then he squared his shoulders once again. "It doesn't matter. The only question is how many others I am going to take with me. That is the one choice—the only choice—I'm leaving to you."

Kellen knew the agents protecting Senator Parker would have weapons trained on Broussard. But she also knew he was too close to the clinic and everyone in it, and they couldn't risk shooting him. Not as long as his finger was on the detonator. The resulting explosion would take him out. And her. That much was certain. But he had said it would likely take part of the clinic and a large number of innocent people as well. None of them could afford to hope he might be wrong.

"In that case, I guess it's just the two of us. Why don't you and I go for a walk and—"

"Kellen, no." Dana grasped her hand, stopping her forward motion. "Are you crazy? Tell me you're not planning on going anywhere with him."

Kellen turned toward Dana. In spite of the darkness pressing in all around her, there was just enough light. She could see the fear on her face. But she could also see the love in her eyes.

She wished there could be another way.

Broussard might yet kill her. If he was quick enough. The odds were against it, but the chance still existed.

It was a chance she had to take.

"Dana, believe me when I tell you I don't want to die. But I won't let him hurt the people that matter to me. All I'm asking is that you trust me."

"I trust you," Dana whispered, closing her eyes and momentarily tightening her hold on Kellen's hand. "But I feel like I've been waiting my whole life for you and I want a hell of a lot longer with you than what we've had. So please, just remember how much I love you and come back to me in one piece."

"I will," she said, and walked down the steps.

❖

Dana's throat felt completely blocked by the scream that had been rising from her chest since Broussard first appeared. For an instant, she remained motionless. Watching Broussard push Kellen in front of him, while maintaining his hold on the deadly switch in his hand. Watching him lead Kellen away from the clinic and along the path that led into the looming forest.

And then the fear that had her held in its grasp released her, and she took a first step to follow. Almost immediately she felt hands grasp her, abruptly stopping her. She heard Cody, Ren, and Annie calling out to her.

Through it all, she heard Calvin Grant's harsh whisper. Telling her not to do anything foolish. Telling her to let Kellen go and have faith that she knew what she was doing. By then, Kellen and Broussard had been swallowed by the darkness.

She turned to stare at Grant, trying to decipher the message in his eyes. Aware he was listening to someone on the wireless in-ear receiver he wore, but unable to hear what was being said. And then there was no more time to wonder, as the explosion shot high into the sky above the trees, orange flames chasing smoke.

Dana closed her eyes, while around her, no one spoke. Images flashed through her mind helter-skelter.

Kellen leaning down to her car window on a stormy mountain road, her smile dazzling.

The first time they danced.

The moment their lips first touched.

"Oh God, Kellen, what have you done?" Her throat tight, eyes burning, she stared in disbelief, as a wave of fear washed over her, threatening to drown her. "What have you done?"

She didn't remember moving. Not really. One minute she was standing on the steps, the next she was rushing down them and onto the path, mindless of the cold and ice and snow. Conscious only of the smell of smoke and the deathly silence that had followed the explosion.

She stopped as she rounded a corner, confronted by a phalanx of FBI agents, while her mind replayed that oh-God moment and tried to make sense of what she was seeing.

"It's called pink mist."

Dana turned and stared at the agent that had spoken. "Pardon?"

"Sorry. Pink mist refers to blood being ejected at high velocity. When someone is blown up by a bomb, the only thing left is a pink mist of blood."

She closed her eyes, but it did nothing to stop the flow of tears. "There should have been another way. She didn't have to go with him."

"Yes, I did."

Dana's eyes snapped open and she saw her then, standing at the edge of the trees. Her face was white, splattered with red. She was breathing heavily and shivering, walking without assistance, but unsteady on her feet. And then her whole body seemed to sway and she dropped to her knees.

Her heart pounding in her throat, Dana ran to her. Just as she reached her, Kellen lifted her arms, welcoming her against her chest. Inhaling raggedly, Dana tightened her hold on Kellen, an agony of relief rushing through her.

"Kellen." Dana closed her eyes and let out a shuddering breath. "God, I thought I lost you. I thought you were blown up. Oh God. Thank you for coming back to me."

Kellen smiled wanly, attempted to wipe the blood from her face, then rested her head wearily against Dana's forehead. "I was not blown up. And just to be clear, I wouldn't leave you. Trust me on that."

"But you're bleeding. Where are you hurt? Let me see."

"I'm okay, Dana. I was a little closer than I'd hoped to be, that's all."

Dana moved away a little. "That's why you told me to trust you? This was planned? You knew this would happen?"

Kellen winced. "Not exactly. Special Agent Grant and I, we figured Broussard would show. The plan was for me to lead him away to where the FBI sharpshooters were waiting."

"You mean they were using you as bait?"

"Not really. Well, kind of. But I'm wearing Kevlar"—she knocked her knuckles against her chest—"so I'd be protected. It's just that no one anticipated the suicide vest."

Dana wanted to know how wearing Kevlar would have saved her from a head shot. But when Kellen closed her eyes and pressed her fingers against her lids, Dana knew she was still seeing Broussard. Replaying what had happened in her mind. "Kellen?"

"He—he told me to get on my knees. Told me to put my hands behind my head while he walked a few feet away from me." Kellen swallowed visibly. "I'm not sure, Dana, but I think he hesitated."

"He hesitated?"

Kellen nodded. "I don't know how or why, but it gave me enough time to scramble off the path and dive behind a tree before the sharpshooters shot him and he...released the compression switch. And then he...oh God—"

Pink mist. Dana held her as Kellen closed her eyes. Held her until the shaking eased and she was sure she wouldn't get sick. "You okay?"

Kellen's eyes were reddened, shadowed, exhausted. But she nodded gamely. "Yes. Your hands are shaking."

Dana laughed lightly. "Yours too."

"I know. It's really over, isn't it?"

"Yes."

Kellen's gaze became intense, searching. "And are you ready for this? For me?"

"More than ready."

"In that case, can we go home? I want to hug Cody and Ren and Annie and Bogart, and then"—she reached for Dana and pulled her closer—"and then I want to love you like you've never been loved before."

"As long as I can love you right back."

"Always."

EPILOGUE

I want you," Kellen murmured as she sank into Dana.
She drove her fingers into Dana's hair and laid claim with her mouth, swallowing her moan. Intense and kinetic, she drank her in. The dark, sultry sounds ignited her even more as her mouth trailed along Dana's throat and then lower.

Never one to be shy, Dana encouraged her. "Taste me."

Kellen obliged.

Dana gasped, arched, offered more. And Kellen indulged, enjoying the sensual feel of her skin, her heat, her taste. She was about to touch her more deeply when Bogart's sharp bark preceded a knock on the front door that echoed in the stillness of the cabin.

Kellen groaned as she glanced at the clock, confirming it was not yet five in the morning, before she pushed up off the bed. She hesitated, watched as Dana stretched, saw the tangled sheets pooling lower, and wanted nothing more than to get back in bed and love her. Again and again. Just as they'd been doing all night.

The knock returned, more insistent this time.

"It better be an emergency or I'm going to let Bogart have at whoever's knocking on the door."

Running a hand through her disheveled hair, she grabbed her jeans and a T-shirt from the floor and slipped them on as she went to the door.

Whatever she might have expected, this surely wasn't it. Two girls stood there. Both young, blond, thin shoulders hunched against the cold. They looked up as Kellen opened the door, fear and hope burning brightly in their eyes.

"Cate sent us," the taller one said warily.

Kellen frowned. "Cate? From Seattle?"

Both girls nodded.

"She said you might be able to help us," the younger one said. "We knew we were taking a chance coming here without her talking to you first, but—"

"Kellen, sweetheart, they look cold," Dana said as she came up behind her, wrapping her arms around her waist. "Why don't you let them in, start the coffee, and light a fire, while I make us all some breakfast. I bet you're both hungry. I'm Dana and she's Kellen. How does scrambled eggs and toast sound?"

"That sounds—" The tall girl froze as Bogart approached.

"This is Bogart," Kellen said gently. "He won't hurt you, unless he thinks you're going to hurt Dana or me."

"We would never do that," the younger girl said seriously. She stretched out her hand and let Bogart approach her, then began to gently rub Bogart's ears. "I'm Riley and she's Jorie. And scrambled eggs and toast sounds really good."

After showing the girls where the bathroom was and leaving clean sweatpants, sweatshirts, and thick socks for them to wear after they showered, Kellen returned to help Dana put breakfast together.

"Who's Cate?"

"An old friend. She runs a shelter for homeless kids out of Seattle."

"She's the one that hooked you up with Cody and Ren, isn't she?" Dana looked at her, a gentle smile playing on her lips. "Why do I get the feeling our family is about to grow?"

Kellen looked at her. "The chosen family would have to agree—"

"I think Cody and Ren would love to have a pair of younger sisters to get into trouble with."

"What about you?"

Dana stood still for a long moment. "I get to vote?"

"Dana," Kellen murmured. "I love you. Cody and Ren love you. Bogart loves you. I can't believe you would actually question that you're a part of our chosen family."

"Okay," Dana said before walking toward the bedroom, leaving Kellen staring after her. Thirty seconds later, Dana returned to the living room, holding a blue backpack in her hand. Without saying a word, she opened the front closet and put the backpack on the shelf beside Kellen's backpack.

"What are you doing?"

Dana smiled. "Just being prepared. I love you, Kellen, and if you ever feel the need to run, I'll be right there with you. Always."

Kellen pulled her into her arms, her kiss devouring Dana. "I can't breathe when you say that," she said, knowing in her heart this was where she belonged.

Old memories of life before Dana faded. They'd be replaced by the new ones they would make together, surrounded by a growing family and held together by love.

About the Author

A transplant from Cuba to Toronto, AJ Quinn successfully juggles the demands of a busy consulting practice with those of her first true love—storytelling—finding time to write mostly late at night or in the wee hours of the morning. She's the author of three previously released romantic thrillers: *Hostage Moon*, a Lambda Literary Award finalist; *Show of Force*; and *Rules of Revenge*. An avid cyclist, scuba diver, and photographer, AJ finds travel is the best medicine for recharging body, spirit, and imagination. She can be reached at aj@ajquinn.com.

Books Available from Bold Strokes Books

Best Laid Plans by Jan Gayle. Nicky and Lauren are meant for each other, but Nicky's haunting past and Lauren's societal fears threaten to derail all possibilities of a relationship. (987-1-62639-658-6)

Exchange by CF Frizzell. When Shay Maguire rode into rural Montana, she never expected to meet the woman of her dreams—or to learn Mel Baker was held hostage by legal agreement to her right-wing father. (987-1-62639-679-1)

Just Enough Light by AJ Quinn. Will a serial killer's return to Colorado destroy Kellen Ryan and Dana Kingston's chance at love, or can the search-and-rescue team save themselves? (987-1-62639-685-2)

Rise of the Rain Queen by Fiona Zedde. Nyandoro is nobody's princess. She fights, curses, fornicates, and gets into as much trouble as her brothers. But the path to a throne is not always the one we expect. (987-1-62639-592-3)

Tales from Sea Glass Inn by Karis Walsh. Over the course of a year at Cannon Beach, tourists and locals alike find solace and passion at the Sea Glass Inn. (987-1-62639-643-2)

The Color of Love by Radclyffe. Black sheep Derian Winfield needs to convince literary agent Emily May to marry her to save the Winfield Agency and solve Emily's green card problem, but Derian didn't count on falling in love. (987-1-62639-716-3)

A Reluctant Enterprise by Gun Brooke. When two women grow up learning nothing but distrust, unworthiness, and abandonment, it's no wonder they are apprehensive and fearful when an overwhelming love just won't be denied. (978-1-62639-500-8)

Above the Law by Carsen Taite. Love is the last thing on Agent Dale Nelson's mind, but reporter Lindsey Ryan's investigation could change the way she sees everything—her career, her past, and her future. (978-1-62639-558-9)

Actual Stop by Kara A. McLeod. When Special Agent Ryan O'Connor's present collides abruptly with her past, shots are fired, and the course of her life is irrevocably altered. (978-1-62639-675-3)

Embracing the Dawn by Jeannie Levig. When ex-con Jinx Tanner and business executive E. J. Bastien awaken after a one-night stand to find their lives inextricably entangled, love has its work cut out for it. (978-1-62639-576-3)

Jane's World: The Case of the Mail Order Bride by Paige Braddock. Jane's PayBuddy account gets hacked and she inadvertently purchases a mail order bride from the Eastern Bloc. (978-1-62639-494-0)

Love's Redemption by Donna K. Ford. For ex-convict Rhea Daniels and ex-priest Morgan Scott, redemption lies in the thin line between right and wrong. (978-1-62639-673-9)

The Shewstone by Jane Fletcher. The prophetic Shewstone is in Eawynn's care, but unfortunately for her, Matt is coming to steal it. (978-1-62639-554-1)

A Touch of Temptation by Julie Blair. Recent law school graduate Kate Dawson's ordained path to the perfect life gets thrown off course when handsome butch top Chris Brent initiates her to sexual pleasure. (978-1-62639-488-9)

Beneath the Waves by Ali Vali. Kai Merlin and Vivien Palmer love the water and the secrets trapped in the depths, but if Kai gives in to her feelings, it might come at a cost to her entire realm. (978-1-62639-609-8)

Girls on Campus edited by Sandy Lowe and Stacia Seaman. College: four years when rules are made to be broken. This collection is required reading for anyone looking to earn an A in sex ed. (978-1-62639-733-0)

Heart of the Pack by Jenny Frame. Human Selena Miller falls for the domineering Caden Wolfgang, but will their love survive Selena learning the Wolfgangs are werewolves? (978-1-62639-566-4)

Miss Match by Fiona Riley. Matchmaker Samantha Monteiro makes the impossible possible for everyone but herself. Is mysterious dancer Lucinda Moss her own perfect match? (978-1-62639-574-9)

Paladins of the Storm Lord by Barbara Ann Wright. Lieutenant Cordelia Ross must choose between duty and honor when a man with godlike powers forces her soldiers to provoke an alien threat. (978-1-62639-604-3)

Taking a Gamble by P.J. Trebelhorn. Storage auction buyer Cassidy Holmes and postal worker Erica Jacobs want different things out of life, but taking a gamble on love might prove lucky for them both. (978-1-62639-542-8)

The Copper Egg by Catherine Friend. Archeologist Claire Adams wants to find the buried treasure in Peru. Her ex, Sochi Castillo, wants to steal it. The last thing either of them wants is to still be in love. (978-1-62639-613-5)

The Iron Phoenix by Rebecca Harwell. Seventeen-year-old Nadya must master her unusual powers to stop a killer, prevent civil war, and rescue the girl she loves, while storms ravage her island city. (978-1-62639-744-6)

A Reunion to Remember by TJ Thomas. Reunited after a decade, Jo Adams and Rhonda Black must navigate a significant age difference, family dynamics, and their own desires and fears to explore an opportunity for love. (978-1-62639-534-3)

Built to Last by Aurora Rey. When Professor Olivia Bennett hires contractor Joss Bauer to restore her dilapidated farmhouse, she learns her heart, as much as her house, is in need of a renovation. (978-1-62639-552-7)

Capsized by Julie Cannon. What happens when a woman turns your life completely upside down? (978-1-62639-479-7)

Girls With Guns by Ali Vali, Carsen Taite, and Michelle Grubb. Three stories by three talented crime writers—Carsen Taite, Ali Vali, and Michelle Grubb—each packing her own special brand of heat. (978-1-62639-585-5)

Heartscapes by MJ Williamz. Will Odette ever recover her memory or is Jesse condemned to remember their love alone? (978-1-62639-532-9)

Murder on the Rocks by Clara Nipper. Detective Jill Rogers lives with two things on her mind: sex and murder. While an ice storm cripples Tulsa, two things stand in Jill's way: her lover and the DA. (978-1-62639-600-5)

Necromantia by Sheri Lewis Wohl. When seeing dead people is more than a movie tagline. (978-1-62639-611-1)

Salvation by I. Beacham. Claire's long-term partner now hates her, for all the wrong reasons, and she sees no future until she meets Regan, who challenges her to face the truth and find love. (978-1-62639-548-0)

A Return to Arms by Sheree Greer. When a police shooting makes national headlines, activists Folami and Toya struggle to balance their relationship and political allegiances, a struggle intensified after a fiery young artist enters their lives. (978-1-62639-681-4)